IRON ROAD

By J.W. Slider

ISBN: 978-0-615-77111-3

Printed in the United States of America

First Printing, 2013

sliderwrites@gmail.com

To foul weather friends and everything
that stays half full.

ONE
POCKETFUL OF SCARS

The wind kicked and threw a blur of orange and brown leaves into Ben Richter's face. He lifted his arm to shield his eyes and leaned hard into the horizon, pushing forward. His feet ached, and the feeling had almost left his hands, lost somewhere in the cold morning air. While he walked, he gritted his teeth and thought about his father, somewhere overseas. Maybe he had another family by now. He smiled for a moment as the thought of his mother came and went. The last thing she'd given him was life, and for that, she was perfect.

His feet slid easily against the gravel of the railway, but the collars of his boots were starting to wear against his legs, and twice he'd had to stop to pad them. He stopped again, noticing a thin line of blood against the leg of his jeans where blisters had begun to form. Kneeling on the damp wood of a railroad tie, he pulled his wool socks up again. As he stood, the ground began to shake, and he heard the whistle of an oncoming train ring out in the distance.

He inched back from the tracks until he was safely tucked away in the tree line. With the train to his right and a stream just beyond the trees, he watched the flowing water until the shaking had passed, then turned back towards the tracks as the last car shot by. Stomping through the brush and kicking ancient shreds of newspapers out of his way, he made his way back toward the grey, winding road. With a final kick, he cleared the edge of the weeds, but something caught his eye: a tiny, filthy coin that skittered across the stone in front of his boot. He took his hand from his pocket, stooped down, and carefully plucked it up.

Ben rubbed the coin between his fingers, taking some of the dirt from its surface, then spit and rubbed at it again. It wasn't like anything he'd ever seen, but it seemed as attractive as it was foreign. *Maybe it'd be worth something. A meal or two*, Ben thought. The first side had what looked like an elaborate maze, and on the opposite side was the face of a man, sharp and angular. He contemplated the gold coin for a moment, then lifted his coat and slid it into the pocket of his jeans. *A few more miles, just a few more, and I'll be somewhere.*

Ben labored on, a 24 year old silhouette against the skyline with wide shoulders and a long stride. He wasn't the scars from his father's belt or what was left of his savings, jammed into his pockets. His shoulders sagged under the weight of those things, but his legs, constant and solid, pushed on. It was a familiar scene on a new canvas. *It's funny how, in some ways, you learn to hate the things you get comfortable with because as soon as you decide to love them, they get busy leaving you,* he thought. The constant pressure of the earth beneath his feet was the one thing that was always there when he needed it.

It was evening when he stepped from the tracks to follow the light from what he figured must be a city. It was farther away than he'd thought, but Ben trudged on, watching the soft glow and outline of buildings grow larger and clearer until he passed a sign that read, "Welcome to Echton." He felt his spirits lift at the thought of a warm meal and a bed and quickened his pace a little. The feeling abruptly left him as he walked past building after building, already closed for the night. He checked his watch, only 6:10.

"Seriously?" he muttered.

"Meeting tonight," a voice said from the darkness of an alley. He peered in the direction of the sound but could barely make out a tall shadow.

"You're not from around here," the voice added.

"Do you know where I could get some food? Maybe just a chair, a beer, and a TV?" Ben asked the shadow. The clacking of footsteps against planking broke the momentary silence, and the figure drew closer until Ben could make out the form of a thin man in a suit with a hat pulled low over his eyes.

"Could see 'bout all that, but you'll have to wait."

"Wait for what?" Ben peered skeptically, glancing around at the clean-cut brick storefronts and ornate grey streetlights.

"Folks to finish up the meeting," the man said.

"Ok, well, is there anywhere I can wait inside?" His socks soaked through and his teeth chattering, Ben was beginning to grow impatient.

The man leaned forward into the light and smiled, revealing a set of jagged teeth.

"Follow me," he said. They walked in silence through the town. When he turned the corner, Ben saw a small crowd gathered outside a concrete building that read, "Echton City Worship." *What could be so important that an entire city had to shut down to have a meeting about it?*

As they neared the door, the man turned, swept off his hat, and with a little flourish, said, "Welcome to Echton." Ben followed the man into what looked like a chapel with tall stained glass windows at its sides and row after row of bodies packed into pews. Some turned to watch him pass, and he grew suddenly conscious of his dirty jacket and torn jeans.

It wasn't that they were dressed much differently than he was, although their clothes were considerably cleaner. It was the way they held themselves, upright and proper. Their eyes would pass over him quickly, but he felt them linger there for just a moment, and it made his skin prickle. Regardless, he was grateful for the warmth of the building that burned his face and hands. They ached and tingled as sensation crept back into them. At the edges of the room, a handful of men in black uniforms leaned against the walls, gazing over the gathered crowd.

The man he was following stopped near the middle of the group and whispered something to two men who were already seated. Ben smiled nervously, looking them over. The first was a frail older man, and the other an enormous mustached man in an overcoat. They slid to the side and opened a spot on the pew for him. He nodded gratefully and lowered himself into the seat. The man to his left extended a gnarled hand and gave Ben a warm smile.

"Henry Smalls," he wheezed.

"Ben Richter."

Henry gestured to the other man, shaking a bony finger at him. "This is my son, Fredrick."

Scooting forward, Ben shook Fredrick's hand, and the big man nodded back politely.

"Nice to meet you," Ben said. He bent down to untie his boots, wincing as his fingers grazed the blisters on his legs. Henry's hand touched his arm lightly.

"That's no good," he said, waving his hand over the crimson stains that dotted his pant legs.

Ben shook his head, "Nothing much to do about that."

"I think you are wrong, my friend. We might be able to do something about this problem," Henry chuckled. "I think I've got at least some thicker socks in stock and they're certainly drier. No charge."

Just then, the lights dimmed, and the crowd grew silent.

"Thank you," Ben whispered. He looked to the front of the room to see a rather fat man perspiring through his suit, standing at a large mahogany podium. The man cleared his throat and began to speak in a rumbling monotone.

"Here we are gathered, in witness of our Lord and Savior, to an emergency Echton city upkeep meeting." The members of the crowd leaned forward anxiously, and Ben could feel the tension in the room. "First, we will deal with some pressing ordinances and township issues; following that, we can move on to - other issues."

The large man beside him frowned, and a murmur spread through the crowd, which again grew silent. Ben couldn't make out anything they were saying, although he thought he heard the name Starns, or perhaps Steagle. Maybe it hadn't been anything at all.

The man pulled a list from his pocket and began reading, stopping occasionally for a quick vote of confidence. The room was warm, and it felt so good to sit. Ben soon found himself drifting off. He fought to regain consciousness, his head falling backwards, then snapping forwards as he woke again. Straightening himself, he pulled at his pant legs, which had risen gradually as he slumped in the pew. His hand grazed his pocket as he sat up, remembering the coin tucked away inside it.

Leaning to the side, he tugged it free and turned it over in his hands. He scraped at its surface lightly with his fingernails and rubbed it with the sleeve of his shirt. It was such a strange little thing, almost as if it had its own gravity. A hand squeezed his shoulder, and Ben looked up to see the thin man standing at the edge of the pew.

"Now, where did you get that?" the man hissed.

"I - I just found it," Ben stammered.

"That's very interesting," the man replied.

He snatched the coin from Ben's hand and turned, motioning for him to follow. Ben looked around, but no one seemed to have noticed them standing in the middle of the meeting. At least none of them were acknowledging it. He allowed himself to be led from the room, but couldn't help but think it strange that no one turned to watch the two make their exit. All eyes remained fixed on the stage, even as he tripped over a woman's feet and almost fell.

He could hardly register what was happening as they reentered the cold autumn air and crossed the road.

"I wondered if a few minutes in our little meeting might

jog your memory," the man said, prodding him forward. "Just passing through, eh?"

"I just found it. I don't even know where it came from." Ben began to protest, but the man lifted a slender finger to his lips and shook his head. Trying to get his bearings, Ben felt his heart beating fast and his muscles tense. As if the man already knew his thoughts, he pulled his jacket to the side so the bronze star on his chest and a grey revolver on his hip shone in the golden glow of the streetlights.

"We're just gonna get ta where we're goin' now. You'll have plenty of time to talk later, " the man said.

Ben watched his feet shuffle along the roadway and frantically tried to imagine where he was being taken. They passed half a dozen storefronts and came to a walkway and the entrance of an aging brick building. The iron doors of a cell groaned open, and the man put a hand on his back and shoved him in. As the cell door slammed shut, Ben was shocked back to reality.

"What are you doing?" he half shouted, watching the man smile and flip the coin in his palm.

"You sit tight. We gonna have a little chat about this, soon as I get back," he laughed to himself and slipped back through the open front door, locking it with a gentle click.

Ben stood motionless, trying to take in what had just happened. He sunk down, scraping his back against the wall and dropping his face into his hands. The cool, hard concrete under him and the iron bars that lined the rest of the room confirmed the obvious: he was a prisoner.

As he sat in silence, resentment started to grow inside him: the thin man in the suit, the coin, and most of all, his horrible luck. He didn't have any kind of identification.

He'd lost any sort of papers he had a few weeks back. *Who can I even call if they give me a call?* He tried to steady his breathing and concentrate, but in the quiet of the cell, everything seemed more infuriating. Tap, tap, tap, something rapped against the back wall.

"What?" he snapped. "What do you want!?" *I can't go anywhere without running into some cop that thinks he's a war hero interrogation specialist.* After a second, the anger faded to a feeling of helplessness, and he slumped back down. The sound resumed, and he swore he heard a voice, although it was so faint he couldn't be sure. *Easy now,* he thought, *it's nothing, keep your head.* The cell was musty, damp, and stiflingly silent, except for the tapping. It seemed to go on forever.

At first, he thought he'd imagined it, maybe a byproduct of the tapping-induced insanity. But no, Ben was sure that something was touching his head or being sprinkled onto it. He looked up, and his eyes were showered with mortar dust.

"Agh," he groaned, blinking furiously. He jumped to his feet and looked at the spot above his head. He couldn't see anything, but then the tapping began again, this time erratic and stronger than ever, and the brick began to shiver each time a tap rang out. He touched it with his fingertips and felt the vibrations radiating through the wall.

"Hello?" he said. It stopped for a moment, and again he thought he made out a voice behind the wall. His pulse started to rise. *Were they just playing games with him?* He pressed his ear to the rough, red wall and listened, but the tapping suddenly stopped.

"You think that's funny, huh?" he said aloud.

In the silence of the room, he now heard only footfalls and a set of voices, growing louder. It took him a moment to realize it was coming from the front of the room, not the wall. He settled himself on the dusty bed at the edge of the cell, pressed his palms into his eyes, and tried to calm his nerves as he heard the door open and shut, bringing the footsteps closer still.

TWO
TRANSPLANT AND BLOOM

Isabel Stanton was seven when she first realized she had a talent for stealing. She'd set a glass in the kitchen sink, and with just a tiny drizzle of water from the faucet, she'd begin to fill it. Next, she'd tiptoe to the opposite counter, one eye on the door, and very carefully lower a tiny hand into the jar of sweets her mother used to keep for the children she tutored. The sound of the water was enough to cover her footsteps and the rustling of the candy as she found the toffee pieces - the only ones she liked, and if she heard a noise from the other room, she'd spring back into position in front of the tap and wait for the glass to fill.

People had always told her that her father, Conrad Stanton, could have been anything, but he chose to be a doctor. He had a knack for knowing when things were off. Yet, neither he nor his wife Maria ever found their daughter with her hand in that jar. It wasn't until a month after

Isabel started nipping candy from the counter that her mother realized the jar was entirely devoid of toffee, and upon entering Isabel's room to ask her about it, found a half-dozen full glasses of water on her tiny desk. Isabel got the worst spanking of her short life and learned that the thieves that get away with stealing regard it as an art, and art must be crafted from many perspectives.

She got her dark curly hair and olive skin from her mother and her intuition from her father. He'd call her his little detective, although in most of the cases he asked her to solve, she was also the guilty party. Conrad would never accused her directly. He let her follow the clues until she'd proven, without a doubt, that she was the only reasonable suspect. If she was thorough enough, sometimes he'd let her off the hook.

Isabel's mother, Maria, was a teacher, a botanist at heart, before she met Conrad, but had nearly ceased her studies to care for their only daughter, taking only a few pupils a year. She still found some time to practice, and when they settled in their first house in Maine, she'd dedicated herself to creating beds of exotic and colorful floral arrangements that encircled their home. In summer, the breeze would carry the sweet, thick floral scent in the windows in the evening and mix with the smell of fresh linens and bread from the oven. Isabel used to lie on the window ledge while her mother made dinner, the smell washing over her like a saccharine fog.

Isabel had only seen her mother cry once: a week after her 10th birthday, when her father announced that they would be moving to a town in Ohio called Echton. She'd dropped in the middle of the flower bed she was working on and sobbed, her whole body shaking as she grabbed at the leaves and flowers around her, tearing them apart.

"You'll have everything you'll need for the most beautiful gardens," he said in a soothing voice.

She paused for a moment and looked up, her hands still filled with leaves and petals. "You cannot imagine what it takes," she growled.

Isabel, who had been hiding behind her father, stepped forward and threw her arms around her mother's neck. "We'll make new gardens," she said. "I'll help you."

Her mother's grip softened as she returned Isabel's embrace, and the leaves slipped from her hands into the wind.

"We both will," her father added, kneeling in the dirt and wrapping his arms around them.

Conrad explained that the mayor of Echton had called him the previous week and told him about their town's need for a doctor. The previous doctor had passed away, and through contacts at Harvard, he'd been recommended to them. They'd offered him a place in town to set up an office, rent-free for an entire year, and promised to compensate him for the cost of the move. Maria and Isabel both knew Conrad's work in Portland was wearing him thin. Moving to Echton wouldn't be easy, he'd said, but it would be worth it in the long run.

The Stanton's first visit to Echton as a family was to move there. Conrad made the trip once before to negotiate a price on their home and see his office on the main strip.

"Not a bad bunch," he told them. "The mayor greeted me himself and introduced me to a realtor right in town."

To Maria and Isabel, everything about Echton seemed foreign. It didn't seem to bother young Isabel, though.

When they pulled up to the big white house on the outskirts of the town, she shrieked in delight and leapt from the front seat of the moving truck.

"It's beautiful!" she cried.

She was a blur, circling the house, running onto its elaborate porch and through the screen door to the upstairs to choose a room. Her father held her mother in the front yard as they listened to the little footsteps and laughter that raced through their new home. Together, they helped the movers unload the boxes, eager to reach town before closing time.

When their black BMW pulled to the side on the main drag in town, Isabel scampered into the grocery store, leaving its heavy wooden door cracked for her parents.

"It's quaint," Maria said, feeling her husband's hand slip into hers and squeeze it lightly.

"It's a little different... but it could be home," he said.

Hand in hand, they followed their daughter's trail into the store. The choices weren't exactly what they were accustomed to, but the man behind the counter seemed nice enough. He introduced himself as Mr. Smalls and welcomed them to Echton.

"That's very kind of you, Mr. Smalls," Maria said, flashing him a big smile.

"Yes, ma'am. You are welcome," he nodded to her.

As her mother and father gathered the bags of groceries, Isabel lingered in the store for a moment, looking over this shopkeeper in his grey suit and vest. He was the first person she'd seen in Echton, and she wondered what occasion had inspired him to dress so nicely. She also noticed the cane he kept behind the counter, its top a beautiful swan carved to flow with the grain of the wood.

"You're probably waiting for one of these," he winked and handed Isabel a lollipop. She'd already taken an assortment of candy from the counter, which now rested in the lining of her socks, but she took the red candy from him anyway, smiled sheepishly, and with a final glance, left the store. *I'm a little old for all this kid stuff, but anyone who gives out free lollipops to a stranger can't be all bad.*

Over the next few weeks, the Stantons were introduced to a number of the town's people. Mr. Hatley, the mayor of Echton or "Social Ambassador" as he called himself, made it a point to introduce them to as many of the town's residents as possible, starting with the sheriff.

"Sheriff Hix!" he chased after the man, one hand on his hat. The sheriff cocked his head towards them, then turned around and retraced his steps, extending his hand.

"Ah, Doctor Stanton. What a beautiful family!" he said, beaming. "Hopefully this is the only time ya'll will have to see me at the big house." He winked, putting a hand on Isabel's shoulder.

"I should think," Conrad chuckled nervously. "Thanks again for your help with the permits for the, uh..." He pointed back at the space where he'd leased his office. Hix just smiled again and nodded, starting back up the walkway and disappearing inside an enormous brick building.

So it went, on almost every visit to town, the mayor's portly form would rush over to them, dragging another hapless acquaintance over to meet "Dr. Stanton, our new physician," adding, "The Stantons were personally invited to join us here in Echton."

Isabel decided that folks in Echton only owned jeans

or overalls and work shirts, stained with grease or dust, except on Sunday when they all decided to up and wear the nice clothes they suddenly had. Her father fit in alright. The town's people seemed to respect a man in a suit and tie, but Isabel was always wary that her clothes didn't look like the other children's. Her colorful dresses and shirts were very different than the black, grey, or white clothes worn by the other girls, and she couldn't grasp how they could stand to wear the same thing every day. She seldom talked to the other kids; it seemed like they were afraid of her. Whenever she stepped from the door of their car, they would stare and whisper, then disappear as quickly as they'd come.

Isabel grew increasingly attached to Mr. Smalls and made every excuse to visit the grocery and talk with him about his time abroad in the Navy before he'd settled down in Echton to open his shop. He never let her leave his store without some kind of sweet, and he told her about his son, Fredrick, who had worked in the lumber industry down South, and was home visiting for a little while.

Fredrick would poke his head in sometimes to help with something, but usually he kept to himself. Isabel figured if he was related to Henry, he was probably alright. She never stole from his store after that first day. Often tempted by the boxes of cookies and funny trinkets, Isabel found it hard to resist, but Henry's warm smile kept her hands in her pockets. Aside from her parents, Mr. Smalls was the only friend Isabel had in Echton.

True to her word, when they'd completed their move, Isabel helped her mother in the garden every day after she finished her studies. They started with a torn and ragged slope but soon broke and tilled the ground into some semblance of a garden bed and set to turning their house into a home. It was a large part of Isabel's education, talking over history and the scientific method in the garden, her hands deep in the soft soil and her knees stained green and brown.

The Stantons had decided that moving in the middle of the year and starting at a new school would be too much for Isabel, so she was to be home schooled until the following spring, a choice she wasn't totally against. She'd wake, nibble on something while she worked on the curriculum her parents had set out for her, and complete her work before noon most days. When she'd finished, she'd gather her mother's tools outside and wait for the second half of her school day to begin.

People from the town would slow their cars each time they passed the Stanton's gardens. They'd never seen anything like Anthurium, Bird of Paradise, or the Orchids in the front pots. Sometimes her mother would try to catch their eye and wave, and they'd always raised a hand politely but would roll up their windows and pull away. Isabel found that none of the people in Echton held your gaze if they caught you watching them. They covered their eyes like a well kept secret.

It took Conrad about a month to set up and finish the licensing and insurance procedures for his office. The day after he'd finished all the paperwork and filed it with the town's clerk, a representative from the sheriff's office dropped by to visit him. He wore a black button up shirt, grey slacks, and a brass badge on his chest. When he first walked through the door, he just introduced himself as "a friend." Conrad sat talking with him for quite some time about the business he intended to open and his history and education. Seemingly satisfied, the man gave him a little smile and a wink, rose to his feet, and added that "the sheriff had a lot of faith in him." He thought it a little strange that someone from the sheriff's office had taken the time to stop by and interview him about his work, but Conrad had bigger things on his mind.

Things were slow at first, mainly a few cases of the common cold and minor cuts, but he waited patiently for Echton to come to him. Often enough, if a man's patience will hold, his pockets will fill, and as things carried on, Conrad saw more and more business. Sometimes he'd hear them call him an outsider or stranger in hushed tones in the waiting room, but he figured it was just a matter of time before he gained the town's confidence. The townspeople started to trust him, and his tiny practice flourished.

By the time Isabel was enrolled in public school the following spring, Conrad was so busy between working at the office and on the occasional house call, he was hardly seen around the Stanton house, except maybe a hurried dinner or momentary sighting during the night. The evening after her first day at school, Isabel found him filling out a calendar on the dining room table.

"Hi sweetie." He paused and grinned at her.

"Hey dad, what're you doing?" She laid her head against his shoulder.

"Organizing my appointment schedule."

"Can I get on the schedule?"

He grinned and capped the pen, tossing it aside.

"How about right now? What are your symptoms?"

"Right now... " Isabel pretended to check her pulse. "I think I'm dying, and the only known cure is ice cream."

She leaned against him and giggled.

He couldn't help but smile. It was like his own mind had come back to rib him.

"Today was my first day of school," she added.

"I know." He put his arm around her. "How was it?"

"The uniforms are weird. I'm not used to looking like a rain cloud."

"I'm sure it's not that bad."

"You wear that itchy grey dress and white frilly thing," she scowled.

He nodded slowly, tilting back in his chair.

"I'm not sure how that would go over with my patients," he laughed. "How about your classmates? They seem like a good bunch?"

"They're ok, but they don't like to talk much."

"And your teacher, Mrs. Garness?"

"A girl got detention today for forgetting some book money she owed." Isabel frowned, thinking about the fifty cent pieces she'd slipped from the girl's bag before lunch. She didn't want to hurt anyone, and silently vowed to return them twofold the next day, maybe with an apology note.

"Sounds like a tough cookie. She teaching anything you can't handle?"

Isabel grinned and shook her head. "Cake," she said.

Her father kissed her forehead and glanced at his watch. "It's time for school girls to go to bed."

"It's not that late," she groaned.

"Late enough. Get ready for bed, Izzy," he said patiently and reopened his bag. She sagged her shoulders, and dragged her feet against the ground, slowly making her way to the stairs.

Isabel felt very alone that night as she looked out her window and thought about Echton. She knew they'd be there as long as her father's business was going well, but her parents never seemed to notice how the people there looked at them. It was like they were a different species that happened to wander into the wrong terrarium. They'd warned her it wouldn't be easy moving to a new town, but she didn't realize it would feel this foreign.

She couldn't help but wonder if maybe she was the weird one, and maybe she just didn't know it yet. Regardless, a little thing like being different wasn't going to hold back Isabel Stanton, and it certainly wasn't going to keep her from going to school. "Knowledge is your greatest asset," her mother always said. Isabel knew, though, that knowledge comes from curiosity, and curiosity can be a dangerous thing.

THREE

A CALCULATED RISK

Isabel thought back on her first year in Echton as she heard Sheriff Hix's voice rumble from the other side of the wall. She had too much time to think, and the isolation she felt now made the memory clear as crystal, even though it'd been over a decade since that night. When she was sure Hix had gone again, she grabbed the thin metal rod from under her bed and went back to work, chipping away at the mortar between the bricks of the cell wall.

She wasn't sure whose the second voice was, but she'd only seen a few deputies come out of that office, and she knew that the main deputy and office clerk's voice was shrill and squeaky, unlike the sheriff's voice or the voices of the others she'd seen, who hardly spoke at all. Working on the wall with a stranger on the other side of it was risky, but she was running out of time. *Maybe I can catch a break,* she thought. *Maybe they brought him here like they brought me. At least I can convince, bribe, trick him, whatever it takes.*

Once she'd decided reaching someone in the jail was her only hope, it'd taken Isabel almost a day to work free a metal strip from the frame of the bed. She'd been scraping away at the brick, taking short breaks to listen through the wall for any sign of the sheriff. When she heard the door slam, she'd held her breath and pressed her ear against the wall. She'd heard the new voice once more, this time louder, before the room went silent.

"Yeah, not a big fan of this place either," she muttered.

At first, she thought she was just imagining things. She'd been in that tiny room for she wasn't sure how long, counting days by the number of times the deputy delivered her small meals, stale and tasteless. It'd been six days, maybe, since she'd been dragged through all those doors and the dark alleyway and thrown into this cell. From the dark red clay on the deputy's boots and the smell of the clematis vines that drifted in each time he opened the thick metal door, she guessed he was keeping her in the basement or a back section of the jailhouse.

She was sure she wasn't the only one either. After her first or second night in the room, she'd begun to hear noises through the other wall, shouting and thumping, but it was so muffled she couldn't understand any of the words. After awhile, it'd faded. Either they'd given up or been moved somewhere else, she was sure. Alone again, Isabel had time to realize her only hope was somehow reaching someone inside those walls.

"Hello!" she shouted. "Help! I need help!" She stabbed the metal into the brick wall, screaming until she was hoarse. Finally, she collapsed into the pile of mortar dust and wept. *I just need to sleep. I can hardly feel my arms to hold them up.* She gave the wall a final stab and swept the dust scattered on the floor into her palm, depositing it in the toilet. Throwing herself down on the small cot in the corner of the room, she slipped the metal rod into the lining of her pillow.

Isabel woke to the sound of distant voices. She shot upright, her mind reeling; she didn't even know what time of day it was. The single light that hung in the middle of the room gave her little idea. She tiptoed to the wall and listened closely. All she could make out were thudding noises and the distinct droning of the sheriff's voice. She sat anxiously, waiting for anything that might tell her about the second voice. It went on for a long time. The sheriff would drone on, punctuated by a muffled thump or crash, and there would be silence again for a moment.

The last week's events echoed through Isabel's head. She'd been thinking, and any way she played it out in her mind, it all didn't quite make sense. Her hair felt matted and oily as she ran her fingers through it, and she could feel a tender spot on the top of her head where she'd been hit. She remembered hearing hushed voices and sneaking into the back of the town hall, then a blinding pain, her feet dragging against the ground, and finally waking up in this room. It all seemed so far away.

Where are my mom and dad? Are they involved in this mess too? Did I do this, or did I just happen to be in the crossfire of something? The people that took her - she hadn't recognized their faces or at least didn't remember them. The little pauses and whispers had to add up somehow, and unless she could get to her parents soon, they'd be caught up in the same thing.

She knew her father would be raising hell until he found out where she was. He'd never think to check in the jailhouse though, and she hadn't seen a soul besides the sheriff or deputy, since they'd brought her here. If she could reach someone who could talk to her father, he'd think of a plan to get her out. *We could be a thousand miles from this place by tomorrow*, she thought, *a lifetime from Echton.*

The room grew silent, no more shouting or thumping. She waited for what felt like a long time but still heard nothing. *Sheriff Hix is probably home for the night, to hell or whatever dark tomb he sleeps in, but what happened to the second voice?* Isabel slowly sat up and felt under her pillow for the metal rod. Cautiously at first, she scraped at the already eroded mortar in the joints of the wall. The first brick was almost free. She reached her fingertips in and tugged at it, then gave it a few more hard jabs with the rod.

Isabel figured it was only a matter of time before they'd be rid of her. As far as she was concerned, she could either sit here and make assumptions about noises and shadows, or she could get out there and do something. *These people - I don't trust a single one of them, except maybe Mr. Smalls. Henry would help me.* She wasn't sure what she'd do even if she did escape, but it didn't matter. She just had to get out of this damp, dirty room.

"Here goes," she said, slipping her fingers into the spaces where mortar used to be at the top and bottom of the brick, giving it a sharp tug. *Nothing.* Isabel paused and remembered to breathe. She tore the case from the pillow on her bed and wrapped it around her hand, then slammed her palm against the center of the brick. It had moved in a little bit. *It must have moved.* She hit the brick two or three more times and saw it had receded maybe half a centimeter into the wall. Working her fingers back into the grooves, Isabel gave a mighty yank, and the brick gave way, throwing her back, bouncing across the cell floor. Pain shot through her tailbone into her back, and she pursed her lips, not daring to move.

She took a deep breath, tenderly lifted herself from the floor, and grabbed the rod from its resting place near the foot of the wall. *A little longer lever would be nice.* Isabel thought back on the physical science lab she'd taken sophomore year and laughed; it was actually becoming kind of useful. A few years away from the gardens had made her soft though. She was tired all the time, and a soreness crept into her bones that she hadn't known in a long while.

The second layer of brick went much more quickly, it seemed. Time didn't really have much meaning either way, save the sliver of a shadow that slipped beneath the cell door and snuck back out again. Isabel chipped away at the brick face steadily, slipping the rod into the wall and scraping, pausing only to clear away the brick dust from the hole and dispose of it. Every so often, she'd pause and listen for any sign of the man on the other side of the wall, but the room was absolutely silent.

When the rod finally broke through from the other side, she started to work it back and forth, breaking pieces of brick away. She created a hole large enough to see through and had started to pull the rod back when she heard a soft groaning. The hair on the back of Isabel's neck prickled, and her heart beat furiously. With a violent tug, the rod was pulled from her hands, and as she reeled backwards, a steady pair of brown eyes met her own.

FOUR
UNTIL THE MORNING COMES

B en woke to a horrible scraping noise; it felt like it would tear his head in two. *That sheriff didn't look like much, but he'd really landed some solid ones. He must have finally knocked me out.* Ben didn't remember the sheriff's leaving or being untied from the chair. He'd lasted a while, the man asking him questions about where he'd come from and all sorts of things about that coin. Ben knew there must be something special about that coin from the way the man had reacted to it. You don't bother giving someone a beating like that unless you think he has something you want.

He spit, red and thick. His hand moved to his mouth and tenderly pushed against his lip, testing the cut he felt on its inside. Groaning, he pulled himself upright and leaned against the wall. Dust rained down on his right shoulder and the tapping, scraping, rapping noise continued, faster and louder than ever. *Is this some kind of continued torture?*

Maybe the sheriff was an even crueler man that Ben had judged him for. Ben turned and saw a metal bar poking through the wall, working away at the brick as tiny pieces tumbled down and came to rest beside him. Every movement was agony, and he thought his left arm might be broken. *Stop whining; it's not so bad*, he told himself.

He was a little banged up, but he'd been in worse shape. Something about not having his mother around; his father had made a point to make him tough. And sooner rather than later, he made sure that Ben knew how to stand on his own. One day, Ben had just come home to an empty house and a note that read, "On your own, kid. Keep your chin up," with the name Jason Richter scribbled below. Ben would make it. He'd be just fine.

With one fluid motion, he reached his right hand up, wrapped his fingers around the rod, and yanked it through the wall, turning to face the hole.

"Enough!" he bellowed. Even the echo of his own voice hurt. A tiny squeak came back from the other side of the wall, followed by a flash of color and a muffled thud.

The silence that followed was ecstasy; he closed his eyes, basking in it. Slumped against the wall, he began to wiggle the fingers on his left hand. To his surprise, they seemed to be working, although the shooting pain that flowed through his arm and back told him that his shoulder was, at the very least, dislocated. He stopped for a moment and glanced through the hole again, but saw nothing.

With his arm pressed against the wall and the front of his coat wedged into his mouth, Ben let all of his weight fall on his shoulder, and with his other hand he pulled it upward, back into place, screaming as he felt it line up.

The bastard could have at least had the decency to leave me some water or something. He gritted his teeth, surveying the empty cell. When he turned to face the wall again, he noticed a bright pair of green eyes watching him through the hole. He leaned forward and stared back at them. If whoever was behind this was taking the time to try to mess with his head after making it so foggy, he wasn't going to play along.

"Is room service complementary?" he growled. He rolled over, hoisting himself upright, out of sight from the hole, suddenly slamming his palm over it. He'd expected a yell, maybe cursing, but the yelp that came from the other side of the wall totally threw him. It was high and airy, a woman's scream.

"It's not polite to stare," he added, softening his voice.

"I need your help."

"I'm not a ton of help to anyone at the moment," Ben said. "Let me get a look at you. I don't trust people I can't see." He propped himself up on his right arm, trying to get a handle on what was hurting more. "Can't even help myself," he muttered.

"Is this okay?" she asked.

"Hang on a minute, yeah?" He took a deep breath, trying to focus. It felt like ball bearings were ricocheting around his brain. Squeezing his eyes shut, he rubbed them gingerly.

"Feeling a little rough around the edges here, little hard to uh..." Ben blinked furiously and shook his head. The swelling in his right eye had almost closed it, but the left was still mostly clear.

"I'm sorry if he hit you."

"'If' is not exactly the point of contention -" he started

as he put his eye to the hole. Ben froze, his mouth partly open. He'd never seen such a strangely beautiful woman. Her dark hair and complexion shone against the brilliant green in her eyes, which gave way to a thin, slanted nose. He guessed from the dirt on her face that she'd been in there for a while.

"Who are you?" he said softly.

"Isabel Stanton. Maybe you know my father, Conrad?"

"Nope, well, I'm not from here, though. I just wandered by, and the sheriff was kind enough to put me up for the night." He smiled wryly, spitting again.

She returned his gaze through the hole and inched closer. Ben patted his pockets, flat against his legs. The realization that the sheriff had taken everything from him was actually a little freeing. There was nothing else he could lose, and the man couldn't possibly know his real name. He hadn't even had an ID, just some old knick-knacks and a little cash.

"This place's a little strange, isn't it? I didn't even know they made jails like this anymore," Ben said.

"I thought the same thing when we first moved here. You get used to it, though. It's just a little behind the rest of the world," Isabel replied.

"A little strange and lot of mean," Ben said, massaging his shoulder with his other hand.

"What's your name?" she asked.

"Ben," he replied. "I'd shake your hand or something, but I don't think it's quite gonna make it through your escape hole."

Isabel laughed, and for a moment, the whole cell seemed to brighten a little.

"You're going the wrong way, just more brick walls and metal over here," he added.

"It would take me a year to scrape away enough brick to fit though," she replied. "That's why I need your help."

Ben paused. He drummed his fingers on the patched knees of his pants and exhaled deeply. "What, exactly, are you hoping I can help you with?"

"I'm really not sure - I just need to get out of here, to get to my family," she said.

Ben paused for a moment, then spoke. "I don't even know how I'M gonna get out of here," he said quietly. He chewed his lip and looked back at her through the tiny hole, listening to the enormous sigh that came from her side of the wall.

"I don't know anything about that coin."

"Coin?" she asked. "What coin?"

"If this is some trick to try to get me to tell you about that coin, I don't even know anything about it," he said tersely. "Stop wasting your time."

"I don't know anything about a coin."

"Well, if it's what you're waiting for, neither do I."

"I don't want to know anything about a coin. I just need to get to my family," Isabel pleaded.

Ben tugged at the stubble on his chin and stared at the pile of mortar on the floor.

"Just let me get some sleep for now, yeah? I can't think with the hammers banging in my head." He gently pressed against the swelling in his face, tonguing the cut in his mouth.

"Ok, just please, soon," she said.

Her voice sounded desperate, and he wanted to

help her, but Ben knew had to clear his head, or he'd do something stupid.

"Any ideas about this hole? If he sees this, we're both gonna be in for a rough morning," he asked. He heard her take a sharp breath and walk the length of the room.

Ben waited for a moment, then spoke again. "Pretty quiet over there. I'm gonna guess you hadn't considered that part. Give me an hour or two to sleep, and we'll see what we can come up with."

"If you're not gonna help me get out of here, we need to fix it. He'll kill me if he sees it!" she cried.

Ben scratched his head and thought about the taste of the blood in his mouth. It seemed strange - what it took to shock him anymore. "So this was your plan? Break through the wall and yell at someone until they help you?"

Isabel was silent.

"What are you in for anyway?" he asked her.

"Really? That's what you wanna talk about?"

"You're not in much of a position to dictate terms, Ms. Isabel," Ben said.

"I can't really say why. I guess I did something wrong, or I heard or saw something I wasn't supposed to."

She's sounding more and more desperate, Ben thought. *Trust and desperation seldom settle well together.*

"I don't know what to tell you," she added.

"That'll do," Ben said, and lay back on the cot, draping the small, rough pillow over his face.

"What about this hole?" Isabel said indignantly.

"Sleep first," Ben murmured. As he did his best to keep his head still, Ben could hear the gliding and striking of Isabel's shoes pacing in the next room. He drifted in and out of sleep, once to see a small white piece of cloth poking through the hole and again to Isabel's frustrated cries for him. *Be patient*, he told himself.

"How can you sleep right now?" Her voice echoed in the cell. Soon, the first rays of light joined her, doing their best to wake him as they shone through the front window of the jail.

"Ben!" she hissed. "Ben, wake up! He's gonna be back here soon."

He lay still, pretending he couldn't hear a word.

"Ben!" she said again. "Damn it!"

This girl must be here for something serious, Ben decided, *for her to make this much noise about getting out. Or maybe she's just like me, in the wrong place at the wrong time. Either way, she's not doing me any favors.* He did his best to ignore the clacking of her shoes against the concrete as they started their march again.

"Such a foolish, stupid girl," her voice came back to him. "Such a stupid girl for trusting a boy to help!" Ben listened as she paced her cell like a caged animal, sometimes pausing momentarily, probably trying to see him. He heard her moan loudly and pause to scream and kick the wall.

"You can't be unconscious. You have to help me!" she yelled, finally resigning herself to silence.

As the light reached Ben's feet, the door to the Echton city jail creaked open to reveal the silhouette of a man wearing a long overcoat. Ben barely opened his eyes, just enough to look over the short man. He was mostly bald, with a thin ring of hair that ran around the outside of his head and met his Coke-bottle glasses in the front. He made a little snorting noise as he kicked the door the rest of the way open and let it slam behind him. Ben sat up slowly, knowing that the noise was intended to wake him.

"Good morning," the man said in a squeaking, nasally voice.

Ben nodded to him silently, shielding his eyes from the light.

"I'm Nathan McCreary, Deputy and First Officer to the Echton Sheriff's Department."

"Thomas Gunson," he grunted in reply. It was the last name he remembered giving the sheriff.

The man gave him a little smile, producing a manila envelope from his breast pocket.

"So I've been reading. Sheriff Hix gave me a copy of his report on you."

"Sheriff Hix," Ben said under his breath.

"Excuse me?" said the deputy, removing his hat.

Ben shrugged and swung his legs over the side of the bed. "I've got a problem, Mr. Deputy McCreary. Maybe you can help me out?"

"The probability is slim." McCreary gave him a thin smile. "However, on the off chance, what is it?"

"My head is pounding, a present from your friend, the sheriff, and there's a girl on the other side of this wall that won't shut up."

"You slime ball!" Isabel screamed.

McCreary was visibly jarred, taking a short step back.

"Sorry, lady, but I don't need problems like you," Ben shot back, jerking a thumb at the hole. "See? She poked a hole right into my cell and has been talking my ear off all night."

McCreary was frozen, totally blindsided. "I should call - uh," he stammered.

"Maybe you could do something about this first?" Ben said. "Sheriff Hix know your prisoners are poking holes in the walls? Is someone supposed to be watching this place? Or you just let the prisoners kind of have the run of it?"

"Well, no, I was at the meeting, and then I..." McCreary trailed off, rubbing his face feverishly. "It was John Kaine's night to watch the..."

Ben could hear Isabel crying on the other side of the wall. He tried to put it out of his mind.

"Just take a look at this! There's a hole in the damn wall of my cell, and you're not gonna do anything about it? She's been making it bigger all night."

"How do I know you didn't make that hole?" McCreary paused and looked Ben over, spotting the metal rod on the floor by his feet.

Ben followed McCreary's eyes to the metal rod, then grabbed it from the floor.

"You mean with this? I took it from her because I was so tired of hearing her scrape apart your jail. How much brick dust do you see over here? Not much, know why? Because I didn't make that hole. Here, take it." Ben slid the metal rod under the bars to McCreary's feet and held his hands up, open toward the deputy.

Nathan stooped down to pluck up the rod and eyed him. He decided that either Ben was a damned good liar or that he was telling the truth. *He didn't look like a good liar.* McCreary slowly approached the bars to get a closer look at the hole, stopping just a few feet short.

"See?" Ben prodded.

McCreary took off his glasses and squinted at the quarter-sized hole in the wall. Ben backed up to the far corner of the cell and kept his hands up.

"Stay where you are," McCreary snapped.

"I don't want any trouble. I just wanna be on my way," Ben said.

McCreary glanced at him and moved a little closer, looking from the rod in his hand to the hole in the wall.

Ben knew it was a gamble, but anyone that introduced himself as Deputy First Officer had to be dying to prove something. He'd met a hundred Nathan McCrearys, and every one of them was just waiting to hold on, white-knuckled, to a sliver of something important.

With his face thrust forward almost into the bars of the cell and the wheels in his head turning, McCreary hardly noticed the tall shadow creeping closer to him, until it grabbed him by the lapels of his coat and pulled his head into the iron bars, three quick thuds until he faded into darkness.

Ben pulled McCreary's keys from his trouser pocket and let his limp form fall to the ground. It only took him a second to find the right set, remembering their bright red border. He felt Isabel's eyes on his back and heard her sniffle loudly.

"Please, don't leave me here," she sniffled.

He cursed under his breath and worked the cell door open, stepping over McCreary's still form.

At 6 AM, the streets of Echton were nearly empty, and no one noticed as a broad shouldered figure in a wide rimmed hat and an ill-fitting overcoat made its way down the street towards Small's Grain and Grocery.

FIVE
BEYOND THIS DOOR

Isabel sat in silence for awhile, too shocked to cry. She'd just have to sit here and wait for the sheriff to find McCreary, see the hole, and come deal with her. She felt it in her bones. She was a missing person, nothing left to do now but lay down and wait. The other set of voices in the cell, they'd probably been in the same situation. Maybe they'd realized they were as good as dead and just gave up on shouting and hollering. It was entirely possible that they'd beaten her to the finish line.

A few minutes after she lay down, the thick metal door to the room shook and burst open. She shrieked as a man's arm beckoned her closer. Isabel froze, not daring to move, but after a moment, Ben leaned into the opening and cocked his head to the side.

He'd already gotten a short look at her, but he stopped breathing when he opened that steel door and saw the entirety of the girl standing inside. She was short, with smooth skin and tiny cuts and scrapes all over her legs, arms, and face, wearing a filthy blue sundress that swayed against her slender legs. Her shoulders were thin, her thick hair barely reaching them. She looked so frail, but she held herself with confidence. Ben had never seen anything like Isabel Stanton. He glanced over his shoulder, then looked back at her.

"Come on, girl, unless you wanna take up permanent residence. Your call."

Isabel didn't know whether to laugh or cry. Instead, she just took Ben Richter's hand and allowed him to pull her into the early morning light.

"Put this on." He handed her an ugly floral bonnet and a long plaid button up. Isabel took it gratefully and pulled it tight, tying it high below her chin and pulling the sides around her face. She glanced around, making a quick effort at brushing the mortar dust from her dress, then threw the coat over her shoulders and fastened it at the top button. As she looked toward freedom, she watched a figure passing the head of the alley slow to a standstill, peering at them. Ben pushed Isabel back towards the cell door and held his hand up in a little wave.

"Oye!" the figure called out towards him. At the top of its towering form, Ben could see a head of thick, greasy black hair protruding from under a skullcap.

"Just cleaning up, sir. Sheriff Hix asked me to clean up some of the brush back here."

The figure paused, flicked a cigarette butt into the gutter and snorted loudly.

"Come over here, boy."

Ben looked behind him at the wall of thick green foliage and rock, then started to inch forward.

"Vinnie! Get over here. We got offload and wash still," another voice called, a little farther off.

The first figure grunted and dismissed Ben with a wave. "Don't let me catch you takin' time off again," he said as he disappeared from the mouth of the alley, rapping a rolled paper against his open hand.

Ben looked to Isabel, who was still watching him, neither daring to breathe. When he decided the men had made it far enough away, he motioned her forward.

"I don't know what to say," she whispered. "Thank you."

He caught her gaze for a moment and found himself grinning like a fool. He'd gotten himself into this somehow, but he thought it fair to give her at least a little of the blame.

"The best thing you can do right now is tell me the fastest way to get the hell out of this place."

SIX

A GUNPOWDER RECEPTION

The rising sun advanced on Ben and Isabel, chasing them toward Echton's main street.

"Probably could have figured this better," he whispered, tossing the keys behind them under a staircase. Isabel nodded, her mind busy at work.

"Follow me," she said. The two made their way across to the cover of a row of store overhangs and set off at a trot.

"I was just over here," Ben whispered. "There's nothing here but an old grocery store and a bank just past it."

"I know."

"What're you doing, then?" he shot back.

"Gonna have to trust someone sometime." She squeezed his arm, then let it go.

Ben tried to walk casually and keep his head low, following her through the faded green door of the shop. Isabel stopped just short of the counter, behind the shop-keep, who was busy behind a broom, and cleared her throat loudly.

"Hey!" Ben snapped, reaching for her arm.

Henry Smalls turned to greet them with a wave of his hand and a broad smile. "You come back to pay for the bonnet and coat, young man? Here I was thinking that money walked out the door with you." Henry chuckled at his own joke.

Isabel pulled back the fabric over her head until her face was almost entirely exposed, then looked up at him.

"Holy Jesus," he gasped.

Isabel replaced the bonnet and pressed a finger against her lips. Henry raised a hand to his mouth, his eyes moving rapidly between Isabel to Ben.

"Lord, forgive my blasphemy. Where have you?" he started, but Isabel silenced him with a wave of her hand and pointed towards the back of the store. Henry strode to the front of the shop, flipped the sign to "Closed" and led them back into the stockroom.

In the cover of the neck high grey shelves, Ben settled himself on a step stool and opened a pack of wafers he'd grabbed on the way in. He nearly swallowed them whole and gulped down a bottle of water afterward. When he'd polished off the snack, he looked back to find Isabel and Henry both staring at him.

"Were you raised by wolves?" Isabel said.

"It's been a little while since I ate. Y'want one?" He brushed the crumbs from his face.

Isabel tore open a package of crackers for herself and sipped from a bottle of water. Ben shrugged and straightened his back, peering through the gaps in the shelves.

"You wanna explain any of this?" Henry said, motioning

Isabel to shut the door. He turned to Ben, who was now busy looking over a can of tuna. "And you. Who the hell are you?"

"Couldn't exactly tell you; I'm not sure myself, " Ben said, working the lid from the can with his teeth.

Henry was silent, studying Ben's face. He looked back to Isabel. "Jesus, Mary, and Joseph, Isabel. I figured you for a run off or worse." Henry's gaze lingered on her.

"I need to get out of here or I might be," Isabel said.

Henry nodded solemnly. The sound of the welcome bell rang out from the front room.

"I locked that door, I swear," he muttered. "Stay here." Shuffling out of the room, Henry left the door open slightly.

They listened as he greeted someone and told them the store was closed for the morning, because he wasn't feeling well. A low reedy voice answered, something about apples out of season. Ben looked to Isabel, trying to massage the stiffness from his neck.

"You trust this guy?" he whispered.

"He's about the only one I do trust here." She frowned, fidgeting with another sleeve of crackers.

"Who are these people?" Ben asked. "Seriously, and what did you do?" He rose and stalked silently towards the door, then circled back towards his seat.

"I don't know. That's the worst part. I guess I got into some things I shouldn't have, but I'm not even sure what they were," she said.

Isabel had never really made friends in Echton, even in all the years they'd lived here. The only person she'd grown close to besides her parents was Henry. She thought it'd change, but it never did. Everyone her own age seemed desperate to keep their distance, like she was infected with some horrible disease, and it would make them like her. She wasn't sure about Ben, but he'd helped her escape from Hix, and for that, she figured she at least owed him a ride out of town. *His face seems honest.* It already looked a little better than it had the night before. The swelling had gone down, and the cut below his eye had closed. *Maybe two people you can trust is enough to get by,* she thought. *Two is a lot more than none.*

She studied Ben in the stillness of the back room, waiting for Henry to reappear. The thick brown hair, cut short against his head, matched his muted brown eyes. His chin and nose were gently sloped, and his nose was crooked at its midpoint, giving him the look of a man who'd been chiseled away at, like an architect had set out to make something brilliant but had found something more interesting along the way.

"Not your idea of paradise, huh?" Ben's gaze lingered on her, and she felt her face getting warmer.

"Wasn't my idea to come here. I'll introduce you to my father, and you two can discuss it." She craned her neck to get a better look at the front room. "Where is he?"

"Probably getting his friends together." Ben swallowed hard and looked from the gap in the door to Isabel. "Where's the back door to this place?" Ben had been on the road for a long while, and if he'd learned anything, it was that people will sell you to the devil if it'll make the breeze so much as sway their way.

"Sorry about that," Henry muttered, slipping back into the room and closing the door. "Thought it'd be more suspicious if I just threw him out."

"Henry, we need your help," Isabel said, placing her hand gently on the old man's arm. Ben noticed he was shaking slightly. *Maybe he was nervous or maybe just guilty.* Henry jumped as though he'd just been woken.

"My help?" Henry fumbled with his glasses.

"I need to get out of here," Isabel slid over until she was looking into Henry's eyes.

"Maybe you should wait here until things've cooled off a little," Henry said, turning to look towards the front door.

"We need to go, now," Ben said firmly.

Henry frowned, speaking slowly, "Of course, it's not safe here," he said, pulling a small set of keys from his pocket and dropping them into Isabel's open hand. "I just don't want to lose you again. Where are you even trying to get to?"

"I'm not sure," Isabel answered, embracing him quickly. "But I promise I'll make it up to you. You can tell them I took the truck by force."

Henry rose, turning toward Ben, who had stood and was adjusting the tiny coat. "You still want those socks?"

Ben smiled and shook his head. "Thanks for the offer, but you've already been very kind. Thanks for the food and all, and I'm sorry about the mess." He swept his hand over the small mountain of wrappers beside his seat.

Henry felt for his glasses and cleaned them with the corner of his shirt, stepping towards the door. "Right, of course. The pickup's out back, just to your right as you go out the door, under the canopy."

Isabel was already halfway across the room, keys jingling in her hand. As Henry watched Ben follow her out, he was reminded what it is to feel truly helpless. He'd told her more than a few times she had too many smarts and not enough sense.

The small, black truck cruised just below the speed limit as it navigated its way through Echton, and Isabel was careful to choose the sleepiest side streets. When they reached the outskirts of town, she gunned the engine, and the ancient machine whined in protest and rattled violently.

"Go easy," Ben shouted over the wind coming through the cracks in the windshield.

Isabel punched the clutch and threw it back into sixth gear, her eyes fixed on the road. The bloodstains on Ben's shirt were a constant reminder that maybe she'd been right about Echton all along, that it wasn't what it seemed. *If the sheriff hadn't hesitated to hurt Ben, what would he do to her father, a man that might actually threaten him?*

"So you weren't born here? Where are you from?" Ben asked. Isabel shot him a quick glance, then pointed to her ear and shook her head.

"Where are you from?" he shouted.

"The east coast, far side of Maine," she shouted back. "We moved here when I was young, but I haven't been home in awhile."

"I've never been to Maine," Ben said as they took a sharp turn, sliding in the mud. "How did you get here?"

"Money, I guess," Isabel replied.

Ben furrowed his brow, drumming his fingers on the armrest and watching her feet as she shifted down.

"My father came here to run his business, said it'd be the perfect place to set up an office," she added. "I left three years ago to go to school."

"Great call on his part. What does he do?" Ben asked.

"Doctor. He's a doctor that thinks he's a private eye

sometimes," she frowned.

"Sounds like you're not far off. It's your detective work that got you locked up, yeah?"

"Mine and his combined, maybe. Between the two of us, we stepped into something. I wasn't sure at first, but the more I think about it, there's no way I did this on my own."

"Something big enough to lock you away for," he said.

"From what I heard, sounded like something they'd lost or were looking for," she shouted back.

"Must have been damned important."

She nodded and glanced in the rearview mirror. *I owe this guy at least some kind of explanation, but I can't explain what I can't put together myself.*

"Almost there now," she shouted. They pulled onto another side road and up a winding gravel driveway. As they neared the house, Isabel undid her seat belt and hopped from the cab before it'd even come to rest.

"Whoa, now," Ben said as he slid into the driver's seat and floored the clutch and break. When he looked up again, she was nowhere to be seen, but the door to the house was open, swinging in the breeze.

The more he saw of her life, the more he felt he was starting to understand Isabel. Even the house was like her, colorful and vibrating with life. Its peaks were covered with ornate gingerbread woodwork and immaculately painted, and its main walk was lined with perfectly spaced rose bushes. It was like nothing he'd ever seen, yet, neither was she.

"Isabel?" Ben said, as he walked inside, glancing around. "Ooph," he said to himself as he looked over the marble countertops in the kitchen and the leather furniture in the living room. "Isabel? Where are you?" He made his way up the stairs, finding nothing but empty rooms and a few open windows.

He finally found her in a large, blue room with an enormous bed at its center and a walk in closet at its far side. Isabel sat on the bed, the floral bonnet bunched up beside her.

"It took my father almost a year to fill this house. He and my mother were so careful with every color they wanted and piece of furniture they brought in the door," Isabel said, her words punctuated by the shutters as they bounced against the siding.

"The car's here, but no sign of either of them," she said. "Not even a trace." Ben frowned and sat beside her.

"I'm sorry, Isabel. I really am... but you have to leave. They could be here any minute," he said gently. "We shouldn't even be here now."

"They're gone. No sign of anyone. No note. It's like they were never even here."

"He was a smart guy, right? I'm sure he had a good reason for leaving," Ben leaned forward a little.

"Yeah, he is. I just don't like this, the sheriff, the mayor, the clerk-deputy-whatever. It's like the whole damn town."

Ben retrieved a stuffed bear that had fallen from the bed when he sat.

"Where would they have gone?" she said. "They wouldn't just leave me. Not like this."

Isabel's mother had gotten lost in the countryside once on the way back from her grandmothers, and her father hadn't slept or eaten until she'd returned. She remembered it still, Conrad pacing the house, muttering under his breath. Her mother had called from a pay phone to say she was spending the night in a motel, but it took Isabel an hour to convince her father not to go looking for her just to be sure she was safe.

"Maybe there's something you're missing. Think harder," Ben said, straightening the bow around the bear's neck. He laid his hands back in his lap after seeing the dirt streaks they'd left in their wake.

Isabel walked from the room and down the stairs, Ben following. Coming to rest in front of the grandfather clock just inside her parent's bedroom, she watched it for a moment, her eyes following the pendulum.

"My father used to say that clocks keep the best secrets," she said, tapping her fingertips on the clock's glass covering. Her father used to hide small things for her inside his pocket watch and ask her what time it was. Isabel still remembered his coming home from work and asking her how long he'd been gone. She would rush to his coat and take the watch from its pocket, flicking its front open to find a coin or a chain, sometimes a beautiful picture folded to fit inside it.

Looking over the clock, she noticed the corner of something white sticking out from floorboards beneath it. Isabel yanked the paper free, then skimmed over it and let it flutter back to the ground.

"Just a legal document, some kind of floor plan."

She tapped her foot, biting her fingertips as she mentally covered every hiding space she could think of.

"We can't just sit here," Ben said, his voice strained.

She reached out and gently opened the clock's front. With the other hand, she stopped the pendulum and ran her fingers along its back. Her fingers curled around it and moved down, working away at something. With a soft tearing noise, she pulled a thinly folded piece of lined paper from the arm of the pendulum and began to open it.

"Move!" Ben yelled.

Isabel froze, the paper about halfway unfolded when the first gunshot rang out, showering her in shards of glass and splintered wood.

SEVEN
VANISHING ACT

M cCreary woke with the sheriff's face inches from his, his acrid breath pouring over him.

"Get up," Hix snapped.

He struggled to his feet, using the bars to hoist himself up. Everything seemed so slow and fuzzy, and the throbbing pain in his face was nearly unbearable. *Where were they? What time was it?* His eyes rolled back in his head, and he stumbled before Hix caught the front of his shirt and jerked him upward, slamming him back against the cell.

"Where are they?"

"Where are who?" McCreary mumbled.

"Where are THEY?" Hix repeated.

McCreary hardly saw the hand that struck him, but the pain that stung the side of his face was very real.

"I don't know!" he said.

"That much is obvious, you twit. You had one simple

thing. What the hell happened?"

McCreary tried to pull himself together. Anything but the truth would work.

"There was another of them that came in here behind me and bashed my head against the bars." He pointed to the area of his face which felt the worst.

Hix grabbed him by the remnants of his hair and tilted his head back, inspecting the marks on this face. McCreary could smell whiskey and coffee on his breath, and see a fleck of something red on his collar. He tried to stop his eyes from darting about.

"I didn't know anyone followed me. I didn't hear a thing, I swear," he pleaded.

"Yeah, I bet you didn't." Hix released him with a shove and began to pace the room. "I want a badge on every bus and train station within 10 miles of here and send McCallister, Johns, and Kaine out to the Stanton place."

McCreary shuddered, trying to clear his eyes. He attempted to put his glasses on, removing them quickly to bend them back into some kind of shape and realizing one of the lenses was missing.

"I mean now!" Hix snapped. "Wake them up. Get them out here. I don't care what they're doing."

McCreary jumped, shuffling over to the desk and snatching up the phone. "Aaron Johns," he said into the receiver, his hands shaking.

When Hix heard a voice respond on the other end of the line, he threw the door open. "Tell them I'll meet them there," he barked, slamming it behind him.

McCreary went through the rounds, flipping through the Rolodex and tracing his finger over the map, hastily crossing off each location as it was assigned. He could afford to put a man on almost all of them. *North,* he was betting. *They'd have to go north because south was all hills and countryside. If the Stanton girl was running, she'd be going north.*

"And just wait there, look for Isabel Stanton or some kid with brown hair and a red plaid shirt," he said.

"Said there were three," a husky voice said from the other end of the line.

"And the third is an older man, black hair in uh…" he couldn't remember what he'd told the others. "I didn't really get a good look at him. I think he had brown trousers on."

He slammed the phone in its cradle, slumping in the chair and sighing deeply. Tilting the roster towards himself, he couldn't believe how many men Hix had left on duty, for something he fondly referred to as "a little border security." About half had been on for the meeting last night, that hellish meeting that would never end. So many questions about trial dates and if there'd been any news. It drove him mad. They were obviously guilty. Hix had spelled it out for him A-Z. It was painful that he couldn't tell them what he'd told McCreary already; they'd understand then. Seemed like everyone in the town had asked him about it, probably thought he was soft. He'd showed them; he'd keep his mouth shut tight.

McCreary rubbed his temples in tiny circles, stood and walked to the center of the room. From there, he could see the dust filtering through the hole in the wall and realized the iron bar was still on the floor where he'd dropped it. He snatched it up, looking around even though he knew he was alone. Casually, he walked to the edge of the cell and tossed it through the bars on top of the bed. He'd make a show of finding it later when Hix was there.

He wasn't sure if he was dying, or if the echo in his skull had just increased, but it was almost as if his entire brain was throbbing. He knotted up his brow, rocking as he scanned the ground for his lost glass lens. It irritated him more than ever that he was always on dispatch and the others only came in to file reports and bother him. They'd stumble in, reeking of liquor, and ask "how the good fight was". *Ignoramuses. It's not my fault the kid jumped me. All this desk work'll make a man soft.* McCreary ran his fingers along the barrel of the rifle Hix kept above the desk.

The jail was quiet, a nice quiet to calm his brain, and he started thinking about places he could lay down. Even a hard mattress like the one in the cell was starting to look tempting. He patted his pockets and jolted back into consciousness. *The keys are gone.*

"Shit," he murmured, rushing through the door and around the building.

The back door was still ajar, and as he pulled it open, he could see the pile of dust and mortar chips at the base of the wall. He quickly gathered any evidence that Isabel had ever been there and stepped outside, tossing a few apple cores and bread crusts far into the bushes behind the jail. McCreary looked for a few minutes but didn't see the slightest glimmer of the key set. *Little bastards made off with them.*

Back at his desk, he tapped a pencil against the dispatch reports, leaning back in his chair. For a moment, he lost his balance and nearly toppled backwards, then caught himself and sat upright. He'd have to sit there until

Hix got back, like a child being punished for something. He made himself busy, flipping back through the log book, pausing to total hours and do little calculations in their margins, but his bitterness continued to grow the more he thought about it. *All these hours, and he won't let me out for a single patrol. I'm a better cop that any of these Neanderthals.*

The town hadn't seen anything more than petty larceny and the occasional fight in ten years, Hix would so often boast. "Prevention not prosecution," he loved to say. He'd snap whenever McCreary made a comment about the budget or the amount of men he had on call. Hix told him it was his business to crunch the numbers, not to ask questions.

McCreary's mother used to say, "Work hard, and keep your head low." She'd been a seamstress, and his father had been a coal miner, born and raised in Echton. He'd made it this far, farther than they'd ever made it. After thirteen years working under Hix, questions were something he'd simply learned to put out of his mind. It seemed to work, so he wasn't going to fix it. He'd just wait until the man making those calls told him what was next.

EIGHT
FIGHT ANOTHER DAY

"Get down!" Ben shouted.

Isabel ran, crumpled bits of paper sticking out between her fingers. "Down here, c'mon!" she yelled over her shoulder.

Holes punched into the wall behind them as shots rang out, and she heard voices shouting outside the window. "They're headed down!" someone called out.

Isabel waited for Ben to get past her, then slammed the basement door and pulled the deadbolt. "Keep moving," she said, flipping the light switch on her way.

When he reached the bottom, Ben looked back at her, frozen halfway down the steps. "What are you waiting on?"

She held the paper up so he could see the small section missing from its middle.

"You can't be serious," he snapped.

She glanced from him back up to the door just as a bullet pierced its center, casting a beam of sunlight into the dusky stairwell. With a tremendous bang, another shot punched a hundred tiny holes around the handle of the small wooden door.

"Move!" Ben shouted. Isabel ran past him to a back corner of the basement. She grabbed the corners of a large cardboard box and started to drag it backwards.

"What're you doing? he said, silently cursing her.

"Help me!" she shouted back. He grabbed the box she was hauling and sent it skidding across the basement floor, then reached for another, sending it flying behind him until a tiny door in the corner of the room was unearthed. Isabel sprang forward and undid the latch on the door.

"This goes to the storm cellar," she said, throwing it open. She scrambled into the small space and motioned Ben to follow her.

As he backed into the crawlspace after her, he could hear the door at the top of the stairs splinter and swing open. Ben reached out and pulled one of the boxes closer, hoping to at least obscure the view of their escape route. He carefully pulled the door shut and shuffled backwards on his hands and knees.

When he emerged from the other side of the tunnel, he found Isabel perched high on the ladder, the top of her head holding the cellar door open a few inches.

"Clear?" he asked.

She dropped back down and shook her head. Ben paced from one end of the tiny room to the other, tearing the shelves apart, looking for anything he could use as a weapon. *There has to be something here, a gun, a knife, shit, even a rock would work.* Finally, he pulled a box open to find a short knife with a long, thick handle, then looked back to see Isabel peeking through the doors again. This time, she gave him a quick wave and pulled her slight frame through the opening. Ben took the ladder after her, the knife clamped in his teeth.

He charged into the open air, quickly falling in stride behind her. When they'd cleared the ground between the Stanton house and the woods, she stopped, and Ben struggled to slow his momentum, coming to a halt inches from her face. Stepping back, he watched her, her eyes welling with tears as she looked back at the tendrils of smoke rising above her home. She stumbled, her hands extended towards it.

"Come on. No house is worth dying for." Ben grabbed her arm and pulled her back upright.

She moved her mouth slowly and stared at the thickening smoke and climbing flames. With Ben's arm around her, he half pulled – half carried her into the forest. After a few minutes, he released her, but as soon as his hand left her arm, she stopped again, turning back towards the dark cloud that hung in the sky behind them.

He touched her shoulder lightly and tried to turn her towards him. "I'm sorry, Isabel."

She looked up at him, then back at the smoke.

"I'm sorry about your house, but we can't stay here.

"Don't tell me you're sorry! I don't even know you! she screamed. Isabel shivered violently, tearing his hand from her shoulder, her eyes beginning to well with tears.

She started to walk back towards the house, and Ben hesitated. *Maybe I should just let her go, let her do what she wants.* He cursed again, then ran ahead to catch her and planted himself directly in her path.

"What are you gonna do? You gonna fight them all?"

She looked past him, raising an absent hand to brush away a falling tear.

"Trust me. We have to keep moving," he said softly.

Isabel sniffled and turned the other way, avoiding his gaze. They walked in silence, except for the snapping of twigs and swishing of fallen leaves around their feet.

"Could probably use those socks now," Ben said as he felt his boots began to wear against his legs again. Isabel didn't respond; she kept her eyes locked on her feet and dragged her fingertips against the bark of the trees.

"Oak, ash, oak, oak, birch, elm," she whispered as they walked. After a few hours, they entered a small clearing, and Isabel grabbed Ben's sleeve.

"This should be far enough," she said, then took a few more steps and plopped down. As Ben watched her wrap her arms around her legs and pull them to her chest, he wondered how long it'd been since she'd eaten a proper meal. She looked so defeated, like a bird kept in a cage too long.

"Just wait here, ok? I'll be right back."

Isabel watched him go and started to rise. "I'm sorry I yelled. I can help - where are you going?" she said.

"It's fine. You sit, and I'll be right back."

Ben trotted off and returned a moment later with a small pile of kindling and larger sticks.

"Just enough to keep us warm," he said as he deposited them next to her. "I'll grab some more as soon as I find something to start this with - you see any rocks? This knife might make some sparks if we can hit it right."

She reached forward, her open hand extended towards him. Ben tugged the knife free from his waistband

and gave it to her. With a gentle click, Isabel popped the handle open, and a bundle of matches, a small compass, and a coiled length of wire were deposited into her palm.

"I'll be damned," Ben said.

"Survival knife," she added.

Ben thought it over for a moment, then decided it might be good for Isabel to have something to keep her mind occupied.

"Think you could get some more of this?" He jabbed a stick at the pile of wood he'd gathered.

"Right, no problem," she said, hopping up.

Isabel watched him disappear into the woods before she headed off in the opposite direction. She returned to their makeshift camp a few times, depositing as much wood as she could carry into the pile Ben had started. On her 3rd trip, Isabel decided they should be set for the night and settled back against a thick oak tree. Its bark was rough against her back, but it felt nice to rest for a moment. *Where is he?* she thought. *I'll just close my eyes for a second, just until he gets back.*

Isabel's eyes rolled and quivered behind their lids. Her mother was tending to the garden, quizzing her about the genus and species of the succulent they were planting. Her father had just pulled up in his black BMW, and she could hear the sound of his loafers sliding against gravel. Isabel ran to him and jumped into his arms, but she fell right through him and landed with a deafening gunshot. She woke, gasping for air, and felt someone holding her. Desperately, she clawed and screamed for help.

"Isabel! Isabel, it's me. Hey, it's Ben," the figure said. Its voice was gentle and soft. Isabel tried to focus, to control the heaving of her chest.

"What's going on?" she said.

"I'm not sure. I just got back, and you were kind of thrashing, so I woke you up," he answered.

"That's embarrassing." Isabel pulled herself upright and felt her cheeks flush.

"Just a bad dream," he said, getting to his feet. He walked to the edge of the clearing and grabbed his coat, smiling broadly. "Hungry?"

Isabel searched his face, unsure if he was simply teasing her or if he'd really found something. Ben lay the coat down and spread it flat, revealing a mound of red and purple berries.

"Where did you find these?" Isabel said as she lunged forward, grabbed a handful of wild raspberries and crammed them into her mouth. Ben grabbed a handful as well and set to work on it, tossing them up and swallowing them, one at a time.

"Since I found strawberries, I'm betting we can't be far from farm land, something had to drop them here. As for the raspberries, I kinda found those on accident." He pulled the leg of his pants taught to reveal a pair of bloody lines where the fabric had been ripped.

"My mom used to call it nature's barbed wire," she said gently. "Does it hurt?"

Ben shrugged and broke apart a few branches from the pile, laying their pieces across each other. He grabbed a match and struck it, cradling the flame as he slipped it under the dry leaves and twigs. A tiny pillar of smoke rose above it, and Ben blew on it gently until the smoldering pile was consumed by flame. Happy with his work, he tucked the rest of the supplies into the knife and set it beside the tree.

Isabel laid more branches on the fire while Ben settled himself across from her and shoved the last handful of berries into his mouth.

"So, what the hell have you got yourself into?" he said between chews.

"Couldn't tell you," she replied. "I've been at U of Maine for almost three years until a few weeks ago."

"I can see why you wouldn't come back."

"It's not my favorite place, but my folks live here." She paused. "It's not that I haven't wanted to. It's just that I haven't had the chance really. I picked a hell of a weekend to visit."

"Uh huh," he replied.

She gave him a little scowl, turning back to the fire.

"This seems too easy," he said warily.

"What's too easy?"

"This whole thing. They should be chasing us. I thought we'd be running again by now, maybe have just enough time to eat something and warm up."

Isabel shook her head, pointing into the distance. "This land preserve goes on for miles, in every direction around my house."

"So they're out looking for us - just not in the right place?" Ben exhaled into his hands, rubbing them together.

"Or just waiting for us to come out," she said. "Not that many ways out of Echton."

"That's comforting," he replied, kicking at a half-buried rock. *This girl is either very smart or very foolish. Either she knows the forest is too big for them to find us, or she's just too damned stubborn to keep moving unless someone's shooting at her.* "What did it say?" he added.

"Huh?" Isabel sat up, watching him through the fire.

"The paper from the clock - what'd it say?"

"You can see for yourself." She produced the note and handed it to him.

"It just looks like marked up gibberish," Ben replied, handing it back to her.

"Sorry, yeah, it's a code. A game my dad used to play with me. The code-key is my middle name, but getting through the translation is a little messy." Isabel looked up at Ben, his face blank. She smiled and angled the yellow paper so the fire illuminated its face, pocked with notes and lines from her deciphering work. "I'll translate, but there's something missing from that stupid hole."

"What's missing?"

"Well, it says they're going to Washington, I think? It's badly smudged. And to come there as soon as I can and stay there if they haven't reached it yet."

"Is that all it says?"

"There's something about waiting for me on the other side at the bottom of the note. I don't know. We have some distant family in Washington, but I can't remember their names," Isabel said, then folded the paper and tucked it away in her coat.

"Damn," Ben said. "Your family went across the country because you walked in on some kind of town meeting?"

"Like I said, that can't be it," Isabel replied. "There's gotta be something else."

"Your dad?"

Isabel shifted uneasily, pulling a leaf apart.

"Maybe he got involved in some things he shouldn't

have?" Ben added.

"Stupid creepy little town. I hate it," she spat. "I never liked it here."

Ben looked on solemnly and reached back for a few sections of wood. They were both quiet for a while, listening to the fire crackle and spit.

"I think there'll be time to hate Echton tomorrow, eh? How about a little sleep?" Ben said.

Isabel smiled and scraped some leaves into a makeshift pillow, while Ben carved out a section of ground for himself. She gazed at the starlight that leaked through the forest canopy until she heard his breathing slow, then pulled the flannel overcoat close around her head.

Her family was somewhere under those same stars, hopefully far from this place. Her father would be pacing the halls, worried sick about her and wracking his brain about whatever had driven them from Echton. It wouldn't be long until he'd be back. They'd be together soon, and her mother would hold her and curse and cry and make her promise never to leave the house again. It made Isabel realize how hasty she'd been be on her own, but at that moment, all she wanted was to be with them, in their arms.

The leaves crackled and rustled as Isabel turned towards the fire. She smiled a little, watching Ben there, his hands tucked behind his head and his mouth open just a little. With her eyes still on him, she dipped into the pocket of her jacket, cupped a golden coin between her hands and raised it to her face. A little past 9, deep in the Echton federal preserve, Isabel's eyes traced over a pointed metallic nose and sharp cheekbones, the lazy flicker of the fire shining on a maze she would soon navigate.

NINE
THE TRANSIENT HORIZON

B en woke early and had begun to stand when he realized his feet were completely numb. He gingerly massaged them through his boots, wiggling his toes and stretching them towards the smoldering remains of the fire. Isabel looked warm enough. She seemed so peaceful, curled into a ball under the enormous plaid coat. *Why do they always have to look so innocent when they sleep*? He wondered. Making every effort to be silent, he crept into the forest to gather whatever scraps of bark or branches he could find.

When he returned to the clearing, Isabel was sitting up, her hair a mess and everything from her neck down covered by the coat.

"I thought you'd left," she said.

"Just for a moment. You aren't rid of me yet," Ben smiled, unearthing a few embers and blowing on them. Isabel grinned, swatting a strand of hair out of her face.

"Alright then. You seem to have this figured out pretty well. What's the plan today, Mr. Richter?"

"Get the hell out of here."

"I can support that." Isabel poked an arm through the neck of the coat and scratched her head.

"We just have to find the best way to do that," Ben said as he coaxed the fire back to life. "There's a rail, west of here, I think. It's what I followed into town," he continued. "Once we get a little way from here, we can find somewhere to rest and eat, then go our separate ways."

"Makes sense," Isabel nodded solemnly. She grabbed the knife from its resting place by the fire and popped open the handle, setting the compass in her palm. "West," she said, pointing to her left.

"As good a direction as any," Ben said.

"You find any more berries?" Isabel asked, hopefully.

Ben looked over at her and smiled, tossing the rest of the wood scraps onto the growing flame.

"We get thawed out, then move," he replied, his hands hovering just above the fire and his feet almost resting inside it.

"Please don't ignite," Isabel said.

"I'll do my best," he laughed.

When the small fire had returned to ashes, Ben retied the laces on his boots and stomped out the embers, sending tiny red showers skittering across the ground. Isabel looked on, busying herself with the rest of the buttons on the coat and fishing the rocks from her shoes. Satisfied with his work, Ben carefully scattered leaves around the site to cover the blackened ground and the indentations where they'd slept.

"Like we were never here," Isabel said.

"That's the idea. Let's go. Faster we move, the faster we can eat something."

He took the survival knife from her, tucked it into the collar of his boot, and with the compass in his outstretched palm, they started their journey west. Isabel told him about her mother, how she used to plant the most beautiful gardens and people would come to see them from all over. Ben smiled and nodded, adding an occasional word to let her know he was listening. He could see how happy it made her to talk about her family or maybe just to have someone to talk to at all. *A bird kept in a tiny cage is bound to sing loudly when you let it free.* He smiled at his own analogy.

"What's funny?" she stopped to ask.

"Nothing, really. I was just thinking about a friend I used to have," he lied.

"Oh. Well, at my first house, we kind of had this maze in the yard. It was like a maze made of pine trees. When my mom first planted it," she dove into another story.

He was actually a little relieved that she wanted to talk, it gave him time to think, and he was tired of the sound of his own footsteps. As long as he could pay enough attention to answer the occasional question, he was in the clear. Ben kept his eyes peeled, searching the woods ahead and stopping sometimes to listen. He'd hold up his finger and Isabel would become quiet for a moment, then as soon as he continued walking, she'd resume her flow of stories.

"What about your family?" she asked. Ben stopped suddenly and looked into the dull blue sky.

"Are we stopping to listen again?" Isabel said.

He shook his head, then looked back at her.

"So what about your family? Where are you from? Isabel trailed Ben silently as he set off again.

"I don't really know my family," he finally said.

"Were you adopted?" she asked.

"My mom died when I was born, but I'm told she was a good woman. My Uncle Richard used to tell me stories."

"Stories about what?" she replied.

"She used to get in a fair bit of trouble I guess. Seems it was always for a good reason, though. Maybe the two of you would have been friends," he teased. Isabel grinned and snorted softly.

"I could probably use a few more friends. Some people I really don't get along with," she said. "What about your dad? Where's he?"

"That's a good question. If you find out, I don't really wanna know," Ben said. "Last time I saw him, I'd just turned 16. He left for Paris with his new girlfriend, Sharon or something. He told me I'd be alright without him. Probably was one of the only true things he ever told me."

Isabel frowned and snapped off a dead limb from an elm, dragging it against the trunks she passed with a soft click, click, click.

"I am. I'm just fine," he added.

"Ben?" she said.

"Yeah?" he replied, turning to face her as he walked.

She launched herself into his arms, the enormous coat sleeves slapping his back.

"I'm sorry," she said.

He laughed and quickly pushed her away, but she swore she felt a tiny wet spot where his cheek had pressed against her.

"I'm fine. Like I was saying, the bastard was right, I've been just fine." He paused and breathed deeply. "Thank you, though." Ben flashed a smile and dragged a sleeve across his face. "Nose is itchy, kicking up all this dust in the leaves or something."

She smiled too, kicking some leaves into the air.

"Like this!? Hey! I had a great uncle named Ben," she said, her eyes bright.

"Yeah? Tell me about him," Ben said.

They walked on through the forest for the better part of the morning, the frost melting around them as the sun climbed into the sky. Ben saw the field first. He waved back at Isabel and then pointed to the south where a sea of grain in the distance was dancing in the wind, a well-worn dirt road just beyond it.

"We keep walking in the tree line until we see train tracks," he added quickly. "I think we're close though."

"Gah, I hope so," Isabel moaned. "My feet are going to fall off. When we see my family in Washington, they better smother me in chocolate, or I'm gonna press charges for abandonment."

"How old are you?" Ben asked.

Isabel thought for a minute, ticking off years on her fingers and biting her tongue.

"Very funny," Ben smirked, navigating to a patch of solid ground. "So, like 83, 84 maybe?"

"22, nearly 23." She stopped, raising herself to her full height.

"Almost 23, eh? I think you're out of luck. The court would probably fine you for not supporting your parents. You're practically ancient," he said, bracing himself for the punch he knew was coming.

"Ancient?" she snapped.

"Do you hear that?" He froze suddenly and held his hand up.

"Hear what?" she whispered.

"I can hear you growing older."

Ben turned to the side, as Isabel's hand sailed harmlessly past his shoulder.

"Also, a train whistle, probably a mile ahead of us, maybe a little more, judging from how it sounds."

She put her hands on her hips and glared at him. "You're lucky there was good news in that sentence, or I'd take you back to town and leave you there," she said.

"You're gonna leave me at the jail?" he laughed. "Come on." He pointed towards the other end of the field. "Should be just past there."

Ben marched on silently with Isabel a few steps behind. The ground had grown soft from the sun's warmth, and their feet began to sink in with each stride, making a soft popping noise. Isabel stopped a few times to retrieve her shoes from the muck, running to catch Ben, but eventually she gave up and resigned herself to carrying them.

"You never told me where you're from," she said, carefully skirting a patch of saw grass.

"Born in some dirt clod town in Iowa. Just came from North Carolina but wasn't there long. I was in Detroit for a little while, a few years ago. I worked in a lumberyard for awhile. The money wasn't bad, and you sleep good at night.

"You sleep well," she said, then added, "What'd you do in a lumber yard?"

Ben glared at her and went on. "Mostly you stack and

restack onto trucks and lifts."

"Sounds like you were employed as a crane."

As they walked, Ben told her more about Detroit. He talked about the people there, and the new car lots that stretched for miles. Isabel listened as he explained how he'd quit his last job after he'd been shorted on his check for time he'd spent on sick leave and how he'd thrown a flat bar through the windshield of his boss's brand new car, something called an Aries. Isabel couldn't really picture herself doing the same, but she decided that at least she could respect the sentiment.

When the tracks came into view, they both quickened their pace, moving just behind the tree line until the very last bit of cover. At the edge of the forest, Ben stopped, raising his arm in front of Isabel.

"Wait. When we break the cover of the trees, we're gonna be really easy to spot if anyone's looking for us. So this has gotta be quick."

"So we run?"

"It's probably another 100 yards to the road and 200 yards past that to the station," he said.

"I'd say we're just about in Reinersville from the look of those buildings." Isabel paused, peering at the structures beyond the field.

"Yeah, it looks like we're about to rejoin the modern world, ideally with fewer lunatics," Ben replied.

"Or at least different kinds of lunatics," Isabel replied. They crept to the edge of the forest and looked beyond it to the dark grey line that would take them to freedom.

"Ready?" Ben said.

"No?"

He took off at a sprint, slowing to a brisk walk as he reached the road. Isabel caught up a few seconds later, clapping her shoes against each other, sending tiny chunks of mud flying. She smiled at Ben, who'd secured an arm over his face to protect himself from the mud showers.

"Keep your head down, ok?" he said from the shelter of his coat sleeve. She nodded silently and pulled her collar higher around her neck. He did the same, buttoning his coat up to its top and tugging a group of burrs from his pant leg. When they reached the station, Ben frowned, looking through the crowd at the station.

"This isn't gonna be easy. Lot of people here. We'll have to jump it a little farther down the track," he whispered.

"Jump it? I'm not jumping anything," Isabel said.

"You gonna pay for our tickets? Because I sure I don't have any money."

"Not yet," Isabel said, slipping away into the crowd.

Ben kept his head bowed, constantly pulling the corners of his coat up to hide his face. He swore for a minute that he saw that deputy he'd hit. Someone tugged at the back of his coat, and he whirled around, one hand up to protect his face and the other cocked back.

"Don't start anything you can't finish," Isabel said, an enormous grin playing across her face. She stepped in close and pressed a small wad of bills into his hand. "Will you get our tickets, darling?" She leaned forward, daring him to tell her no.

"Yeah-fine," he mumbled.

As he made his way up to the counter, Ben realized that he didn't really have any experience buying railroad tickets. He couldn't remember the last time he'd paid to ride a train or ridden in a vehicle intended for people. He quietly stepped into the ticket line and tried to read the tiny lettering above the window. Skimming through the rows of arrivals, he spotted a 12:15 to Boulder.

"That'll do," he muttered, stepping up the counter.

"Can I help you?" the attendant said, flipping her hair around her finger.

"Yeah, uh, the 12:15 to Boulder."

"Just you?" she asked.

"Ah, sorry. Two tickets, please."

"36 dollars." With a sharp pop, her gum exploded and receded into her mouth.

Ben fumbled with the bills, peeling off thirty dollars from the money Isabel had handed him. He'd ask her about the money later. *She must have been hiding it in her dress or underwear or something.* He drummed his fingers on the counter, skimming over the notices beside the window until his eyes came to rest on a face that looked a little like Isabel's.

"Wanted for Murder and Assault of Law Enforcement," the headline on the sheet read. When he really thought about it, the woman on the right side of the sheet was a dead ringer for Isabel, and her "accomplice," as he was listed, was a poor rendition of what could have been him. Strangely enough, there was a third man at the bottom of the sheet with a broad, flat nose and small, beady eyes. He was listed as accessory to their escape and guilty of assaulting an officer.

"OK, you're all set, sir." The attendant slid a pair of thick yellow tickets across the counter. Ben bit his lip. It had to be them, small red letters just below the headline read "Echton Township Sheriff's Dept." He scanned over the print at the bottom of the notice, his pulse quickening.

"Sir?" she repeated, her voice growing sharper.

Ben forced a quick smile, grabbed his change and the tickets and headed back to the platform where Isabel was waiting for him.

He handed her a ticket, and they stood together, hands in their pockets and eyes on the ground. He debated telling her, but thought it better to wait at least until they were moving. They watched a train pull into the station, and Ben checked his watch, just a few minutes after noon, Colorado was only a few steps away. Bodies surged forward as a conductor stepped from the train and announced the first boarding call. He tapped Isabel and motioned to the newly formed lines.

"I like that coat," a voice said from behind him. "You borrow that from a friend? It looks familiar."

We were so close, Ben thought, his chin tucked down until it was almost touching his chest.

"Shame you got it all muddy. How'd you get that mess all over your coat?" the man said.

This time Isabel noticed as well. She grabbed Ben's sleeve and turned slowly to look back at the man's legs and the holster that hung from his belt, letting out a tiny squeak. Ben felt his arms and legs tensing under the pressure of Isabel's grip, his hands clenched.

"Turn around slow. There won't be no trouble," the man said. The passengers had all but disappeared from the platform, and the conductor was calling out the train's departure. Ben grunted as the nose of a gun dug into his back. He turned to Isabel and mouthed a single word.

"What's that? Didn't quite catch it," the man snickered.

Ben turned slowly, lowering his right hand to his hip. The train started to slide away from the platform, screaming its departure.

"Nice and easy, keep them hands where I can see them," the man said. He wasn't particularly tall, but well built around the shoulders with a ragged beard and short black hair. His charcoal coat was flared out where his hand held the gun, a bronze star shining on his chest. *Sheriff Hix must run a pretty tight operation,* Ben thought.

The man motioned him forward and Ben followed, Isabel watching him carefully. He took a slow step, then lunged and brought his hand down on top of the gun, firing a bullet into the ground and dragging the man forward, then sent his other hand crashing into his face.

The man was still for a moment, his chest dotted with blood that now streamed from his nose, then wavered, stumbling. Before the echo from the gunshot had died, Isabel and Ben were sprinting down the platform.

"The other side! The other side!" Ben shouted over the churning of the train's wheels.

The end of the orange railcar exploded in a shower of sparks, leaving a shining grey crater where his head had just been. Two more hits, both to his left, even the gunshots were drowned out by the deafening roar of the train as it picked up speed. Ben grabbed Isabel by the collar, pulled her to the right side of the car and pointed at an iron bar that protruded from its side.

"We have to jump!" he screamed in her ear.

The train's wheels were picking up speed, and he knew they'd lose it soon if they didn't get a hold on something. Ben sprinted ahead and grabbed the bar, swinging himself up over the railing and onto the thin platform that connected the cars. "Isabel, come on, faster!" he shouted, leaned over the rail.

Her eyes wide, they flashed from the roiling machine parts to the tracks behind her and to Ben on the platform. With the wheels rumbling and surging at her feet and the wind screaming in her ears, Isabel Stanton held her breath, jumped, and missed.

TEN
BROKEN PARTS AND HELPING HANDS

There are two ways to do things, Fredrick Smalls thought. *You can bide your time and let them fall into place or drive them in with the hard part of your head, and it's only a matter of time before something breaks.* As he watched a string of black cars pull through town, he wondered if Sheriff Hix had ever considered the first. Something about their familiarity was unsettling. Being so early in the day and after the town meeting last night, he couldn't help but wonder where they were headed.

His father had been furious with him for coming back after he'd worked so hard to get him out of Echton. He'd bought the bus ticket, offered to pay for the rent and everything else if Fredrick would just move somewhere else. Henry had done just about everything except carry him there himself. He never fully explained why, just said there were better things for Frederick – other things.

"I don't know." Henry would pace in front of the kitchen window, his hands clasped behind his back. "Your mother would have wanted more for you."

It was the worst excuse. Fredrick couldn't stand it when his father would mention his mother. He hardly remembered her, but in a fit of anger, Henry had once yelled something about her leaving them both to live in a big city. They'd never spoken about it again, and from his side, that was fine. She was gone, and it didn't really seem like she'd given a second thought to him, so he wasn't about to lose any sleep over her. It seemed like something his father would always bring up but never wanted to talk about.

"I want you to go to a good school, get a good education," Henry would say.

His persistence seemed strange to Fredrick-- on the borderline of obsession. Yet, after a while, he was convinced and moved south to Memphis. The irony of the whole thing was that he ended up flunking out of the school he'd been accepted to and took a job with a milling company, the same kind of work he'd have taken in Echton. Henry sounded less than enthusiastic but seemed to take it alright when Fredrick told him the news.

"At least it's a change of scenery," he said.

The work wasn't so bad, and the pay was good. So, he saved his money and waited, with time leftover to learn about the engines in the mill. Fredrick even tried his hand at picking up French from a man named Bernard who ran the shop until one crisp Autumn morning when the phone by the front door rang a dozen times before Bernard snatched it up, and after a moment, extended it towards him.

"From a car accident?" Fredrick said, the receiver

creaking under the pressure of his grip. That afternoon he put in his notice to the foreman and was on his way home before the paperwork was on file, a blur in a beat up pickup he'd been working on. He barely made it, the car choking and sputtering the whole trip, but by midnight he was pulling into their driveway.

Despite his insistence, Henry needed someone to take care of him, and Fredrick knew it. His arm was broken, his collarbone shattered, and the bruising around his face was horrendous. When Henry had become more stable, Fredrick offered to help out around the shop and thought he'd even take a crack at putting the car back together for when his old man was well enough to drive.

He went to sheriff Hix to ask where the car had been taken but was told by a man named McCreary that it'd already been scrapped because the damage was too extensive and that a check for the parts would be mailed to him. When he mentioned it to his father, Henry's face grew pale and his gaze distant. Fredrick had always found Hix to be a strange man, but never really had any reason to cross him. At his father's urging, he wasn't going to start then. With the help of one of his father's friends, a thin woman whom Henry called "Aunt Kathryn," he finished replacing the parts on the pickup with the rest of the scrap money and decided it would suit them just fine.

A few days after Fredrick finished the truck, he'd awakened to the sound of his father's voice in the hallway. He thought he'd imagined it, but after a moment, realized he wasn't dreaming. The voices moved away towards the front door, but he caught a little of the conversation as he quietly rose and tiptoed towards the living room.

"Thanks for your cooperation. Pity about your accident," a low, gruff voice said.

"Tell your boy we said welcome home and to keep his nose clean," another added.

Fredrick walked into the dining room just as the front door closed and found his father propped up in an armchair, turning something in his hand that reflected the flicker of the TV. "Who's here?" he said.

"Jesus," Henry started, clutching at his chest. "No one. Too hot to sleep so I had the TV on and thought I heard somethin', so I went outside a minute."

Fredrick scratched his head, peering at the object as Henry fumbled with it, but his father quickly slipped it into his pocket and began to teeter back towards his room.

"Sorry if it was a bit loud. I'm alright, son." Henry pulled him into an embrace as they passed, holding him for just a moment longer than usual.

It all got Fredrick to thinking, and he tried to put it together in his head as he settled back into bed, but as he played it over and over, he realized he had no clue what had been real and what hadn't, so he closed his eyes and tried let it go. He soon forgot about that strange night as a week turned into a month, a year, five years, and frail as Henry was, Fredrick continued to make new excuses to stay. The evening the caravan rolled through, Fredrick was checking a filter on that old truck, cursing under his breath.

"Burns oil as fast as gas," he called to Henry, who'd settled into a rocking chair on the porch, a cigar burning in his hand.

"Scrap," Henry called back. "If you'd let me buy a new one, you could stop pissin' with it."

Fredrick waved him off and looked up as the cars sped by, his eyes coming to rest on something that had been tossed from the last car and landed, smoldering, beside their driveway. Something about the casual flick of the cigarette reminded Fredrick of that night, so long ago. There was something that made him uneasy about any man who played with fire so casually.

ELEVEN
TANGENTS AND TRICKS

It was in the way Ben's eyes narrowed when she jumped, Isabel knew immediately that the train was moving too fast and the rail was too far above her. He threw himself forward, clamping his hands around her wrists and yanking her up towards him. With his body bent across the railing of the car, he braced his legs against the platform and tried to steady his feet. With a quick jerk, he pulled her over the side of the rail, then wrapped an arm under her and let her down against the railing. She stared forward, her eyes wide and body rigid, taking short, rapid breaths. Ben crouched down beside her and softly laid his hand on her arm.

"It's alright. Everything's ok," he said, shouting over the roar of the train's wheels.

The floor beneath them shook and groaned as the train took a long, winding turn. Ben laid a hand against his brow to shield his eyes from the wind, watching the trees fly by as the train roared around the bend. Suddenly, he heard laughing. It took him a moment to realize it, but Isabel was laughing hysterically at his feet. He wasn't sure what was so funny, but couldn't help but join her. His whole body felt numb.

"You alright?" he shouted.

She nodded, feeling her face with her fingertips and looking over her legs and arms. Ben stood and tried the handle of the train car, jiggling it open and slipping half-way inside.

"Come on!" He pushed the door the rest of the way open. The inside of the car was stacked high with long wooden crates, stamped "PRODUCE" in faded red letters. They carefully navigated the rows of boxes, finding a small opening near its center and settling themselves on the floor. Ben stared hard at Isabel, a smile still lingering on her lips.

"What?" he said.

"That was amazing! He had the gun, and you hit him, and we were running, and he tried to shoot, but the train -" she stammered. "Just, did that really just happen?"

She shook her head and lay back, propping herself up on the rough wooden floor. They sat in silence, both settling into the luxury of the solid ground beneath them, embracing the warmth of the train compartment. Hidden between the rows of crates, her legs resting against Ben's, she couldn't help but close her eyes for a little while. She felt like she belonged on that train, melted into the cracks in the floor-boards, somewhere between urgency and exhaustion.

Ben rolled his neck and cracked it. He knew he had to tell Isabel about the notice at the train station before they split, but he didn't know how. She wasn't used to getting her hands dirty, that much seemed obvious, but she seemed resilient, tough enough to sleep on the ground and eat wild food. He flexed his feet against the crate they rested on and watched her, her chest rising and falling gently.

"Isabel?" he said softly. She stirred. He scratched his nose and glanced around the compartment. "You awake?" he said a little louder, this time watching carefully. She looked so frail when she wasn't moving. Ben thought for a moment, then spoke.

"I think you're asleep, but I'm gonna say this anyway. It's just – I'm sorry for whatever happened to you, and you're gonna be ok." He draped his coat over her legs and sat upright, trying to distract himself from the pain in his face and sides.

Ben walked the narrow aisle they'd first stepped into, looking over the tops of the boxes and rapping his knuckles against them. He came to a short, square crate near the edge of the compartment and shook it. Removing the knife from his boot, he wiggled it under the lid of the box and carefully pried its corner up, pulling the loose nail from its top. He repeated the process on the next corner, then pulled the lid free to reveal a field of smooth green apples.

"Beautiful." He pulled an apple from the box, turned it over in his hand, and sliced a piece from it, savoring its tartness. When he'd finished, he tossed the core casually behind him, sending it skipping across the tops of the crates. Ben grabbed an armful of apples and returned to find Isabel. He found her glaring at him violently, a neatly sliced apple core in one hand, the other wiping apple juice from her face.

"Sometimes birds drop those - it's how apple trees

get all over the place," Ben said, struggling to keep the corners of his lips from rising.

Isabel made a sour face, whipping the apple core at his head. It bounced harmlessly off his shoulder and landed in his hand.

"If it were up to me, birds would drop you somewhere," she snarled. Isabel knew she couldn't act mad much longer, that she'd break and laugh, so she gave Ben a final glare and tucked her head into her knees. He tossed the core to the side and lowered himself down beside her, slicing a piece of apple off and offering it to her.

"How about a forgiveness bribe?"

Isabel grabbed blindly for the apple slice, head still tucked into her arm.

He pulled it out of her reach and clucked softly. "Can't eat what you can't see."

She raised her head and did her best to muster a fierce glare but laughed instead and snatched the fruit from his hand. They finished the apples quickly and set about searching the rest of the compartment. Sifting through a few dozen boxes, each lid was pried open and set back in place.

"I'm gonna die if I have to eat another apple," Isabel groaned when they opened the sixth box of green fruit.

"I don't think we have much choice, Izzy," Ben said flatly, setting the lid back in place.

"Don't call me that," she said, finishing another apple and tossing the core to the far end of the compartment.

"Nice choice of cars – Izzy," Ben sunk the knife into an apple and raised it up to eye level.

"What do you think we'll -" Isabel started, but Ben held a hand up.

"Hear that?"

Isabel shook her head.

"I don't hear anything," she whispered.

"I disagree," he replied, moving to the door of the compartment. "We're slowing down."

"That was fast," Isabel said.

"We're not there. It's only been a few hours. We're maybe on the west side of Indiana at best," he replied, glancing back at her. She was watching him too, a half dozen apples balanced in her lap. "We're probably stopped to detach cargo that stays here or gets transferred," he continued, "Which is...usually the last few cars on the train."

"Like the one we landed in," she finished his thought.

Isabel walked over and stood at his side, her ear pressed to the wall beside his. A tremor ran through the floorboards, and she grabbed for the crate beside them.

"Careful," Ben said, catching her other arm.

She nodded quickly, and both strained their ears against the train car's sudden calm. The wheels had completely stopped, and it was quiet for a long while, broken only by the sound of an engineer's voice, pacing outside the cars. The compartment shook again, this time more violently, and threw them into the wall. They regained their footing as they felt the car move beneath them begin to roll, come to a sudden stop, and shake again.

"What's going on out there?" Isabel whispered.

"I have a suspicion, but we really won't know until we get out there."

"Get there? Get where? You mean Colorado?"

"Yeah, maybe Colorado," Ben whispered back.

"What?"

He held a finger to his lips and shook his head.

Isabel followed him back to the clearing in the boxes and hunkered down, her back against a tall, dark brown crate. They waited silently until the rhythm of the wheels began to accelerate. Settling back down, Isabel leaned back, groaning weakly, her hands on her legs.

"You hurt?" Ben said.

"Just sore, I think," she whined. "I don't know."

Ben leaned forward, pulling her foot toward him.

"What're you doing?"

"Wait," he said, tugging her shoe off and smoothing his palms against the bottom of her feet, rolling them in small circles. She inhaled sharply, trying to relax the rest of her body.

"Amazing you don't have any blisters," he said, examining her toes. "Give me the other one."

"I normally just don't wear shoes." She started to replace her shoe, but he tapped her hand and shook his head.

"Leave those off for as long as you can," he said and laid his jacket over her legs. "The other foot," he repeated.

She complied, resting her left calf on his thigh. Ben slipped the other shoe off and wrapped his hands around her foot, beginning to work the knots from it.

"Where did you learn that?" she said, her eyes following the tiny circles his thumbs made. Ben tucked the jacket over her other foot and smiled.

"A woman I knew in Gainsville used to do that for me when I couldn't stand anymore."

"Someone you were seeing?" Isabel asked.

"A doctor that worked for a guy I used to work for. She was supposed to fix us up so we could meet quota," he spoke softly. "More expensive to replace a worker than to try to fix one and send him back out."

"Oh...well, it's being put to good use now," Isabel said.

Ben did his best to smile, realizing that hearing about ancient problems of his was probably the last thing Isabel needed at the moment. He sighed and straightened his back against the crate.

"Don't worry about it," he said. "I probably got you in more trouble than the help was worth."

"I don't know if I could have been in any more trouble," Isabel replied, twirling an apple stem between her fingers.

Ben grimaced and took a deep breath.

"What?" Isabel said.

"At the train station," he started, knotting the fabric of his coat between his fingers.

She leaned forward, waiting for him to continue.

"There was a warrant."

Isabel gasped sharply, grabbing his sleeve and pulling him a little closer. "For my dad? What did it say?"

Ben let his head back against the crate.

"It wasn't for your parents."

Her face grew blank, then contorted in rage. "That dirtbag! You can't be serious. A warrant for what?"

Ben shrugged and held his hands up. "It was for both of us, and some other guy I'd never even seen before. Maybe I read it wrong. I don't know. I was in a hurry."

"Ben, what did it say?" she snapped.

"Murder," he blurted out.

Her jaw dropped; her knuckles, drained of their color, clenched against the bright red of the plaid coat.

"Murder?" she yelled.

Ben moved in a flash, his hand clamped over her mouth. His voice was steady but firm.

"You need to be smarter than this. We don't know where we are or who's in the next compartment of this train. I need you to be smart, or we are both going to jail or worse. Nod if you understand." She nodded, her eyes moist. He gently pulled his hand away from her face and sat back against the crate. "I'm sorry, Isabel. You just don't know."

She watched him for a moment, then turned away, her shoulders shaking. Ben felt a weight growing in his stomach. Isabel was the first girl he'd met in awhile, but in the back of his mind, he knew that if he was going to help her, even for a little while, he might have to hurt her feelings a little. He reached a hand towards her, but then pulled it back, holding it to his chest.

"Maybe we should both get some rest and have some time to think," he said. Isabel pulled her knees to her chest and tucked the tails of the coat under her feet.

"I'll take first watch," he added.

Ben sat, watching the gravel flash through the cracks of the floorboards. He thought about Isabel's family somewhere in Washington. Well, maybe they were in Washington, maybe somewhere a lot worse. He couldn't see a point in even suggesting it; it wouldn't matter either way. He knew the girl with the bright green eyes was totally lost. He could see it in the way her head was bowed. *It's not my problem, and she'll probably have a better chance of making it if we're apart. The warrant is for both of us together.*

He wasn't sure what to make of her. *Was she the girl who'd cried and paced her cell, screaming for his help, or the girl that nearly insisted on going back into gunfire for a scrap of paper? People are seldom a single way,* he thought. *It just depends on how things hit them.*

Isabel tapped his arm. "You sleep, I'll watch," she said. Her eyes were bloodshot, and her face looked drained. Ben wondered if she'd slept at all. He turned on his side and looked up at her.

"If we stop again, we need to get off. It won't be long until they open this car to inventory it," he said. "That'd be a little hairy."

Isabel brushed her hair out of her eyes and nodded. Ben checked his watch, *maybe five or six hours they'd been onboard. If they were lucky, they'd be west of Missouri by now. The further from Ohio, the better.* He closed his eyes and tried to clear his mind, let it all slip away. The train was an old friend, and he welcomed it as it rocked him to sleep.

Isabel's mind had been racing for hours. She hadn't slept, just closed her eyes; she doubted she would until she was with her family again. She kept going over what she knew and trying to put it all together. *There was a warrant out for her arrest, for murder. No doubt it'd been Hix that issued it.* Maybe it hadn't been so bad at first, but once he'd kept her without charges or bail, she knew there was no turning back. *What am I missing?* All she remember hearing in the conversation was something about record keeping and something that was lost and had to be taken care of. She wracked her brain. *A problem that had been taken care of.* The words refused to leave her mind.

Is it my father they want, or do they think I heard something, or was it both? Isabel looked over at Ben, watched his eyes flit about under their lids, restless as he always seemed. *If her father had heard something, it might explain why they took her, but why hadn't they taken them both and thrown them in together? And why had he left without her?* Isabel mulled over the same questions in her mind, again and again, until she felt nothing; it all added up to nothing. She had to get to Washington and find her parents. That much was clear. It was really the only thing that was clear.

Her fingers traced over the face of the coin she'd taken from Henry when they'd said goodbye. *It was strangely heavy, and somehow connected to all of this*, she suspected. She'd noticed him fingering something in his pocket when he was speaking to the man in the other room, and remembering Ben's mention of a coin, couldn't help herself. It had something to do with Ben or the reason he was there. There was no way to know if it was the same coin, but it seemed too big a coincidence.

Isabel woke with a start. She frantically scanned the room and found Ben still sleeping next to her. Then it struck her, they weren't moving. The ground under the floor wasn't a white-grey streak anymore, but a thousand tiny gravel pieces. She grabbed Ben's coat and shook him awake.

"What?" he groaned.

"Ben, we're not moving anymore. The train's stopped."

"Not moving," he repeated, his eyes shooting open. They both rose and tip toed to the end of the car.

"We gotta scram before they throw open that big door," Ben whispered. He curled his fingers around the edge of the door they'd entered and slid it open, peering into the dusk.

"Come on." He pulled her outside the car. Ben came down with a soft crackle as the rocks gave way under his feet, Isabel landing just behind him. They both froze, trying to take in their new surroundings.

A woman's voice in the distance called out: "Those two freights are in, C14 and C18."

"Yes, ma'am," another voice answered her.

The sound of footsteps grew closer, then a loud clank and the grinding of iron against iron. The car they stood behind rolled backward a few inches, then came to rest. Ben mulled over his choices, forest to his back, and it looked like three more lanes of track beyond the one at their feet. The air was warm and dry. *Arizona maybe?* He wondered.

"Follow me, quiet as you can, ok?" Ben whispered.

Isabel walked a half-step behind him as he navigated the length of the car, carefully stepping between rail ties. They paused at its end, seeing two open lanes and then another line of railcars. A breeze rustled the brush behind them, and Isabel noticed, for the first time, the ringing in her ears. Ben's warm hand closed around her arm, urging her forward.

"Keep up."

"Sorry," she murmured.

They reached the next row of cars and slipped into the shadows between them.

"Twenty feet, maybe," Ben whispered. He paused to listen to the voices from down the line, giving Isabel a tap on the leg.

"Go."

She rolled over the coupling between the cars and took to running as fast as she could, then waited for him on the other side. He was close behind her, catching up as they ducked through a side door, to a room stacked high with wooden signs. Racing past stack after stack of them, she followed Ben until he threw open another door and they were in some kind of reception area, its walls lined with ancient armchairs.

"This way," Isabel said, leaning to her left. He followed until they cleared a door that deposited them into the front lot of the building.

"Good call on going left," Ben panted.

Isabel shrugged and smiled, falling into stride beside him. They put a little more distance between themselves and the depot they'd just slipped through, but paused a few hundred yards up the road.

"Where are we?" she said.

"I'm not sure," Ben replied. "It looks like a decent sized city, though."

From where she stood, she could see a dirt road that continued for a few hundred yards, then gave way to pavement. Hundreds of lighted windows shone in the distance above rows of well manicured trees. Isabel and Ben shed their coats, set off towards the city, and soon found themselves between rows of apartment buildings and shops.

"Is this The West?"

"Something like that. I haven't been out here much, but it definitely matches what I've heard," Ben replied, kneeling to grind a pinch full of sand between his fingertips. He swung his arm in a wide arc, tracing the skyline. "All those people crammed in together. Pretty wild, huh?"

"I've only seen pictures," Isabel replied. "Summers in Echton get hot, but not like this, especially at night."

"I don't think Echton counts as a city," Ben laughed. "What's next in your master plan?"

"I'm starved," Isabel said.

"Yeah, the apples didn't exactly do it for me, either."

"How about that?" she asked, pointing to a neon-lit storefront a few blocks ahead. "KT's Cafe."

Ben pulled the money from his pocket. "Dinner's on me." He waved it at her.

"You mean on me?" Isabel replied, snatching it from him.

"Mind if I borrow a little of that?" he asked.

"For services rendered." She split the stack and handed him half of it, grinning as she added a little curtsy.

"So how'd you get it? Hidden in your clothes somewhere? I figured the sheriff would've searched you when he brought you in."

Isabel hopped onto the base of a light post and swung around it. "One of them did. It was disgusting." she shivered and hopped down.

"So where's the money from? Your house?"

"Found it at the station," she grinned, her eyes running along the rooftops as they walked.

"You found it?"

"In a few people's wallets."

Ben shook his head in disbelief, chuckling to himself. *You're just full of surprises, aren't you?* Isabel surprised Ben again that night, polishing off half of a roasted chicken, mashed potatoes, a plate full of vegetables, and nearly half a pie. He sat, watching her, chewing his turkey sandwich thoughtfully.

"Do you have a newspaper?" he asked the waitress. She brought the morning's paper to him with Isabel's third slice of peach pie, piled high with whipped cream.

"Monday, October 28th," he read aloud. "Reagan

seems to have done A-ok in the last debate and we are, in fact, somewhere in Oklahoma. I'm guessing Tulsa. He flattened the paper and pointed to the header, which read "Oklahoma Gazette."

"Tulsa, nice," she said between mouthfuls.

"There are probably about a million busses a day that run from here out towards California, and if you can get out there, it'll be a cinch to get up to Washington," he added.

Isabel paused, setting her fork down.

"Where are you gonna go?" she said.

"I'm not sure. Maybe down to Texas. I heard they've got a labor shortage down there." Ben pulled absently at the hair on his chin. Isabel furrowed her brow and slouched down in her booth.

"What about the warrant?" she whispered.

"Hell, that picture didn't even look like me, and they don't have my name either." He crossed his arms and leaned back.

"What about me?" she asked, her voice even lower.

Ben looked into her eyes. "You're gonna be fine, Isabel. As soon as you find your family, you'll call the police or whoever and get it all straightened out."

"I'm sure you're right, I'll be OK – I just have to get to Seattle, that's all."Isabel faked a smile and sat back, tapping the fork against her plate.

Ben did his best to keep his face blank, but his chest ached. He kept telling himself: *She's not your responsibility; don't get involved; don't get involved. She's going to be fine.*

"Ready?" he said. "I'll help you find a bus."

Isabel threw a final forkful of pie into her mouth and nodded emphatically. She counted out a 40 percent tip while Ben asked the waitress about a station in the area.

It was a quarter to 8 when Ben helped Isabel buy a pair of tickets, one to Santa Fe with a transfer to Santa Clarita, and a separate ticket to Amarillo. The bus depot was nearly deserted, just a few sleeping passengers on benches and a man in the ticket booth. They sat and talked for a long time, joking in hushed tones about their camping trip and the hospitality of the Echton City Jail. It was the first time he'd had a chance to explain how he'd ended up there, and she agreed that he'd come into some pretty terrible luck.

"Got all your luggage?" Ben said.

"I think I've got everything I came with." She slapped the ticket against her open palm.

"I've gotta take off in a few minutes here." He checked his watch again. Isabel glanced up at the station clock.

"I'll be ok," she smiled.

"You sure?" he said.

"Totally sure." They looked on into the darkness until the high beams of a greyhound bus came around the bend and idled into the station. The word Amarillo shined in neon on its front. Ben stuck his hand out, and Isabel took it gently.

"It's been a pleasure, Isabel Stanton, and I hope you find your family."

"It's been a pleasure, Ben Richter. I hope you find whatever it is you're looking for." She squeezed his fingers and smiled. With a final glance, she watched Ben disappear around the corner, and a few minutes later, heard the Greyhound's diesel engine roar and watched its lights fade into the distance. *This is ridiculous,* she thought, *how can you miss someone you've only known for two days and has only been gone for five minutes?* Yet, as the air cleared, Isabel wondered where Ben Richter was and if he was thinking about her too.

She checked the clock again, 10:30. She had almost seven hours until her bus would leave for Santa Fe. Her footsteps echoed softly as she headed back into the city, passing rows of shops, closed for the night. She'd pause, peering inside their windows at beautiful dresses, and new appliances, tags dangling and turning lazily in their cases.

After an hour or so, she decided she'd go back and try to get a little sleep. For a nice tip, she was sure the desk clerk would promise to wake her up in time for her train. Isabel knew she couldn't be that far from the station, maybe 15 or 20 city blocks.

As she set off, she noticed that her footsteps sounded strange against the buildings, like they were multiplying. *It's only an echo. Don't let your imagination run away with you.* She paused to get her bearings. *North until I hit Lance Boulevard, then a right,* she recited. When she started to walk again, she heard another pair of footsteps begin that nearly matched her own. She shook her head. It was certainly something she was imagining.

Isabel stopped again. This time the footsteps kept going, a soft scuffing against the pavement. It seemed like they were growing closer. Isabel started to walk faster, as did the footsteps. She finally broke into a run, cutting through a side alley. If her memory served her right, she was only a few blocks from the station. She was in a full sprint when she noticed a dark shape looming ahead of her.

She skidded to a halt, taking a quick left behind another set of buildings and ran straight into an aluminum fence stretched across the alleyway.

"No, no, no," she said, whirling around to find the shadow standing in the opening she'd slipped through.

"Lost?" a gruff voice asked.

"No, I'm alright, thank you," Isabel said, trying to push past the man. He was fairly large, and in the moonlight, she could see a scar across his neck and a thick head of blonde hair. He extended a hand towards her.

"Come on now, love. We can still be friends." A withering smile crept across his face. "That's a nice dress. You got a purse to match that?"

Isabel tried again to push past him, but he grabbed her by the back of the neck and threw her to the ground. She felt the impact resonate through her body. It wasn't like the train. *This was not adrenaline. It was sheer terror.* She hardly felt the burning in her knees or the blood trickle from her nose. A second man spoke from behind him.

"This the one?" the second man said. She couldn't make out his features, but could see little bits of his dark skin in the moonlight, and the calm in his voice made her tremble.

"Yeah, this's the one. I seen her pay for that bus ticket with a big old wad of cash." The blonde man crouched beside her. He was balding with a small crooked nose and a belly that hung over his waistline.

"Let's see it then, darlin'. Where's that money?"

Isabel spit in his face and lunged for him, her hand leaving three red lines on his cheek where her nails had dug in. He kicked her in the ribs, sending her backwards, gasping for air. It felt like lightning was arcing through her lungs.

"If you don't give me what I want, I'm gonna take it," he said, smiling and reaching towards her.

TWELVE
FROM THE DARKNESS

Her throat was tight. The air just wasn't coming. Isabel crawled backwards, trying to put space between herself and the two men. *Maybe I could get over the fence if I can distract them somehow.*

"Where's your friend? Guess you weren't worth sticking around for," the blonde man jeered.

"Yeah, where's he now? Shame he left you here all alone," the other man said from the edge of the alley.

"We'll keep you company," the blonde man added, grabbing her legs and dragging her away from the fence.

From behind him, Isabel heard a soft thud, followed by a wheezing sound, like air leaving a tire, but the blonde man didn't seem to notice or care. He knelt down and grabbed a fistful of her hair, pulling her upward as he stood.

"That's enough," a new voice growled, a sharp metallic twang ringing out as something struck the brick.

"What's enough?" The blonde man said, tossing Isabel back to the ground and giving her a quick kick to the stomach, sending another wave of pain through her ribs and chest. "The hell are you on about?" he snapped over his shoulder.

Isabel struggled to pull herself upright, gasping for air and struggling to focus her eyes, blinking furiously at the darkness that filled the alleyway, the air thick as tar. The other man was still there, but something large was at his feet, and she swore she heard it moan.

"I said it's enough," the new voice repeated, like a nail on a glass. The shape of a boot rose and came down hard, landing with a sickening crunch. Finally, the blonde man took notice, turning to face his partner.

"Are you listening, Goddammit -" he barked, but by the time he'd realized the shadow wasn't his partner, Ben was already in front of him, a steel pipe crashing down on his shoulder. He gave him two quick jabs with his left hand then unwound the bar into the side of his head with a dull thud. The blonde man moaned and stumbled backwards.

Isabel crawled over and flattened herself against the opposite side of the alley as Ben grabbed the man's coat and threw him into the wall. The blonde man crumpled, his legs folding beneath him. Ben turned to Isabel, tossing the bar aside as he closed the gap between them. He knelt down, wrapped his arms around her and carried her into the light outside the alley, carefully letting her down.

"You ok?" he asked, gently placing his hands on either side of her face and inspecting it.

She nodded, wiping the blood from her nose with her coat sleeve.

"Just your nose?"

She shook her head and put a hand over her ribs, clenching her teeth as she shifted her weight. The sharp pain had given way to aching, and her breathing was growing easier. Ben carefully ran his fingers over her side, pressing lightly.

"Hopefully not broken, but you're gonna have some bruising. Why did you think it was a good idea to - " he started, but then cut himself off, his lips pressed tightly together. "You're OK now, alright? No one's gonna hurt you. Wait here, I'll be right back," he said, disappearing back into the alley.

Isabel still couldn't fully grasp what had happened as she watched his outline recede into the shadows.

"You're lucky. If she was worse off, you'd be dead," Ben's voice reverberated in the alley.

She'd never heard anyone speak like that before, harsh and cold as winter. Then came a thud, a high-pitched yelp, and a few seconds later, Ben emerged with two wallets in his hand, in the process of emptying their contents.

"I shouldn't have left you. You can't just go wandering around back streets in a big city, Izzy," he said softly.

It hadn't quite sunk into Isabel's mind. *Was it Ben who'd just knelt down and was now carrying her back towards the bus stop? Or was she already dead, and this was something else?*

"Where are we going?" she said, staring at the flecks of blood on his shirt. "How are you here - those men..."

Ben shook his head, looking back at her. "I guess I just missed my bus."

Isabel blinked hard, the lights of the station coming

into focus a few blocks ahead.

"Think you can walk?" Ben asked.

"Yeah, I think so. Can we just sit for a minute?" Isabel asked. "What happened? I don't remember what happened."

"Where I'm from, we call that getting jumped," he said, letting her down again on the grass beside the sidewalk.

"Fighting?"

"Yeah - I mean, sometimes. It's not always that, but the world's full of people that wanna take whatever you have." He plopped down beside her, dropping his head into his hands. "I've been on my own for as long as I can remember. My dad didn't leave until I was 16, but all he did was come home and ask me where I'd been and why there wasn't any food in the house, or slug me until he felt I'd had enough. I don't even know if I can blame the guy. Seems like he probably blacked out most of it." He cracked his knuckles into his open palm.

Isabel tried to stay still to calm the aching in her sides, breathing slowly as she lay back in the grass.

"Did you kill them?" she asked; she didn't actually want to know, but couldn't stop the words from coming out.

"No, I don't think so," he sighed. "They'll be alright in a few weeks, probably cornering someone else in an alley, but it's gonna be a hell of a morning after."

"Oh." Isabel didn't like either thought, but the pain in her ribs and face wasn't exactly inspiring any sympathy.

She thought about her father, his freshly starched shirts and immaculate lab coats. She couldn't remember a time when he'd even raised his voice to her. Even when he was frustrated, he'd just shake his head and sigh. *Something as strong as hate can so easily bend a person's mind.*

It confused her how Ben could seem so warm and genuine, but turn to violence so quickly. *Maybe it was what he knew, what he'd needed to know to get by.* Strangely, she was grateful for his willingness to fight, because she didn't know if she could. She couldn't decide if that made her the one who was really guilty.

"Your father shouldn't have hurt you," she said.

"Yeah, well, he shouldn't have, and I don't really enjoy hurting other people, but sometimes you have to hurt someone else so they don't hurt you."

Ben tongued the nearly-closed cut inside his lip and stared off at the smattering of lighted windows in the distance. Isabel rested her hand on his arm, and together, they sat in silence, feeling the weight of the world against their skin. Ben looked to his wrist, twisting it until he could read the watch face.

"What time's that bus coming?" he asked.

"6, I think," Isabel said, pulling the passes from her pocket. "Yeah, 6:10."

"We'd better get going somewhere better lit," Ben said, standing and offering her his hand.

"We?" she said, a weak smile playing on her lips.

Ben smiled back and carefully helped her up, an arm under her shoulders. "You know, I hear Washington is nice this time of year."

THIRTEEN
CHANGE OF PACE

Exhausted didn't cover it; Ben was asleep before the 6:10 to Santa Fe pulled away from the station. They'd had enough time for Isabel to sneak to the bathroom and wash her face, but it was beginning to swell, and she could still see flecks of blood dotting Ben's shirt. *We'll have to get rid of that,* Isabel made a mental note. She was tired, more tired than she'd ever been, and she could feel it down in her guts. *Soon I'll be with them,* she promised herself. *Soon I'll see them and know that they're ok, and they will know that I'm ok, and everything will be fine.*

It was getting hard to think, but as the bus rumbled along the worn Oklahoma roads, she couldn't stop her mind from wandering, always racing, but ending up back where she'd started. Her ribs and face throbbed, and she couldn't have slept anyway, too tangled in what she knew and didn't know, trying to fit it all together. *Dad must have found something or seen something he shouldn't have, or he had to leave town because I saw something, but what did I even see? What did I hear that I wasn't supposed to?*

She couldn't believe Ben had come back. Isabel grew spiteful for a moment. *If he hadn't left in the first place this never would have happened.* His head rested against the bus, trembling gently as the window vibrated against it. The thick brown hair, the stubble grown long from days of neglect - - she didn't understand him. His methods were a little unorthodox, but she couldn't argue with the results.

"Thank you," Isabel whispered, gently laying her head against his shoulder. She couldn't be sure, but she thought she saw his lips curve into smile in the reflection of the window.

Isabel woke with a start and found the bus nearly empty, Ben still slumped against the window. It'd been pretty sparsely populated when they'd first boarded it, but now there were only handful of other passengers.

"Glorieta," the driver shouted over his shoulder. The door hissed and shuddered its way open, letting a short, portly woman out, and the smell of exhaust came flooding in. The doors closed and the bus swung back onto the road and started to accelerate.

"Next stop is end of the line?" a man behind her called up to the driver.

"Bout thirty minutes," the driver called back.

Isabel patted Ben's cheek.

"Time to get up, sleepy boy."

"Where are we?" Ben opened one eye.

"Almost to Santa Fe," she replied.

"Have I been out that long?"

"Yeah - You kinda drool a little when you sleep."

"Your problem, not mine," he laughed, dragging his sleeve over the sides of his mouth.

Something further up the road caught Isabel's eye, a line of white against the dull grey and brown.

"I was thinking new clothes before we get to Santa Clarita," she said, still watching the road ahead.

Ben stretched his arms and tugged at his shirt collar. "What's wrong with these?"

Isabel stared hard at him.

"Oh you know - nothing." She pointed to the tiny red dots on his shirt. "Blood? I think, and we both smell like livestock. I've been wearing this dress for a week, and you've probably been wearing that shirt for a year."

Ben laughed and pulled his collar up to his nose. "Only about 6 months. Let's be fair."

"We're getting new clothes in Santa Fe," she replied, rapping her knuckles on the armrest. Isabel leaned out into the aisle, seeing the white object in the distance much more clearly. At least some of what she'd seen had been cars, spaced across the road. White cars with a bright blue stripe across them, and some kind of yellow fencing. *Police,* a voice screamed inside her, sending chills down her neck and back. It was probably nothing, just an accident or some kind of road cleanup, but panic tugged at the back of her mind. She turned to Ben, nodding her head towards the front of the bus.

"What?" he said.

She nodded again. He grabbed the seat in front of him and raised his head above its top. Ben was silent, his body rigid, as he lowered himself back into the seat.

"Why would they have a road block?" Isabel said.

"I don't know," he said, chewing on his fingers.

Isabel leaned into the aisle again just as the bus started to slow. The outline of men in black uniforms loomed ahead. *I need to pull it together,* she thought. *I should be thinking of a way out of this.* She looked through the window of the bus, at the red dust and dried plants that stretched to the foot of mountains on the horizon. Just beyond the line of white, buildings rose into the sky, tall, clear, and beautiful. Ben tugged at her sleeve.

"We have to get out of here," he whispered.

"To go where?" she said.

"I don't know, but I'm not going to prison, or worse, back to that damn town in Ohio with all the -"

Isabel held her finger to his lips. The bus had come to a complete stop, and the door creaked open. She could see the options evolving in Ben's head, his hands opening and closing, cracking as he clenched them.

"No," she whispered. "Just follow my lead."

His eyes lingered on her, then turned to the door of the bus. A large man in a black and grey uniform with a grey hat made his way up the steps and stood, adjusting his belt.

"Sorry about the disruption folks, just looking for someone, might have got over this way."

He paused to clear his throat and dabbed at his face with a white handkerchief. Sweat gathered and ran down his neck where the hat met his clean-shaven head. "If you could just produce an ID as we make our way down the aisle, we'll make this that easy."

It was the first time Isabel had seen Ben look nervous. His eyes darted around the bus as the trooper started to make his way down the aisle, stopping briefly to glance at a thin black woman's ID. Her skeletal hand extended into the aisle. The trooper nodded, smiling sheepishly and continued on towards them.

"I hope this is a good plan," Ben whispered.

Isabel laid her hand on his and intertwined their fingers, squeezing gently. The trooper stopped just in front of them, a thumb hitched in his belt and the other hand extended towards her, palm up.

"Identification?"

Isabel stared at him blankly for a moment, then frowned. She pointed to her ear and shook her head. The trooper took a long look at her, turning to the bus driver.

"She got a hearing problem or somethin'?"

The bus driver shrugged and let out a long sigh. The trooper turned back to them, pointing to Ben.

"You hear all right?"

Ben stared back, his expression blank.

Isabel touched her finger to her chin, brought it back to her ear, then turned her hands in front of her in what she imagined looked like sign language. The trooper strolled back to the front of the bus and poked his head out the door.

"We got anyone here that speaks hand talk?" he shouted to the men standing at the barricade.

Isabel stood and tried her best to look confused. The trooper made his way back to their seats, a piece of paper and a pencil in his hand. He extended the paper to Isabel, the word identification scrawled in all capital letters in its center. Isabel shook her head, pointing at the pencil in his other hand.

She removed her hand from Ben's, and with the

paper resting on the seat, scribbled the word "robbed." The trooper glanced at the paper and furrowed his brow. She gestured to him again, bringing her hands in a wide ark, then continued writing. When she'd finished, she handed it back to him.

"Robbed in Tulsa by a big blonde haired man and a short dark-skinned man. Took my purse and his wallet, money was wired to us for bus tickets," he read aloud.

When he looked up, Isabel gestured to the bruising on her face, and Ben looked on, puzzled as ever. Isabel could feel his skin trembling slightly. She tried to keep her breathing steady and her expression sincere. The trooper took a hard look at them, then reached for his radio.

"Sir, can you come in here and let me know what you make of this?"

Isabel looked on expectantly and tapped her foot, while another officer made his way onto the bus. The second man was taller and thinner, with a thick head of hair that flared out beneath his cap. On his breast, a metal rectangle read "Sgt. Johns." They held a quiet conversation, then he took the paper from the first trooper and read it over, looking to Isabel and Ben.

"Probably those same bastards - robbed that gas station up there a few weeks ago," the sergeant said. He turned back to Ben and Isabel. "They're lucky they're in this good'a shape if its the same guys."

Sergeant Johns held Ben's gaze for a long moment, turning back to the first trooper.

"Shit Ronnie, guy we're looking for is about 6-1 and's got long black hair, and the lady don't match her description neither. Let these folks alone." He crumpled the paper in his hand and pointed to the other passengers. "Give 'em a quick look over. Let's get this thing movin'."

The trooper nodded, his face red.

"Sorry about that, oh - erm," he stumbled over his words. Isabel just smiled and nodded, tapping her hand against her chest.

He moved quickly through the other passengers, returning to the front of the bus.

"Sorry 'bout that folks. Thank you for ya'lls cooperation." He tipped his hat and descended the steps of the bus. Ben shook his head, hiding his grin in the collar of his coat.

I must be sweating more than that officer was, Isabel thought. *They weren't even looking for us.* Relief flooded through her body, washing away the tension. She breathed deeply and looked toward the city again, pillars of smoke and steam rising on the horizon. They were both careful not to say a word until the bus pulled into the station.

"End of the line," the driver shouted. They left the bus last, letting the other passengers gather their things and make their way down the aisle. Isabel waved to the bus driver and flashed him a smile as they made their exit. He just grunted and swung the doors shut behind them.

Ben looked over Isabel, head to toe, as the bus pulled away. Isabel bowed low and smiled demurely.

"You didn't tell me you know – whatever it was you just did," he said.

"I don't know sign language, but it was convincing, huh? That guy didn't have a clue what to do with us, and you heard him, they were looking for some tall guy with long hair and a woman that doesn't look like me."

"Well, that narrows the suspects," he laughed. "It's

not exactly a good idea to let the police know that you've been lying to them, just because they're not looking for you."

"True," Isabel said. "Shall we move on?" She fished another pass from her coat pocket and looked over it. "We have a few hours before our transfer leaves."

They took a quick left out of the bus station and found themselves only a few blocks from a crowded market. Isabel led the way, weaving in and out of vendor's stands, through the labyrinth of bodies and chatter. It reminded her of Maine, when she used to go to the farmer's market with her mother and they'd walk through the stalls, her mother's dress tightly gripped in her hand. Everything seemed much smaller now, but the colors were just as beautiful. Isabel stopped to buy two apples and a small loaf of bread.

"Not in the stealing mood?" Ben nudged her playfully.

"Not from them," she replied.

The bread split easily, steam rising from its middle. Isabel handed half the loaf along with an apple to Ben.

"Just like my mom makes," she said, then cheerfully added, "You'll get to meet her soon and my dad. Funny that the first boy I ever bring home is a wandering ne'er-do-well that broke me out of jail."

"I prefer delinquent," Ben said. "At least that way it sounds like I have a career ahead of me." He paused, looking over the fruit. "Ugh, not sure if I'm ready for more apples."

"Don't be a baby. They're good for you," Isabel chided.

He tossed the apple from hand to hand before biting into it with a loud crunch. "How much do we have left?" Ben mumbled, his mouth full.

Isabel flipped through the rest of what she had, waiting patiently for Ben to produce the cash in his pocket and add it to the pile.

"Plus the contents on those two wallets...it's enough."

"Enough?" he said.

"For a new set of clothes, and for the sake of all mankind, we need someone to hose you down. You smell awful." Isabel crinkled her nose and ducked away through the crowd.

"I smell awful? You should smell yourself," he called after her. She waved a dismissive hand and continued through the crowd until she broke into the open on the other side of the market and stopped.

"It's strange being here," she said as they crossed to the sidewalk. In their first few days outside Echton, it had been hard for Isabel to register exactly where she was, or how she'd gotten there. It was strange enough to come back to Echton after being away at school.

"Welcome to Santa Fe, I guess," Ben said, pointing up the street to a sign loosely affixed to a dull green storefront. "How about this?"

"Griffith's Used Goods," Isabel read aloud.

"We'll stand out less if we don't have brand new clothes," he said. Isabel frowned, scanning the other stores.

"Fine, but we're not putting anything on until we get some sort of shower," she said, scowling at the dirt caked onto her slip on shoes.

The bell chimed cheerfully over their heads as Ben let himself in, leading them past rows of dresses, sorted by size. Pots and pans lined the walls on thick wooden shelves, and toys were neatly sorted along the wall.

"Can I help you find something?" an elderly woman squeaked from behind a counter by the front window.

Isabel flashed her a smile and shook her head. She was definitely still hurting, maybe more than she had been last night, but it was nice to know she'd be clean soon.

"We're just gonna look around," she replied.

The woman smiled back and resumed her work, pecking at an ancient tallying machine, pausing to scribble something down. Ben sighed, pulling his coat off and folding it over his arm.

"Come on," Isabel said.

"Come on what?" Ben scoffed.

She knew he would never admit it but had a strong feeling that Ben had no idea how to pick clothes out for himself. Judging from the condition of his jacket and pants, he hadn't bothered in quite awhile. She grinned as they headed up the stairs to the men's section. He might not know it yet, but she had him pretty well sized up.

"In a suit - I'd say 42 regular, but I feel like you're probably not a suit guy," she laughed at the scowl on his face, and continued down a few more miles. "You probably weigh what? 170, 175 pounds? Probably a 32 inch waist."

She left him in the dressing room with the pants and a pile of shirts, most of which she called "industrial."

"My mom used to do this for my dad all the time. He wouldn't buy clothes for himself, so we'd buy them for him and just leave them in his dresser for him to find," she explained as Ben tossed the pants and shirts back over the changing room wall as he tried them on.

"This's fine," he'd grunt, or "Nope," when he came to something he didn't like or fit into. Isabel sorted them into two piles and continued to bring fresh replacements until she was satisfied that he'd have enough to get him by.

"Christ, I should have stayed with Hix. At least he was honest about torturing me," Ben cried out, flinging open the changing room door.

"It's a wonder you're on your own," Isabel said. "Find a suitcase and the rest of the clothes you need. I have to pick out a few things. Then we can go."

Isabel left Ben with his pile of clothes and headed back downstairs. She threw a few dresses over her shoulder and grabbed a few new pairs of shoes, heading for the corner marked "Dressing Room." She unbuttoned the coat and let it slide from her shoulders, landing with a gentle clank that made her pause.

She'd grown so used to its weight and steady tapping against her leg as she walked that she'd completely forgotten about the coin. Isabel sat on the short wooden stool in the corner of the room and ran her fingers over the coat's hem until she felt it, tediously pushing it back up to the slit she'd cut when she first hid it. Then, pinching its edge with her fingertips, she pulled it out and held it up to the light.

If the coin had anything to do with her family or the town, she couldn't find the missing link. She felt like she could draw a connection between everything else, however improbable it all seemed. Isabel wondered if Henry thought he'd lost the coin, or if he realized she'd taken it. Maybe he knew when she took it that morning. She hadn't been herself, hungry and tired, clumsy at best.

She hadn't noticed before in the dim light, but the words 'Mutuatus Vita' were pressed into the metal around the bottom of the coin. *It sounded like Latin or Greek,* she thought. She'd ask her father about it when she saw him. He knew a little bit about everything. *Be patient,* she told herself, setting the coin on the stool between her legs.

Isabel slipped her old sundress off, pausing to examine the purple splotches on her ribs and prod them tenderly with her fingertips. She carefully pulled on a light green cotton dress, wiggling it down her body. *Not a bad fit.* She smoothed the cloth against her legs. She tried on a half dozen more dresses, draping a few over the door that seemed to fit her figure. She'd just pulled the last dress over her head when she heard a knock at the door.

"You done yet?" Ben's voice echoed in the tiny room.

"Almost," Isabel answered. She snatched up the coin and clinched it in her teeth, then started gathering the dresses that littered the floor.

"What are you doing in there?" Ben asked, chuckling. "You find a rabbit hole?"

She took the coin from her mouth. "Are those shoes out there?"

"I don't see any shoes. C'mon we don't have much time to get back," he said.

"Oops," she said, spying them in the corner, peeking out from under her coat.

"Almost done, just give me a second," she said, setting the shoes on the pile of dresses. She had the door halfway open when she realized she still had the coin in her hand. She quickly pulled it back shut.

"Do I need to come in and save you from yourself? It sounds like a real struggle in there."

"I don't ALWAYS need saving," she replied coolly, replacing the coin in the lining of the coat. She opened the door to find him sitting, cross-legged, between two aisles of women's blouses.

"You wear anything except those dresses?" he said.

"A lady wears a dress. Did you find a suitcase?"

He gestured to the pile of clothes set beside him, a plain grey case teetering at its peak, a second case for her beside the pile.

"Happy?" Ben said as they approached the woman, clicking away on her adding machine.

"Over the moon. Just over the moon," Isabel replied.

They left Griffith's Used Goods, a suitcase under each of Ben's arms.

"It's almost 2:40. Train leaves at 3, right?" Ben said. Isabel checked the tickets again.

"Yeah, 3:15," she replied. The market was emptier now, a few people milling about the stalls and stacking crates. On their way back through, Isabel bought a handful of cucumbers, carrots, and another loaf of bread, wrapping it all in brown paper, and tucked it under her arm. By the time they made their way back to the station, it was a little after 3 PM. Ben parked himself into a short wooden bench, sliding the two cases beneath it. Isabel joined him, peering down the street in search of the bus that would take her ever closer to her family.

"Ca-li-forn-i-a," she sang the word under her breath.

FOURTEEN
A LITTLE WARMTH

On one hand, Ben could count the number of times he'd felt truly at ease. At his Uncle John's farm, listening to the crickets in summer, John smoking on the porch. For such a mean drunk, his old man had some pretty decent family. He remembered the first time he'd gone out to his uncle's after his father left, just the two of them and the dog, named Dog.

"I ain't gonna name it," his uncle told him. "Damn thing's just gonna die anyway."

"They bothered to name you, didn't they?" Ben chimed in, escaping to the safety of the front porch.

His uncle puffed up his chest and started to stand but then sat back down and laughed, a soft rumbling laugh. "Looks like work starts a little earlier than usual tomorrow," he said, winking and taking a long, slow drag on his pipe. "Care to make any other observatioooons?"

He always had the same grin on his face when he thought he'd won an argument. John always said there was one rule he'd learned from living in Iowa: there's nothing a little more work can't fix.

Ben would just smile. He spent a lot of time with John after his father left, working during the day, drinking beer and listening to the radio when the sun went down. He'd fought with John over something stupid. He couldn't even remember what it'd been, but Ben had packed his things, hopped a train and hadn't been back.

He knew he would, eventually, come back to John's and say he was sorry, and his uncle would laugh and shake his hand. Ben missed the farm and the warm softness that would settle into his body, knowing that he'd be alright when he slept that night, that it was OK to sleep with both eyes closed. He thought of John now, as the same gentle warmth crept over him, his arm rubbing against Isabel's in the back of that stuffy Greyhound bus.

They'd probably have to hitch or catch a train up the coast. The barren landscape shot by, a blur of brown and tan with flashes of white. It'd be good to see the Pacific. Ben had heard so many stories about California, he wasn't sure what to believe anymore, but it couldn't be worse than this. He made a face at the cracked clay and sand.

They'd stowed their cases away, settled in, and almost immediately after the bus started rolling, Isabel had drifted off, leaving Ben to his thoughts. He was calm, but wary, a lot of questions still unresolved. *Even if they found her family, what were they supposed to do about Echton?* It hadn't even looked that much like him; he could always split, but Isabel was dead to rights on that poster at the train station. *Well, if her dad is half as smart as she made him out to be, he'll think of something.* Isabel stirred in her seat, her eyes fluttering open.

"Where are we?" she said.

"Not sure, maybe somewhere in the desert coming into Cali. I think this bus is a straight shot. We haven't stopped anywhere yet - nowhere to stop, it looks like."

"You been up this whole time?" She arched her back and raised her hands over her head.

"Yeah, a fair bit of it," he replied. "How much money do we have left?" Isabel produced the billfold from somewhere inside her dress, deftly thumbing through it.

"12 dollars," she said.

"Not bad." Ben smiled, then was silent for a few minutes. "So who's this family we're looking for in Washington?"

"I remembered their names yesterday, but you were sleeping, and I totally forgot to say. My Aunt Sarah and Uncle Thomas. My aunt's real name is Gretchen, but she hates the name Gretchen, so everyone calls her Sarah - That's her middle name."

"Got an address for them or anything?" Ben said.

Isabel thought for a moment. "Nope."

"No problem. We'll just pick a corner and yell their names until someone turns around."

"Or, option number two, we can look them up in a phone book," Isabel smirked.

Ben settled back in his seat and closed his eyes. "I'm passing out. Don't know how much sleep we'll get tonight. We get lucky, we might catch a ride that way and be there by morning."

Isabel leaned over him to get a look out the window.

"Sure, sure," she murmured.

Ben had spent a fair bit of his life on trains and busses, even an airplane once when he was coming back north from Gainsville. His best sleep always came knowing there were a set of cylinders firing away, carrying him somewhere else. He glanced over at Isabel, her fist tucked up under her chin, eyes on the passing scenery. *We'll be in California soon enough*, he thought, California was somewhere else, and somewhere else was fine with him. Sure enough, after what felt like only a moment, Isabel was shaking him awake.

"C'mon. We're here," she said again.

Between the sleep and fleeting thoughts of home, Ben's mind hardly registered the change in landscape. He followed Isabel down the bus steps and into his first few steps on Californian ground. The sun was warm on his face, and the air was fresh but thick.

"I think I'm gonna die if I have to spend another minute in a motor vehicle," Isabel said, hoisting her case onto her shoulder.

"I wanna get a look at that ocean," Ben said. "That breeze's coming off the water, I'd bet. We just have to follow it there."

"We can't play around and set up camp," Isabel protested. "My family is probably worried sick about me."

"You said it yourself. We need a break. Just a few hours, I promise," Ben replied, setting off down the road. "Come on, Izzy."

She sighed and fell in behind him, peeling the coat off and throwing it over her back. They walked through the city for awhile, watching the cracks in the concrete pass under their feet, snacking on the provisions she'd bought in Santa Fe.

"Any idea what Santa Clarita means?" Ben asked

"No idea...Saint something?" she answered.

He nodded, shifting the case to the other hand. They ran out of sidewalk after a mile or so, but Ben could see the slight imprint of where a trail had been. He looked back after a few hundred yards to find Isabel struggling to pull her case through the brush that surrounded the trail.

"You alright?"

"This thing's heavy," she said.

"Yeah, maybe you shouldn't have gotten so many dresses." He offered his hand. Isabel pulled the case up to her chest, and he slipped his fingers around the handle.

"If you insist," she said, stepping around him and pushing on through the weeds. They continued their trek, winding their way through a stand of trees, the ocean scent growing stronger.

"Hey, wait," Ben swung one of the cases to his right. "Can you hear that?"

"What is it? Me growing older?" Isabel grumbled, pausing up ahead. "Water," she said. "I can hear it!"

"And I'm guessing it empties right into the ocean," he said. "We're on the right path."

Ben shouldered the cases, following Isabel through the dense foliage until he came to the edge of the trees. *The West Coast isn't all that different from the east, except everything seemed a little bigger here,* Ben thought as he looked out over the rolling blue horizon, down to the waves that crashed against the sandy shore below. Isabel stood at the edge of the cliff, inching forward to look over the drop-off ahead. Ben joined her, setting the cases down and taking a deep breath of the sweet, salty air. He knelt, scraping at the edge of the cliff with his fingernails. It crumbled, sending a tiny shower of earth cascading down towards the beach.

"The ground's really soft here. I'm betting it won't be as bad over there." He pointed down the ridge to a patch of trees that seemed to meander its way down to the beach.

"Sure, probably," Isabel said, then lowered her legs over the side of the cliff and started to work her way down, sliding and catching herself every few feet.

Ben took the knife from his boot and tossed it into his case, then carefully lowered the cases over the cliff. He watched them bounce and slide down its face and heard Isabel yell from below.

"That's my stuff!"

"Yeah, I sent it down for you," he shot back, letting himself over the edge in the same spot she had. He took his time, choosing his hand and footholds methodically, riding the loose gravel and sand down when the rock face became less steep. When he reached the bottom, he pulled his boots off, setting them beside the two cases and looked around for Isabel. She stood farther up the beach, the surf lapping over her bare feet and surging up around her ankles.

"I forgot how beautiful the ocean is," she said.

"Yeah," he said softly, adding, "Still want that shower?"

She followed his gaze farther down the beach to where the stream they'd been following poured from the lip of the cliff into a pool at its base, making its way out to the ocean.

"No kidding," she said.

"Go ahead, it should be fresh water. I'm gonna go for a swim," he said.

Isabel glanced up and down the empty oceanfront and eyed him suspiciously. "If I catch you peeking at me, it's gonna be a swift path to vengeance, Ben Richter."

"Don't flatter yourself," he scoffed.

He pulled off his jeans and shirt, tossing them on top of his jacket, then waded into the surf. It was much colder than he'd thought, but he wasn't going to turn back now that Isabel might be watching. He took a deep breath and plunged his head under the water, then reemerged, clearing the salty water from his eyes and flattening his hair against his head. Ben lay back and let the waves carry him as they swelled and rushed towards the shore. Weightless, it felt like flying after so much crawling, washing away the dried blood and the soreness and the cuts that catalogued his last few days.

Back toward the cliff, Ben could make out Isabel's outline under the waterfall. Her dark skin gave contrast to the wall of rock and sand behind her. She was turned away from him, her hands combing through her hair as the water poured over her head. Ben pretended not to notice the subtle curve of her hips and legs. He just bit his lip and took a deep breath, then turned the other way and kept swimming, doing his best to keep his eyes on the water and to keep his teeth from chattering.

When he reached the shore, Ben walked towards their luggage, brushing the water droplets from his skin. He glanced back at the waterfall, but Isabel was nowhere to be seen. His heart raced as he jogged back towards the water. When he was standing in the surf, he could finally see her tangled mess of dark hair shaking in the wind. She'd found a small indentation in the cliff face, protected from the ocean breeze, and was using one of the dresses she'd bought to dry herself. Ben shook his head and sighed, walking back towards the case and their clothes. *I don't even know this girl, and I've got myself more tangled up than the seaweed on this beach.*

The sand was warm between his toes, and as he sat there, pulling his new clothes from the case and deciding which to wear, a strange calm came over him.

"Have a good swim?"

Ben started at the sound of Isabel's voice. "Shit! Don't do that," he grumbled, resettling himself atop his case.

"A little jumpy, aren't we?" Isabel laughed, tucking the wet dress and the dirty one she'd been wearing into her case. She'd put on a light green cotton dress, and though he tried not to think about it, it was almost the same color as her eyes. Isabel gestured to the waterfall up the coast. "It's not bad once you're in there."

"Yeah, I should probably wash the salt off anyway." Ben replied. He grabbed the new clothes and another shirt to dry off with and headed down the beach. After a quick rinse, he ducked back into the indentation Isabel had found and threw the new clothes on, shaking the sand from his pants. *At least they were comfortable,* he thought, tugging the shirt down.

When he returned, Ben found Isabel sitting on her case, gazing into the blue expanse, where the waves rose and broke, rolling towards the shore.

"I feel a lot like that." She paused. "Tossed around and flipped upside down, trying to get my feet under my head and a breath in between."

"Or just waiting for the wind to die down," Ben added.

He tossed his dirty clothes into his case, snapped the lid closed, and offered her his hand.

"I think those trees are our best way out of there." He helped her to her feet and gathered his socks and shoes. They walked down the beach, suitcases on one hand and their shoes held loosely in the other.

"What's the first thing you're gonna do when you see your parents?" Ben said. He decided he'd keep asking until it happened. It was better to say when than if.

"Hug them, I guess, then demand a tropical vacation where they can explain what the hell happened while our lawyer sorts this all out," she replied.

Ben smiled, sweeping his arm in a long arc. "You already have your tropical, sort of," he laughed. "I understand though, if I were in your place, or could even be in your place - I understand."

"Do you think you'll see your dad again?" she asked.

"Honestly, probably not. I don't know that I'd want to, though. I think I'd probably knock him out if I did."

"It'd be well deserved."

"Yeah, maybe. I think it hit him pretty hard when my mom died, and maybe he saw her when he looked at me, so he didn't wanna look at me." Ben watched his feet slide through the sand, dodging shell fragments.

"Maybe he saw himself when he looked at you, and it was his own eyes he didn't want to see," Isabel replied softly.

They were both quiet for a long while, walking in the surf as the wind whistled in their ears.

"Are those steps?" Isabel cried out. Ben followed her gaze to just beyond the trees, where a dark haired man and a blonde woman were trotting up the hillside.

"No shit," Ben said. "How about that?"

As they got closer, he could see that the hillside had been outfitted with a long series of wooden steps.

"It's kind of liberating, isn't it? Being able to just go wherever you want, whenever you want?" Isabel said at the base of the hill.

Ben pulled one sock on, teetering and hopping on the other leg. "It's not bad." He slipped his foot into the leather boot and knotted its laces.

Isabel shook the sand from her shoes and slipped them on, steadying Ben's shoulder as he worked on his second boot.

"You don't have to worry about anyone else, but you also don't get to worry about anyone else," he added.

"Doesn't sound so bad," Isabel said. She hopped up the first step and started taking long strides up the incline.

"I suppose I'm carrying these?" Ben pointed to their cases at his feet.

"Sorry, I can't hear you! I'm too far up the mountain!" she shouted back. Ben laughed and cursed under his breath, taking hold of their luggage and starting the ascent.

The walk back into the city seemed to go faster, Isabel bounding ahead and Ben following steadily behind in the path she traversed. When they reached the sidewalk, Ben finally felt warm again, between the heat of the sun on his back and the bulky cases he'd been struggling to keep from slamming against his legs as he walked.

"Hungry?" Isabel turned around, walking backwards.

"Starved," he said, setting her case on the ground and continuing down the path.

"That's my stuff. You can't just leave it!" she cried.

"I totally agree. Someone better carry it before wild animals chew it all to pieces."

It took Isabel a moment to grab the case and catch up to him. She held it with both hands, tight against her chest.

"There aren't any wild animals around here," she said, unsure if it was a question or a statement.

"Nothing worse than me," he said.

"I can't really imagine anything worse than you," she replied, pushing her way past him.

Ben smiled as he watched her struggle with its weight, then gave chase, passing her again. They both laughed, Isabel doing her best to catch him, until he stopped so abruptly she nearly ran into his back.

"How about that place?" Isabel said, pushing him out of the way. A dingy looking diner sat a few blocks to their left, just beyond a traffic light and a bay of pay phones.

"You have impeccable taste," Ben replied. "You wanna try to look up their number before we go to Seattle?"

They reached the diner, and Ben carried their bags inside, sliding them under a booth and plopping himself down. After a minute, Isabel slid in across from him, setting a small yellow piece of paper between them. Ben pulled it closer, scanning it quickly. "555-234-3423 Thomas Stanton, 5th Ave S., Seattle, WA"

"I think this is them," Isabel said hesitantly.

"Did you try?"

"No change," Isabel said. "After we eat, I'll call."

They ordered two cheeseburgers apiece and set into them, finishing the first burger without a word. After a few minutes, the waitress returned to check on them, but hesitated when she saw the empty plates.

"Is it OK to take the dishes near ya'll right now? I don't wanna lose a finger."

Ben grinned between handfuls of fries.

"I promise we have all our shots," he laughed. Isabel giggled, her mouth full of burger.

"Can I get you anythin' else?" the waitress added, carefully stacking the empty plates at the table's edge.

"Yeah, I think so. What's the best way to get up to Seattle from here?" Ben said.

"The best way to get up to Seattle," the woman echoed, scratching her head with a pen. "Be back in a minute, sug." She disappeared back through the kitchen doors.

"Who do you think she's talking to? What if she recognizes us?" Isabel whispered.

"Well, with our luck she'll probably rob, then murder us. Who cares if she recognizes us?" Ben winked at her.

Isabel finished her meal, dragging the last of her fries through the ketchup at the edge of her plate and tossing them into her mouth. Ben watched her, her eyes darting around the room and settling on him. After a few minutes, the waitress emerged from the back room and headed towards their table. She planted herself at the edge of the booth, her hands on her hips.

"Gordy says that fella over ta' the end of the cafe's goin' up that way." She nodded to a man at the end of the counter, clad in an immaculate set of dress clothes, brandishing an enormous cup of coffee at some invisible foe he'd taken to arguing with. His gnarled golden hair met a neatly tailored pinstripe vest and a matching set of trousers, giving him an air of wild elegance. Ben frowned and looked back to the waitress.

"Oh honey, he ain't bad. A little strange, but he ain't bad," she said sweetly. "He's in here every once in awhile, talkin' 'bout the good days."

"Well, that makes me feel better," Ben said. He glanced at Isabel, who looked anything but convinced.

"Well, take it for what it's worth, sug. You could always take a bus from uptown, but nothin's gonna take you there tonight," she said, clearing the rest of the plates. Isabel stared across the table, shaking her head.

Ben shrugged and scooted out of the booth, walking over towards the other end of the restaurant.

"Damnit, Ben!" Isabel whispered.

He settled on the stool next to the man and extended a hand towards him.

"Ben. Heard you're going up towards Seattle."

The man looked up at him, his face blank for a moment. Then he grinned, a wide toothy grin.

"Derek Schafer," he said, taking Ben's hand.

Ben glanced back at Isabel, her face frozen in horror, then waved. "Don't mind her. She must have something stuck in her throat." He turned back towards Derek. "So you're going up towards Seattle?"

"Right that way," Derek replied. His voice was thick and raspy, but he spoke gently, his words carefully formed. "Something I can help you with?"

"I wouldn't say no to a ride. We're just trying to get to our aunt's place."

Ben set the last of their money on the counter and held Derek's gaze for a moment, trying to read his face. Derek smiled again and drained the last of his coffee.

"Who am I to keep a man from his family?"

FIFTEEN
FLEETING GLANCES

"You've got to be kidding me," Derek heard Isabel mutter as they stepped outside. He looked back to find her watching them, as Ben tried to make conversation, talking about the east coast and fishing. They rounded the back of the building and headed towards a row of trucks parked at the edge of the lot.

"This is my baby." He affectionately patted a white truck with a jet-black trailer. "We've been through a lot."

"Wow, she's a beaut'. How long you been driving her?" Ben asked, circling the front of the truck.

Derek paused, tapping his fingers against his vest as he counted backward. *This guy Ben seems nice enough, but this lady looks like she's about to have a stroke.*

"8 years, in April," he replied, giving them a big smile. Readjusting his vest and trousers, he popped the door open and pulled himself up into the cab, motioning them to the other side. He was doing all he could to make himself seem friendly, but it seemed like half the people he met these days didn't trust a soul any farther than the end of a gun. The vest was brand new, the first day he'd worn it after his old one had sprung just a few too many holes. He wondered if they'd notice, if anyone had noticed. By the time Derek saw Isabel's head pop into the truck, Ben had already settled in and looked quite content.

Isabel followed him up, pausing to examine the leather seats and rear section of the truck's cab. Derek had always prided himself on its immaculateness, a small sleeping area in the back, with polished steel countertops and walls he'd papered with a mixture of concert posters and portraits. *All said and done, I haven't done half bad in making the place a little artistic.*

"Welcome to my estate," he said, following her gaze. Isabel pointed to a poster above the sink just behind them. It was a man in a suit, with slicked back hair and a dimpled chin. Derek had always thought the smile on his lips made it seem as if he was hiding something.

"Who's that?" she asked.

"John Herbert Dillinger," he replied.

"The bank robber?" Ben said.

Derek ran a hand through his long blonde hair, smoothing it against his head.

"The money extraction specialist." He felt a surge of irritation, but pushed it back down and forced a laugh as he turned the key, the cab shaking lightly as the engine started. *Everyone thinks they're some kind of expert on criminal history.* Isabel sunk into her seat beside Ben, eyeing the foot bench that separated Derek from them, where a long black lever extended up to his right hand.

Derek knocked the lever forward, trying to seem casual as the truck eased out onto the road.

"Where you two from?" he asked, watching as Ben and Isabel's eyes met for a moment.

"Coming from Michigan. We've been living there the last few years, and we decided it was time for a change. This is my sister, Isabel," Ben said.

"Nothing wrong with a little change of scenery," Derek chuckled. *Pretty tight-knit family, close as those two are sitting.* Ben laughed uneasily, and Derek wondered if he'd been too obvious. He'd never had a very good poker face.

"Who's John Dillinger?" Isabel blurted out.

"Bank robber in the 30's right? My uncle used to tell me about how much trouble those cops in Chicago had with him," Ben added.

Derek nodded, taking a wide left turn and pulling the knob back towards him. It made him realize how seldom anyone saw the inside of his truck. He wouldn't admit it, but he loved talking about that picture, even if half the people he talked to got it wrong.

"Dillinger was German. Story goes he's a relative of mine, somewhere on my ma's side. Anyway, he robbed about a dozen banks before they got him. The police sur-rounded him in some old house and shot him in the back."

"Why the picture?" Isabel said. She leaned forward and watched Derek absently change gears, his hair dangling into his eyes.

"I dunno, really. I always thought he was interesting. The man had style. More than most folks would know what to do with. Just because you make a living stealing money, doesn't mean you haven't got something worth admiring." Derek paused. "John Dillinger died when he was 31, but that son of a bitch sure knew how to live," he laughed.

To his surprise, he heard Isabel laughing too. It was a pleasant change to be in such interesting company.

"I think I like you, Derek," Isabel said.

Ben smiled too, watching her." She won't even admit she thinks I'm alright. I think you're making some pretty good headway."

Derek tried to keep his cheeks from flushing, grinning while he fiddled with the knobs on the AC.

"Tell me more about this Dillinger guy," Isabel said.

He spoke; pausing occasionally to see if they were still listening. Each time he stopped, Isabel leaned forward expectantly around a now sleeping Ben as the truck chased the highway up the coast. Derek told Isabel how Dillinger had systematically robbed Chicago blind and the way he dressed, talked, walked, and acted until he didn't have any more to tell. *Jesus, this girl has questions I don't know if there are answers for.*

"Why do you drive a truck?" she said suddenly.

It caught him off guard, and he saw Ben's eyes open and his head shake almost imperceptibly.

"It's ok." He patted the dash, then waved a hand out at the horizon. "Every day I get to say good morning to a different sunrise, and it gives me time to think, and I love to think," he answered, grinning.

"I think maybe I've had too much," Isabel sighed, leaning forward on her elbows.

"Hell, I just can't stay in one place for long enough to set roots," he'd told them, jerking a thumb at his sleeping quarters. "That's enough for me right there."

Ben nodded appreciatively and began telling Derek a story about a truck he'd ridden in on his way to Carolina.

"I wouldn't mind traveling," Isabel interrupted. "I've never been anywhere but Ohio or Maine and the in between."

"And Michigan," Derek added, winking.

"Doesn't count," Isabel said, blushing. "We live there."

"Speaking of the in between," Derek said, swinging the truck in a wide arc from the highway. He couldn't hold it any longer and could use a cup of coffee or two. They kept it short, taking everything to go and piling back into the cab.

The road was almost completely deserted, and the last sliver of sun cast everything in a golden light as the truck eased back onto the highway and gathered speed. The more he looked at Isabel, the more Derek thought of his daughter, who he'd left almost 10 years ago, sleeping in her cradle. He wondered if her mother was telling her about her old man. Sometimes he couldn't tell if the thought was pushing him farther from home, or pulling him back.

"Shit," Isabel said.

"Hmm?" Ben grunted.

"I never called our, uh, our aunt and uncle."

"Won't be long. Few hours more, we'll be up there, and you can call then," Derek replied. "It'll pass before you know it," he added softly.

He reached for the radio, turning the knobs until he found a gentle melody that flowed easily through the speakers. In any other company, he'd have gone for rock, but it just didn't seem to suit the moment. He decided it was justified when he noticed Isabel nodding off, her head resting between Ben's shoulder and the soft leather seat.

He and Ben talked for a while, complaining about road construction in Michigan, the truck quivering slightly as Derek pulled left against the wind. After awhile, they too grew silent, the truck like a piece of the hills that had taken to moving. A force of its own.

"Hey kid," Ben said, shaking Isabel's leg. She sat upright, rolling her neck to the side, and gently prodded the side of her face.

"Where'd you get that?" Derek asked. *How did I miss the swelling under her other eye?* He glanced over at her, then back to Ben. For a brief moment, anger flared inside him. *This better not be your work, kid.*

"Robbed, well, they tried anyway," Isabel said. Not everyone is the gentleman Mr. Dillinger is."

"Hmm." He thought for a moment, but decided Ben didn't seem like the violent type. He gave her a gentle smile, relaxing his shoulders. "At least we can get you where we're going, eh?"

"Yeah," she smiled back.

"You already slept through half the trip," Ben laughed. "We're about an hour and a half from Seattle."

The sky was dark, save for an occasional pair of headlights that broke the horizon and shot by.

"It ain't all that bad," Derek told Ben. "It ain't all peaches though, either."

Ben nodded and smiled, patting Isabel's arm. Isabel arched her back, stretching. Shaking his head, Ben watched the Seattle skyline drawing closer.

It was around 4 AM when Derek dropped them in front of a bus station in downtown Seattle. He shook Ben's hand firmly, kissed Isabel's, and refused the money they'd promised him, pressing it back into Isabel's hand.

"Don't need it," he said pointedly. "You two got me thinking about my kid and I... Well, never mind that. I just hope I could at least help you along the way a little."

Isabel stepped forward and held him in a quick embrace. "Thanks," she said, her face buried in his vest.

Derek blinked away a tear he felt try to escape. With a quick wave, he was back up the steps of the truck. He'd felt Isabel's hand against his chest as he stepped back, a brief moment of human contact in what seemed like an eternity without. With the open door of the truck inviting him back in, he knew he'd better be on his way. *Home,* he held the word in his mind. It was a nice word to think about.

SIXTEEN
RUMBLE, RAMBLE, INTO TROUBLE

———————————

Turning to Ben, Isabel held his gaze until his face split into an enormous grin.

"You were wrong. Admit it," he said.

"He wasn't such a bad guy," Isabel replied. "But you're lucky we aren't both in a ditch somewhere."

"Not much left to steal," Ben said, shrugging.

"We don't have anything left to steal." She showed him her open hand, watching the tail lights on Derek's truck disappear over a hill. "It's in his breast pocket. He'll find it in a little while."

"No problem. I wasn't hungry or anything," Ben said.

Isabel turned and started down the street, holding the crumpled yellow note with her family's address.

"5th Ave S., Seattle," she read aloud.

They looked over a map of bus routes, and after realizing it was only a dozen blocks, took off on foot. *They must be quite the pair to see on a Seattle morning,* Ben thought. Isabel's strides were short, but she made up for it in speed, and that morning, she had to restrain herself from running down the street. She would see them soon, so very soon. Ben lingered a few paces behind, watching a single car meander its way down a side street behind them.

Isabel took a sharp left onto 5th Avenue, scanning the rows of houses for anything that looked familiar. As they drew closer, she recognized the house, but didn't see any cars in the driveway. *Maybe they're pulled farther back or something.* Ben was the first to spot the cruiser, masked by the bushes at the end of the road. He darted forward, grabbed Isabel, and pulled her into a narrow gap between houses.

"What?" she whispered.

"Police." Ben nodded back towards the street.

"So? There's no way they're looking for us. We're a few thousand miles from Echton."

Ben frowned and peeked out at the car again.

"Humor me," he whispered.

"Fine," Isabel said. "My aunt's place is only a few more houses up."

They crept back around the house, slipping through an opening in the fence and across a tidy green yard. Isabel stopped just before the white house she was sure was her aunt's. The gold lettering beside the mailbox confirmed it.

"What?" Ben whispered.

"Nothing... I just thought I'd be able to tell they were here when I saw it. It's silly."

"Maybe it's the wrong house?" Ben set their cases down and looked over his shoulder. Isabel shook her head, then shot across the driveway, flattening herself against the wall of the house and creeping towards a stairwell at its rear.

"A little warning, maybe?" Ben muttered. He slid the cases under a shrub and followed, his eyes moving back and forth between the road and Isabel. Just as she slid around the corner, Ben heard something moving down the street, wheels against pavement. He ducked in after her, barely making out the nose of the cruiser as it rolled by.

"Wait," Ben hissed, but Isabel was already gone, shooting across the back lawn. The passing seconds were agony as he listened intently for anything that would tell him what she was doing. Ben tried to think of something to do. He had to warn her, but his mind wouldn't seem to focus.

Everything was moving too fast. He crept around the house, following in Isabel's footsteps, but didn't see any trace of her. *We shouldn't be rushing into this,* he kept thinking. *We need to slow down.*

On his toes, Ben peered through a back window of the house, but couldn't make out much, except a bare dining room table and some china sets in cabinetry. The sun had just begun to rise, casting the side of the house in a pale glow that continued to move closer to his feet. He'd always loved this part of the day, when the sunrise illuminates the world, but now it seemed like a butcher's blade bearing down on him. He moved down to another window and was just reaching up towards it when he heard a thunderous crash from inside.

Ben threw himself beneath the window ledge and lay there, frozen. Maybe it was a cat, a stack of boxes, a trap she'd come into; possibilities flew through his head, but it came down to the probability that either Isabel had found someone, or someone had found Isabel. After a few seconds, he raised his head above the ledge again and saw a towering, dark haired man in a long coat, standing just beyond the door leading from the kitchen. The man's head jerked about, a snub nose pistol in his right hand. He waved it wildly, stalking around the room, looking behind and under things. Ben couldn't place it, but the man looked entirely familiar. Oddly enough, it was the first thought that entered his mind.

His instinct was to run, but then he still hadn't found Isabel, and he couldn't just leave her there. Ben pulled himself up using the window ledge and angled his head, trying to see the far end of the room. The man was drawing closer, tearing open cabinet doors and kicking away pots and pans. As he pulled his head back from the window, Ben caught a quick glimpse of green as something moved across the room. He lost it for an instant, but as he moved back to another window, he saw Isabel, flattened against the wall just a few feet from where the man was walking. Wherever he walked, she tiptoed just a few steps in front of him, barely out of sight, her jaw tightly set, face drawn in desperate focus.

In this moment, Ben realized a few things: The sheriff had some deeper connections or deeper pockets than he'd thought; Isabel's family was never in Seattle or were already in Hix's hands, hidden away somewhere; and they were both probably dead if they didn't leave this house in the next 60 seconds. He watched Isabel continue her silent evasion, as they both disappeared into the next room.

Ben strained his hands against the smooth white finish of the windowsill, stretching to catch another glimpse. Even if he could be inside, he wasn't even sure he'd be able to help, but he also knew there was no way Isabel would stand a chance if that yeti in a coat caught her. He would just have to wait, and any second, Isabel would come bursting through that back door, and they'd make a run through the backyard. *That would be the best way.* He turned to mentally map out their escape route but only saw a towering wall of black cloth, broken by the silver handle of a revolver and a baton.

Ben looked from the man in front of him, to another making his way up the driveway, then raised his hands and dropped to his knees. He thought about Isabel, trapped inside the house. *Trouble on the inside, trouble on the outside. Please keep your eyes open, Isabel.*

"Good kid," one of them grunted, bringing Ben's arms behind him. He felt cold steel close around his wrists, ratcheting tightly until it stung his skin.

"Bad choice," the other snickered. He smiled as he pulled his baton from his belt, thrusting it into Ben's side.

SEVENTEEN
CHASING SHADOWS

She'd only been inside the house for a few seconds when Isabel realized something was wrong. The air was colder than it should have been, or the house was quieter. She couldn't tell what it was. Her brain screamed *get out*, but she wouldn't let herself. She paused in the doorway of the house for a few seconds, then crept forward, stopping to peek into the living room. She didn't realize what she was seeing at first. It looked like a mountain of clothes and blankets, but the slow rising and falling of its middle told her differently.

The man sleeping on her uncle's couch looked peaceful, but in a way that made her uneasy. She couldn't think of any guest of their family that would be sleeping with his boots up on their furniture, or his hand wrapped around the handle of a gun, protruding just slightly from the breast pocket of his coat. Isabel tip-toed in closer to get a better look at him, but as she left the kitchen, her foot snagged the corner of a rack, sending a shower of cookware spilling onto the floor. She cringed and darted away from the crash, towards the dining room.

When the pots and pans came to rest, it sounded like the man had fallen off of the couch, and now she heard him breathing heavily as he crossed the room towards her. She slipped back through the dining room, careful not to step on anything, and watched him from the opposite side of the table. Through the reflection in the window Isabel could see the gun fully now, hear the clicking of the chamber as he opened and checked it.

It was almost like a dance, her movements mirroring his as he made his way towards the kitchen, then into the dining room. She kept herself just one step ahead, hoping that eventually he'd be forced to check outside, where Ben had, no doubt, already realized what had happened and had hidden or run away. Isabel wasn't sure how much longer she could do this before she tripped or made another noise, and she hoped desperately that the man would settle in one place or leave altogether.

After a few minutes, her wish came true. From the back window, she heard the sound of laughter and muffled voices, and the man walked over to the back door and opened it, shouting to someone outside. That moment was all Isabel needed, and as he leaned out the door, she shot through the living room, behind the couch and made her way up the stairs. She knew she should leave through the front door, running as fast as she could until she found Ben, but they hadn't come all this way for nothing. She had to see if her parents had left a note or a clue, or if they'd even been there.

Isabel was sure she wouldn't have much time before the man returned; she'd have to work quickly. She cracked the doors of every room until she came to one that she assumed was a guest room, then decided that was a dead end too. It was empty and everything seemed to be in order, the bed neatly made and a thin film of dust resting on the desk. Isabel stepped back out and easing the door shut, she walked over to her aunt and uncle's room. It, too, was made up, except a few drawers in the dresser that were slightly ajar. Isabel spotted her uncle's planner atop a pile of change, and she carefully liberated it, as well as a pile of notes under it, tucking them into the small, leather-bound book.

The door slammed downstairs, and Isabel stopped breathing. Heavy footsteps rumbled through the house, pausing for a long while, then clomping away again. Leaning out the door, she could hear a voice speaking to someone about a delivery, something that was headed their way. She allowed herself a peek from the window and saw an enormous black car parked outside, a pair of black police uniforms standing by its trunk.

"Shit," she whispered.

One of the men gestured to the house, then slammed the trunk shut, and both got into the car. Isabel felt the hair stand up on the back of her neck. It was what she wasn't hearing that worried her. The easiest way to leave was downstairs, she knew, but she doubted she'd come out of that game a second time. She decided on the fire escape at the far side of the house.

Where the hell is Ben? Isabel made her way across the hall and through one of her cousin's bedrooms, carefully choosing her footsteps and cursing every squeaky floorboard. She twisted the doorknob slowly and let herself in, closing the the door behind her. When she pushed the white lace window trimmings out of her way, it was impossible not to think of her mother; her aunt had the same style. She bit down on the schedule book as she raised the window sash. It shuddered and stuck as she tugged at it, and every few seconds, she'd pause and look over her shoulder.

The cool morning air flowed into the room as she poked one leg outside, then, balancing on the narrow metal platform, slid the rest of her body through the opening. Pressed against the slick, white siding, Isabel hardly dared to breath. She swore she heard the rattling of the doorknob. Then, footsteps began to vibrate through the floor, drawing closer until they stopped, and a thick hand pressed itself against the window. She tried to make herself as flat as possible.

"I said if you're gonna smoke inside, close the goddamn windows," a voice said, muttering furiously.

When the sash slammed shut, she nearly fell off the ledge, swinging her arms madly to regain her balance. Isabel didn't dare move until several minutes after the footsteps faded away.

Too close. She let her head fall back against the house and surveyed her surroundings. Anyone who cared to look would have a clear view of her standing on that fire escape; her green dress was a startling contrast against the brilliant white of the house. Below was a faded red ladder, leading down to a break in the bushes. As Isabel swung her feet over its edge, she realized its path took her directly past the main windows of the house. She couldn't jump. It was too high and would be too loud, but she had no way of knowing where the man was or even if he was already waiting for her.

She scanned the trees and bushes around the house. No sign of anyone waiting there but also no sign of Ben. *Where are you, Ben?* A wave of nervous energy passed through her. Slowly, she lowered herself down the ladder, then froze a few rungs above the window. She stuck her legs through the ladder, wrapped them around its sides, and lowered her head towards the window. Isabel pulled her hair back tightly with one hand, and with the other, shielded her eyes, as she lowered herself the final inches until she could see inside the room.

The man's legs were barely in view, just inside the living room. She saw them straighten, then relax, propped up on her aunt's coffee table. It was a chance she'd have to take. Isabel took the ladder three rungs at a time and landed softly between the bushes.

"Ben!" she whispered. Crouched between the thick green shrubs, she could hardly see but knew that also meant that any searching eyes wouldn't find her.

"Ben, are you here?" she whispered again, a little louder. A few houses away, a dog was barking, and somewhere close, she heard a door slam. *Not even a glimmer of Ben.* Settling herself deeper into the bushes, she flicked through her uncle's schedule book until she came to October. *Nope, no, no,* she thought as her fingers traced over the tiny notes that covered the pages. She finally came to the last few days of the month, which were each marked with a large red X.

Isabel continued on to November, noticing that, like the last few days, the entire first week of the month was marked off. On November 8th, a tiny note read "Keys."

The keys, she mouthed the words, wracking her brain. It could be some kind of clue or a trick. Whoever was taking up residence in her family's house had to have taken them somewhere, and when she found her aunt and uncle, her mother and father would be with them.

Staying low, Isabel crept towards the garage.

"Ben!" she tried one last time, but heard nothing. She reached the garage, turned the corner, and let herself in the side door. Just inside the dusky, cobwebbed space, was a large black car, with brightly polished chrome trim. Isabel weighed her choices. She was alone as far as she knew. Ben had probably realized what had happened and left for the train station or somewhere nearby where she would know to meet him. She could find him later, or he would find her. All she could think about now was finding her family. She glanced over the notebook a final time, then set it aside on a shelf, walking towards the back of the garage.

Even as she popped open the trunk to the car and crawled inside it, Isabel knew she was taking one of the biggest gambles of her life. With the thought of her family alone with Hix, she didn't hesitate.

EIGHTEEN
MIDNIGHT HOSPITALITY

Vinnie pulled into the motel, the wheels spinning as they rolled over the edge of the parking lot.

"Honey, I'm home," he muttered, throwing it into park and turning the radio off. For a moment, he swore he heard something thump inside the trunk. *I swear I pulled out that club tire.* He made a mental note to check before he went out again. He wasn't in the mood to be chasing shadows; he just wanted to get the hell out of Washington, and the sooner, the better. He'd been a little shaky and a lot of pissed off all day after that kid had almost snuck up on him, but with him taken care of, he figured the other would come around soon enough.

"Wher've yew been, Vincent? Feels like I've been waitin' all goddamn day," a voice wheezed from behind him.

"Waitin' at that house all day like we was told to, 'til 8," he said, recognizing Glenn's accent instantly. *Jesus,*

I've been here two minutes, and he's already on my case.

"I said forr. Idtiot. Forr o'clock."

"Yeah, well the boss said 8 o'clock. What the hell's the matter, anyway? You in some big rush or somethin?"

"Yeah, I'm in some big roosh, to put my foot up yur ahss." Glen walked towards him. He was about a decade older than Vinnie, and for as long as Vinnie could remember, he'd thought that made him the boss man. *There will be a day when I'll look down at your corpse and smile.* It was an idea Vinnie relished, and he had to raise a hand to his face to hide the smile that spread across it.

"Well, I'm here now, ain't I? What's the big emergency?" Vinnie said.

Glen leaned against the car, a smug grin on his face. "I'm starvin'. Go watch ta kid so Brian and I ken get somethin' ta eat."

"Shit, I'm hungry too, Glen. That kid'll be alright for a few minutes. He even awake yet?"

"No chances on this one, boy," Glen replied. "Boss says it could blow up if we don handle it right off."

Vinnie grimaced as Glen parked his girth on the trunk of his car. *I am gonna punch this ugly fat bastard in his ugly fat face.*

"Get me a cheeseburger and a milkshake or somethin', alright? And get off my car, you fat mook. You'll scratch it up." He made half an effort at faking a smile and looked toward the motel room, wondering what sort of shape the kid was in after an afternoon with Brian and Glen. *Hix has gotta get me shifted out of this bullshit. There isn't any money in it.*

"Grab Bri and tell 'im I'm waitin' fer 'im out here,

will ya?" Vinnie heard Glen say as he stepped up the curb towards the row of doors, their paint a faded blue-grey.

"Oye, Brian," he called as he popped the door open to find a brooding figure hunched over on the bed, watching the corner of the room intently. As Vinnie drew closer, he could see what Brian was watching, a young man cuffed to the register, blood crusted on his face and chest.

"He ain't hardly breathin'," Brian said. "Can't we just be rid of him? He ain't gonna tell us anything he hasn't already. We been at it all afternoon"

"Maybe you been too soft with him," Vinnie snorted. He stooped down to get a good look at the kid, but his face was so swollen that he could have been anyone.

"He's told us plenty, but it's a different story every time. Glen mighta broke his arm when he told us he was there alone."

"The kid doesn't matter. She's the one he wants. Hix said he stays with us until we find her. Then we can lose him somewhere. Alright? Those instructions come down from the top."

Brian shrugged and lowered his long legs over the side of the bed, setting his feet into his shoes and stretching toward the ceiling. He was a full head taller than Vinnie but rail thin. Vinnie watched Brian disappear through the door, calling after him.

"Cheeseburger and a shake. Chocolate!"

As the door clicked shut, Vinnie saw his outline flash across the window toward Glen and away into the darkness. He removed the gun from his pocket and set it on the nightstand, then lay back, propped up by the headrest. He sat in silence for a long while, then plucked a cigarette and lit it, relishing the burning that filled his lungs. Smoke rose lazily into the air as it poured from his nose and mouth. Vinnie picked up the phone with his other hand.

555-323-43...34? he thought. He could never remember the last two digits. Oh well, he'd call the office troll and make him transfer the call.

"McCreary," he barked into the receiver. "The sheriff around? I got something for him."

A voice on the other end of the line squeaked something about holding, and Vinnie tapped his cigarette on the edge of the nightstand, showering ashes to the carpet below. A new voice came through and Vinnie glanced over at the unconscious figure in the corner.

"Yeah, about 6 foot tall, 160 - 170, brown hair." He paused to listen. "Nah, I don't think he's got anything. Bri and Johns picked him up and he's been w'Glen all day." He put the phone down and walked over, giving his captive a kick in the ribs. He waited a moment, then returned to the phone. "He ain't gonna be up for awhile I'd guess. No, no sign of her. We're runnin' the same routes as usual."

"Jesus, boss, this Houdini stuff ain't us. I wanna get back to the work." As he started to sit back down on the bed, a rock came hurtling through the window, spraying shattered glass across the room onto both beds. Vinnie froze for a moment, his mouth slightly agape, then shook himself back to reality.

"Something I gotta take care of. Sorry, boss."

With a quick jerk, the door flew open and slammed against the wall, the echo sounding into the night. Vinnie strained his eyes and ears but heard nothing but the hum of a distant engine on the highway.

"Vinnie! I like your car, Vinnie," an airy voice called from somewhere in the lot.

"My car?" he echoed, moving closer, until it came into view. "I'm gonna kill you, you little bastard!" Vinnie bellowed, glancing over the deep gouges in its hood.

It took him a minute to register it, but all the scratches looked like they spelled something.

Mutuatas Vita, he thought it read.

"Come get me," the voice said, and he saw movement in the corner of his eye, a thin hand, waving at him in the darkness. He wondered if it was a trap, if there were more of them out there than just these two. *No way she's smart enough to set up something like that.* McCreary had said something about a third, but Stetson had only seen two at the train station. Maybe the third split before they'd even left Echton. Vinnie didn't mind his chances. He had one and could take the other two if he had to. *Even if the third guy took McCreary out, that's not saying much.*

"You lookin for trouble, sweetheart? I'm gonna teach you a lesson." He ran toward the sound of her voice, kicking up gravel. The figure disappeared as quickly as it'd come, leaving him glancing about wildly, ducking low to look for a glimpse of moving feet.

"Come on!" he spat and started back towards the middle of the lot, cracking his neck.

When he'd reached the row of doors, he stood under the light, where he could see a little better, and looked around, realizing that she was almost in front of him. There, he could finally see her, at least the outline of the girl they'd been briefed on, the one that'd been wasting his time for the last two days. Her dark hair cast a pointed shadow on the ground, and the way she stood so close told him that she might be faster than he'd thought, or at least she thought she was. She blew him a kiss and turned to run in the opposite direction. She was trying to lure him away from the room, he knew it. *You wanna play, sweetheart?*

"Mommy and daddy have been missing you," he said, charging towards her. Suddenly, his left leg was jerked from under him and he found himself face down on the gravel. Struggling to get his breath back, he rolled onto his back, gasping for air. He could see the cuff of his pants caught in some kind of snare, tied to his car. He gave the leg a few hard kicks, until he heard the ping of the wire snapping, then pulled himself to his feet and pocketed a newly freed tooth. Raising a hand, he wiped away a trickle of blood from his mouth.

"That was a nasty trick," Vinnie said, his eyes sweeping the lot again.

"Shit," the voice in the darkness said quietly.

"I hope you had a better plan than that," he laughed, turning to duck back inside the room and snatch up the gun. He gave the boy in the corner an extra kick on his way out. "You're friend's a shithead. She's as good as dead," he told him.

"Where you going?" the voice rang out, almost sing song, from the other end of the lot.

Vinnie was sure someone must have heard them by now, but he didn't care. *If they wanted to get involved, he'd kill them too and burn the whole damn place down.*

He walked towards her, the pistol gripped loosely in his hand, his thumb playing over the hammer. To his left, he heard the crackling of shifting rock and whirled around, towards the noise, letting off a shot and shattering the window of a car across the way. *Nothing but a shadow.*

Vinnie roared and kicked a motorcycle over, cutting between two trucks and making his way towards the road where the light was better. He didn't care about the details. Now it'd become personal, and he vowed to himself he'd see her die before her parents ever saw trial. *The money will keep flowing, and she'll be six feet underground.*

As he cleared the opening between the two trucks, Vinnie saw a shadow flash by just ahead, followed by a blinding wave of pain. As he faded in and out of consciousness, he saw a girl in a green dress toss a length of something behind her, then reach towards his hand.

NINETEEN
IVE HAD WORSE

Not really what I had planned, but that's ok, Isabel thought, retrieving the gun before she walked towards the open motel room. She was shaking, and her fingers were numb from the impact of the wood as it struck his face, although she imagined he was feeling much worse. She nudged the door open with her foot, gun held tightly in both hands.

"Ben?"

A weak groan answered her from the corner of the room. She raced over and knelt down beside him.

"Are you ok?" She dabbed at the blood on his face with a bit of her dress.

"Well, that should take care of it." Ben managed a weak smile. His skin on his face was raw and swollen, his shirt stained crimson.

"Can't keep you out of trouble, eh?" Isabel said, trying

to smile too.

"Keys," he said, weakly.

"What are the keys? That was written in my uncle's planner. Did they tell you what the keys are?" she said.

Ben held his arms out, hands still bound by the handcuffs. "Keys."

"Oh!" Isabel ran to the dresser, snatched up the keys, and carefully opened Ben's restraints.

"Thanks," Ben croaked.

"We have to get out of here. They'll be back soon," Isabel said. She started to help him up, but the look on Ben's face told her something was wrong. She whirled around to see Vinnie framed in the doorway, red streaks running from his nose. There was no way it wasn't broken, judging from the angle it now occupied.

"No more running," he said, lumbering towards them, jaw set in a terrible grin.

She picked up the gun and trained it on his chest.

"You don't know how to use that. Just give it to me," Vinnie snarled.

"What're you gonna do? Charm it out of my hands?" Isabel straightened her arms, stepping forward.

"Easy now," Vinnie said, halting his progress. She glanced back at Ben, who was pulling himself upright, using the table as a crutch.

"Can you walk?" she whispered over her shoulder. He shook his head slowly. She looped her arm under his shoulders and helped pull him upright, the pair of them hobbling forward together.

"We're gonna go for a drive." She waved the gun at Vinnie. "Get your keys."

The big man didn't move, just stared at her, his hands slowly beginning to rise from his sides.

"I said now, goddamnit!" Isabel squeezed the trigger, firing a shot into the bed a few feet to his left.

"OKAY, okay, I'm moving," he said, shuffling awkwardly, snatching his keys up from the nightstand, and tossing them towards her.

"Now!" she snapped.

Vinnie stepped through the door, Isabel and Ben following close behind. Isabel stumbled under his weight, catching herself against the car. Lunging forward, Vinnie made a bid for the gun, but Isabel jerked her arm back and aimed it at his face.

"Not the smartest thing," she said, "but you don't really seem like the smart type."

Vinnie snorted, standing motionless by the driver's side door, his face flushed red.

"Mutuatus Vita," Ben said suddenly.

"What?" Isabel glanced back at him.

"The car, it says 'Mutuatus Vita'. I've seen those words before."

"We're not keeping secrets from our boyfriend are we?" A sadistic grin crept across Vinnie's face.

"I've seen that before. What's it mean?" Ben repeated, his eyes glossy.

"I - I don't know," Isabel stammered, looking back to Vinnie. "Shut up and get inside," she yelled, arcing the gun from Vinnie's face towards the car. Ben searched Isabel's face, as she helped lower him into the car.

"I'll explain later," she whispered in his ear. Isabel handed Ben the gun and hurried around to the other side of the car, sliding in behind Vinnie.

"My partners are gonna be back any second, and I wouldn't wanna be you," he chortled.

"Drive," she said. Ben leaned forward and pressed the gun into Vinnie's neck.

"You heard her."

As they pulled away into the night, another black car with two men in it turned into the far end of the lot and parked in front of the motel room.

"Don't even think about it," Ben growled, increasing the pressure on Vinnie's neck. Vinnie stiffened and continued down the road, accelerating slowly.

"Where you think you're going? Somewhere we won't find you? And the next time we find you – Mmm. You're gonna think this was a Hilton vacation," Vinnie said.

Ben stared hard at Vinnie through the rear view mirror. "Just keep driving," he said.

Isabel thought for a moment, looking over the swelling on Ben's face and the blood on his shirt. He looked worse than when she'd first found him in Echton. It was obvious that he'd been through hell in the last few hours. She couldn't help but feel that she was responsible, just as guilty as the ones who'd done it.

"Pull into this lot up here on the left and kill the lights," she said, tapping on the car window.

Vinnie made a wide turn and eased the car to a halt. They were in a small clearing, bordered by trees, and barely lit by the streaks of light that leaked from the road.

"What now, sweetheart?"

"Now you tell me why you're here, and who you're working for," she said stiffly.

Vinnie laughed, his broad shoulders shaking in the front seat. Ben slowly let down and re-cocked the hammer of the pistol. The man in the front seat seemed totally unphased.

"It doesn't shoot twice if you cock it twice," he said. "You ain't so smart yourself, Stanton." Vinnie said. "And who's your friend? Where'd you find this guy?"

"I'm asking the questions," Isabel replied. "Where's my family being held?"

"Somewhere. If you want I could take you both there."

"Where are they?"

"Could be anywhere, really."

"You better start giving me some answers I like, or things are going to get really ugly for you," she snapped. "How'd you find us here?"

"Kid, you only got a half dozen places you'd be hiding out, and after that little train stunt you pulled, your dear aunt and uncle's place was the only one anywhere near Colorado. Like I said, You really ain't as smart as you think."

Vinnie grinned, watching her through the rearview mirror. The hole where his tooth used to be made Isabel feel a little better about their complete lack of progress.

"How do you know where my family lives?"

"It ain't exactly Einstein work," Vinnie said, sneering at her. "I got a chart of the whole family tree back at the station. I'll have them leave it in your cell for you."

"How about the people in the house you were in, where are they?" Ben said.

"You got a lot of questions, and I don't exactly feel inclined to answer any one of them. See, I don't think you're gonna use that pistol - just wave it around like some new toy."

"Poor bet to make," Ben said.

"It just happened to be empty when you got there?" Isabel interjected. "What are the keys?"

"Keys? Keys to what? Yeah, it just happened to be empty. You see any relatives drinkin' coffee with me inside?"

Isabel's nostrils flared, her face a mixture of confusion and indignation. She glanced over at Ben, frowning.

"Who sent you here?" Ben said.

"I'm just an ambassador, a man of the law." Vinnie started laughing again, that sick laugh that told her he knew something she didn't. "Sheriff Hix sends his regards."

"What did you do with my parents, you stupid goon!" Isabel screamed, kicking the back of his seat. Ben gently grabbed her wrist, shaking his head.

"Usually, when I look for something, I check where I lost it," Vinnie said, eyes on the rearview mirror.

"Well, this has been helpful," Ben said. "Get out of the car." He kicked the door open and pulled himself to his feet.

"I can take care of this," Isabel said.

"Sure you can, but I'd like to," Ben replied coolly. He limped around the car, keeping the pistol trained on Vinnie as he eased himself from the front seat and started towards a crop of trees.

"Get on your knees," Ben said. Vinnie hesitated, looking Ben over. "I'm not going to kill you, although, I really should."

"That's right, you ain't gonna shoot me, and we both know it. Anyway, if I gotta come after you, it's just business, kid. It's nothing personal," Vinnie said.

Ben pressed the gun into the middle of Vinnie's back as he knelt, watching him carefully. Ben pulled the pistol back and lowered it to the right of Vinnie's head.

"Right. Just business," he said and squeezed the trigger until it clicked.

From where she sat, Isabel could just barely see Ben's back and part of Vinnie's shoes. When she heard the gunshots and saw the flashes of light, she leapt from the car and called Ben's name. As she strained her eyes, she saw Vinnie clutch at the side of his head and groan in agony and Ben crack the butt of the pistol across his head, then hobble back towards the car.

"What was that?" Isabel said, eyes wide.

"What'd it sound like?" Ben replied, easing himself back into the passenger side. "Can you drive?" Isabel nodded and slid in beside him, pulling the seat forward and throwing the car into reverse.

"Jesus, Ben."

"He's not dead, if that's what you're wondering. Although, your sympathy seems to be a bit generous these last few days. Drive a little faster, if you'd please," Ben replied, shifting his weight and taking a sharp breath. "Maybe it'd be different if you were the one being used for a punching bag."

Isabel tore out of the lot and onto the open road.

"Thank you," Ben added.

"What'd you do to him? I heard shooting."

Ben shook his head and closed his eyes, trying to steady his breathing. "Something to remember us by."

"And thank me for what? What you said is absolutely true. I'm the one who keeps getting you into this stuff. At least, I should be able to get you out of it," Isabel added.

"Doesn't always work out that way," Ben said, cradling his left arm.

"Are you ok?" Isabel asked.

"I'll be fine, just need to take it slow for a minute."

"Or see a doctor." She eyed him suspiciously.

"I'll be fine, but we need to lose this car."

Isabel nodded her agreement. It was getting late. The clock on the dashboard said 8:88. *Well that's helpful.* The sky was a deep purple, and they hadn't seen another car since they'd started driving.

"Got any ideas about what to do now?" Isabel said. She wasn't sure if Ben was furious or planning something, and either way, the silence in the car made her uneasy. She pressed her hands flat against steering wheel, waiting for him to speak. As the adrenaline left her system, she finally had time to realize that the board she'd hit Vinnie with had cut little grooves in her hands, and they stung like hell now. *Add it to the list of aches and pains.* The new pains actually kind of distracted her from the older ones, so having another wasn't the end of the world.

"Well, if they hadn't gotten a good look at me before, they sure as hell have now," Ben said, holding his ribs as he laughed softly. "My next wanted poster will at least be better looking."

"Ben...I am so sorry."

"I'm fine, but I think we should find somewhere to get off the road and get rid of this car."

"Yeah. You see anything?" she replied.

"The sign back there said five miles to the next town. Somewhere called Mirrormont. We can leave it there."

"Are you sure you don't need to see someone?" Isabel glanced over towards the passenger seat.

"I'm fine," Ben replied, pausing for a moment. "What does 'Mutuatus Vita' mean?"

"No idea, why do you ask?"

Ben pointed at the hood of the car, where the words were carved in sharp relief against the shiny black paint.

"Got nothing to do with me," she lied. "I saw that on his car too. Seems kind of strange."

Isabel felt Ben watching her for a long while, then he lay back, his head resting against the car window. As they drove, Isabel told him about how she'd hidden in the trunk for hours and tricked Vinnie with the trip line. She was careful to leave out any mention of the bike spoke she'd used to carve the words into the car, making something up about noticing them when she got into the car at her aunt's. *It'd worked perfectly though, made Vinnie mad as hell when he saw it.*

They'd been driving for a long while when they passed a billboard that read "Welcome to Mirrormont," and Isabel pulled the car behind a factory building. With strips of cloth from the bottom of her dress, they wiped its interior clean, taking extra time to make sure any prints on the steering wheel and car handles were polished away, and tossed the keys into the weeds.

"Where'd you learn this stuff?" Isabel asked as she helped Ben to what looked like a major road.

"I haven't exactly been a model citizen. Or a model anything, really."

"Who really is?" she said.

"I suppose. I still haven't exactly made a ton of great decisions...Can we rest for a second?"

Isabel nodded and helped lower him onto a curb.

"You really think your family was gone by the time those guys got there?" Ben said.

"My uncle's planners said "Keys" for a few days before this and about a week after. Got any idea what that means? It sounds like some kind of code, or maybe something he was involved in." She paused, watching Ben, who had begun to giggle.

"I heard you say that in the car, but I wasn't gonna ask questions...Your aunt and uncle ever go on vacation?"

Isabel stared hard at him. 'They went down to Arizona last year, I think, I'm not really sure. What does that have to do with anything?"

"I'm thinking maybe the "Keys" stands for the Florida Keys, a little string of Islands at the bottom of Florida." Ben lay back against the bench and cracked his neck. Isabel was silent; then she began to laugh. It started as a giggle and rose until tears leaked from her eyes and her mouth hurt from smiling.

"They're on vacation, and I'm breaking into their house, trying to interrogate hired henchmen in some ridiculous bullshit conspiracy." She wiped tears from her eyes. "The Keys," she repeated, doubling over and clutching her sides. *I don't know if I should laugh or cry,* she thought, *but laughing feels a lot better.*

"Maybe your folks knew that? So they wouldn't have to get them involved if they hid in their house?'

"Yeah, could be. I wonder how much they really know. Using the train we hopped to narrow our possible locations was – well, it actually showed some degree of skill," Isabel said, biting her lip.

Ben shrugged, pushing himself to his feet again.

"Either whatever you did is worse than you thought, or this Hix guy is part of something a hell of a lot larger."

"I should call Henry. Maybe he can tell me something."

"Well, you're not going to do it right now. So how about helping an old man get to somewhere he can lay down and die?"

"Don't make those jokes. It's not funny." She pulled Ben back up, and started towards the city.

They made their way through back streets and alleys until they came to a small residential neighborhood. Ben picked out a corner house, with a red "For Sale" sign in its front yard, a few hundred feet back from the road.

Isabel was exhausted, dirty, and hurt everywhere, but she felt strangely at home. If someone had told her, even a month ago, that she'd be comfortable with breaking into an unoccupied home with a boy she'd known for less than a week and secretly hoping that he'd sleep by her that night, she'd have called them crazy. Now, she found comfort in the way her fingers knew their path as they worked open the lock on the back door and the way Ben's hand felt on her arm as she helped him inside.

TWENTY
NEW NAME TO AN OLD FACE

***

Not *a bad way to wake up,* Ben thought, as Isabel raised her head from his chest and crept over to peer out the window. His eyes barely open, he watched the ideas churning in her head as she took in the landscape. He wondered what those eyes saw, especially when they turned to him. Rain was streaming down the windows and hammering against the roof. It took him somewhere else for a moment, somewhere simpler. Ben took a slow, deep breath, enjoying the sweet scent that leaked in through the cracks in the door and the windows.

"How are you feeling?" Isabel said over her shoulder.

"I've been worse. You ok?" Ben cracked his neck and pulled himself upright. In truth, his ribs ached, and the swelling in his face, coupled with the pressure from the storm, was shaping up to sponsor a perfectly excruciating headache. *A coma sounds pretty nice. Maybe they could have just finished me off.* He staggered upright and opened the back door, gathering rain in his hands, washing the dried blood from his face and chest, Isabel's hand steadying his back. It felt a little better, just to have something cool against his skin.

It wasn't until he reentered the house that he noticed the tears rolling down Isabel's cheeks. Ben wrapped an arm around her and pulled her close.

"It's wet enough outside. No need for those in here."

"Where do we go from here?" she said. "They weren't even here. Where am I supposed to look for them now? Where are we supposed to go?"

"We lay low for a day or two. Then we keep moving," Ben smiled. "We call your friend Henry in a little while and see if he can tell us anything we don't already know."

"It doesn't even matter." She leaned against the wall and slid to the floor. "I've been thinking and thinking, and it doesn't matter. Jesus, no matter where we go, it's like they're already there."

Ben settled himself beside her and dipped his head, trying to catch her eyes and ignore the pain shooting through his sides and neck.

"C'mon now. One of us can sneak into town and grab something to eat. I'll go, and you can relax a little and see if there's anything good in here."

"You're hungry?" she asked.

"Starved. Aren't you?"

"Yeah, I guess I am."

"Just sit tight. I'll be back in no time," he said. Ben made a few steps towards the door before Isabel caught him and laid a hand on his chest, her fingertips tracing the bruises on his neck and caressing the side of his face.

"You're in no shape to be going anywhere," she said.

"What if someone sees you? You heard the guy, I'm a nobody to them; no one's gonna know who I am."

"A nobody that looks like he's been in a prize fight. It's a chance I'll have to take," she said and silently slipped through the doorway.

"Stubborn," Ben said, wincing as he tested each of his ribs for noticable breaks, a point of painful familiarity. *I'd bet at least two of these are broken. I'm lucky it's not more.* He checked the time, 10:17. If she wasn't back by 11:30, he'd go looking for her.

The small rectangular rooms in the house made him think of a dollhouse he'd seen in the corner of Isabel's room. He and Isabel were the dolls now, being tossed around blindly by something they could hardly grasp even when it dipped its ugly head inside to shake them.

Ben spent a while considering what they'd really gotten themselves into as he systematically lowered the blinds in the house. *If anyone get suspicious, we're cornered.* He considered their options. *No escape tunnel in this place.* Ben wrapped his hand around the edge of the stairwell and caught the light switch, flipping it up and down again. He waited patiently, but no light came on. Stepping back into the hallway, he made his way past the kitchen into a large green room with a single window. Light spilled through the dusty pane and split at its center, one shaft stretching toward the door and the second illuminating a small stack of boxes, splitting at their sides.

Their labels were smudged and half peeled up, scrawled in red marker: "Derek and Allison's Christmas."

He pried the lid from the first box to find stacks of plastic plates and dusty silverware. Tossing it aside, he took a look in the next box, the same label on its lid. It was topped by a layer of crumpled newspaper and the corner of something brown and solid. Plucking out the newspaper, he uncovered a series of hardbound leather books with gold lettering that read "Encyclopedia of American History." The leather binding was cracked and fading, but Ben could just barely make out the inscriptions. He wrapped his fingers around the third book in the box and started leafing through its pages.

Satisfied, he set it back on top of the pile and carried the entire box into the room they'd slept in. As he traced his finger over the handwriting on the lip of the box, he thought of the man who'd driven them to Seattle and wondered where he was now. *Maybe that's our ticket back east. Catching a ride with someone would be easier and safer than taking something public.* With a resounding thump, he dropped the box, sat down, and propped himself up against the wall, pulling the books close.

How about you, Christmas Derek? You a fan of Mr. Dillinger? His fingers scrolled idly through the pages until he came to the section he was looking for: "Dillinger, John." It outlined his life a little differently than their new friend had, albeit in a much more concise fashion. In his opinion, Derek had done a much better job. Ben's eyes followed his index finger across the page until they came to a few names he'd heard before and a few he hadn't. At the end of the section about Dillinger, it mentioned other famed Chicago crime figures: Capone, Moran, and a man named McLellan.

Ben flipped backwards through the encyclopedia, until he found the heading for Capone and skimmed through it. Capone's operation made Dillinger look like an amateur. *The man must have been sharp as a razor and ruthless to run that much liquor through a major city during prohibition. Both men were a little baby-faced,* he thought, not really what he thought a killer would look like. *They must have been more intimidating in person.* Ben shrugged and tossed the encyclopedia to the side. He'd have to see if Moran or McClellen were a little more intimidating. He tapped the spines of the other sections, then pulled another volume out, flipping through it rapidly.

"McLellan," he said aloud, licking his finger and pulling a few more pages to the left. When he came to "M", the name met him at the bottom of the third page. There were just a few words after it, references to gang violence and robbery, followed by a footnote about the disappearance of the group's leader, Sean McLellan, along with his son - "Suspected foul play." *No kidding.* As Ben looked over the next page, his eyes lingered on a photo at its top left corner. The photo of the gang boss struck him as peculiar, something about the nose, strong cheekbones, and curly hair. *McClellan.*

"Hungry?" Isabel said.

Ben's body went rigid, and he dropped the book. "Stop doing that. You know I hate when you do that," he said, leaning back against the wall.

"Well, you don't have to eat if you don't want to."

Isabel set a large brown bag beside him and opened its top. Ben leaned forward and sniffed at it appreciatively.

"What in the world is that?"

"Chips and soup, freshly donated from the front seat of a delivery truck in town," she replied, winking.

"I see we're remaining low key." Ben pulled two large

Styrofoam containers from the bag, handing one to Isabel.

"They never even thought about seeing me."

"You're soaked," Ben said. "Take my shirt."

He removed the stained button up and tossed it to her. Isabel began to protest, but Ben quickly pulled a bundle of plastic cutlery from the bag and waved it menacingly.

"I'll do it. I'll come at you."

"If that comes near me, I'll eat the hand you're holding it with, I'm so hungry," she said, pulling the shirt around her shoulders and plunging a flimsy spoon into the soup.

For a few minutes, they ate in silence, picking at the homemade chips, dipping them in the soup, and listening to the rain on the roof. Wiping a greasy hand on his pants, Ben reached forward and tapped the encyclopedia.

"You know, I was reading about that Dillinger guy. He's a real piece of work. Everything Derek said was pretty much true, but he and this guy didn't exactly see it the same way."

"Yeah?" Isabel said between mouthfuls. "Thinking of becoming a gangster? Probably more lucrative than being a delinquent."

"Being a roadkill scraper pays better than whatever the hell it is I'm doing now," Ben laughed, tiny pieces of broccoli stuck in his teeth.

"But would the girls be as pretty?"

"Fishing for complements, are we?" He tossed the empty soup container back into the bag and dropped the last chip in his open mouth. "I think if we lay low through today, we could probably slip out of here tonight."

"And go where?"

"Ever been to Michigan?"

"That's a lot closer to Ohio than Washington."

"We're about as far from Echton as we can get right now, and not really any farther from it at all." Ben shrugged and ran a hand through his hair.

Isabel's hand hovered over the encyclopedia, tracing the gold lettering spread across its cover.

"How many of these are there?" she said.

"A whole set, I think." Ben motioned to the ragged cardboard box on his other side. "I just glanced over some stuff about that Dillinger guy and a few other Chicago outfits. Pretty dry, though."

Isabel frowned and pushed the book to the side.

"What else is in here?"

"A few more boxes in the bedroom over there that I didn't open, and I didn't go into the basement. You can't see a damn thing down there."

"Well let's see what we can scare up, eh?"

Ben rose and arched his back, his arms extended behind him. Just as he was bringing them down, he felt the coolness of Isabel's hand on his side.

"You're moving better today."

"Yeah, not so bad at all. Just a little sore." It wasn't totally a lie. He was feeling better than this morning, but it still felt like a tornado had played pinball with his body and left him for dead. He did his best to manage a sincere smile.

"I'm sorry, Ben," she said quietly.

"I'm alright," he said, shaking his arms lightly at his sides. She did the same, laughing and mimicking his every move, until something shiny dropped from her dress and rung out as it struck the floor. Ben stepped back as Isabel lunged forward, throwing herself on top of whatever had made the sound.

He knelt down beside her and wrapped his hand over her closed fist. When she looked up, her eyes were wide and her lip quivering. Ben looked into them and squeezed her wrist lightly, sending the coin clattering back to the floor, face up. He stared hard at the likeness imprinted there for a silent moment that stretched on and on.

"I know that face."

TWENTY ONE
AN AMERICAN RELIC

"Where did you get this?" Ben said. Isabel reeled, her hands grasping blindly at the molding on the door.

"I - I just found it."

"Liar!" Ben yelled, raising himself up to his full height, hands clenched at his sides.

"I didn't mean to hide it. It just - " Isabel stammered. His voice sounded like it had before in the alley, but then, it hadn't been focused on her. She dared a glance at the open door across the room.

"Where did it come from, then? You didn't notice it in your dress until just now?"

Isabel was silent. Her mouth moved, but nothing was coming out. She didn't want to lie but couldn't bring herself to tell him the truth.

"What do you people want from me?" He advanced on her. "Seriously, what are you looking for that you think

I have? I have nothing! I've never had anything. There's never been anything to take!"

"I'm not!" was all she could manage.

"You're a damn liar, and you know it. Last person I saw with that coin was Hix, and he was beating the hell out of me. What were you hoping to get with this, all this dragging me all over the country with that bullshit about your parents? You were one of them all along."

"I'm not. I swear," Isabel said, shaking as she backed away slowly, arms up to protect her face.

"Tell me the truth." Ben lunged forward and grabbed Isabel's hands, pulling her to within an inch of his face. "Tell me the truth right now, or I leave you where I found you. Alone."

"I took it from Henry in the shop," she blurted out.

Ben stared at her, his jaw set tight.

"I noticed the shape in his pocket when he walked in, and I took it from him when we said goodbye."

"That's convenient," Ben spat.

"It's the truth!" Isabel added quickly.

"Even if that's the truth, it means you've been keeping it from me this whole time, and that still makes you a liar. I helped you through all of this and you lied to me."

"I know," she said. "I know I did, and I'm so sorry." Tears began to escape down her cheeks and dot the carpet.

Clear as oil. Ben couldn't decide if he wanted to hug her and stop her from shaking or throw her from him and leave her there. He gritted his teeth and released her hands, stepping backward.

"I can't - what were you thinking?" he said. "Unbelievable. You were carrying that thing this whole time and didn't say a word." He stared at the back of her hand for a moment, noticing the indentation where the coin he was holding had been pressed against it. Briefly, he forgot Isabel and changed his focus to the object in his hand, inspecting its pale yellow surface and the face imprinted there.

"What did you say before?" Isabel said, tentatively.

"You ever keep something like that from me again and we're done," Ben snapped. "And if I find out you're working for them or even remotely helping them," he took a deep breath and let it out. "I've taken too many punches for you to lie to me."

"I'm sorry," she pleaded. "I really wanted to tell you, but I knew after I took it that if I didn't tell you that you'd be mad, but I didn't wanna tell you yet because I didn't trust you, and before I knew what happened, it had been more than a few days, and I just couldn't tell you anymore." The world spilled from her mouth like a waterfall.

Ben bit his lip, too preoccupied to process Isabel's explanation. He walked back over to the encyclopedia and tore through its pages until he came to "M." He turned the book to Isabel, holding the coin just to the left of the simple black and white portrait.

"Who is that?" she said, pulling the picture closer.

"Sean McLellan," he replied. Taking the book back, he flipped the page over and started to read aloud.

"McLellan. The McLellan crime family's rise to prominence in metropolitan Chicago began in the late 1930's. Predominantly run by Sean McLellan and his sons Edwin and Eidsel, the McLellan gang was well known for funding their operations by stealing and killing other gang members. Their history included a lengthy war with mob boss Al

Capone. Edwin McLellan was killed by law enforcement offi-
cials in 1943. Sean and Eidsel McLellan were never brought
to justice but are said to have perished in a roadside bomb,
allegedly planted by rival gang leader Bugs Moran."

"So what does it mean?" Isabel said. "Can I see?"

Ben pulled the coin closer, looking over its other side
and mouthing the words at its bottom.

"You haven't had enough time to see it the whole time
you were hiding it from me?" He snapped, tossing the coin
to her. "What does 'Mutuatus Vita' mean?"

"I honestly don't know," she replied, tapping the coin
with her index finger and looking over the face she knew well
but had just come to recognize. "I don't speak Latin or whatever
that is. I just thought it might mean something to those guys."

"Didn't seem like he knew what it meant either."

"It really didn't seem like it...but maybe he was putting us on," she replied.

"How does something like this end up in Echton,
Ohio?" Ben wondered aloud, shuffling his feet. "And why
does Hix want it so bad?"

Isabel ran a hand through her hair and watched him
pace across the room and return to the other side. "Maybe
it's just chance?" she offered. "Maybe it was just because
it's gold - Is it gold?" She tossed it in the air.

"Let me see." Ben took the coin back from her, and
bit its edge, leaving a small canine tooth impression in its
face. "I think that's a yes," he said, glancing back over the
page of the encyclopedia, then tearing it out.

"Maybe there's more in Echton, and Hix and whoever
he's working with just don't know where to look?" Isabel said.

"If that's the one I had before, I just found it in the

weeds by the railroad tracks."

"Maybe my parents found out where the rest of it is."

"That could be," Ben said. "What was it you heard before they took you to that cell?"

"Just something about keeping something that should have been burned but wasn't. I'm not sure what they were talking about. It still doesn't make any sense," Isabel shook her head. "Maybe a map to where it's hidden? Or something about where it is?"

Ben began to pace again, gnawing at his fingernails.

"I've got a friend, the same one I was going to say we should visit." He paused for a moment. "She knows a little about everything, bit of a history buff, I guess. I'm sure she could tell us something about this. It'd at least be somewhere safe to lay low."

"Where is she?" Isabel said.

"Remember when I asked if you'd ever been to Michigan? We can't move yet, but tonight we split as fast and quietly as we can," Ben said.

"How?"

"Leave that up to me." He tucked the coin in his pocket, patting it lightly. "Now, we've just got a day to wait through."

For awhile, they talked about motives and possibilities, and Isabel told Ben all about Echton and that there were probably a thousand places where someone might hide something valuable. He wondered how her parents could come across something that seemed so shrouded in secrecy but then reminded himself: *If they're anything like her, it wasn't much of a stretch.* After a few hours, they'd exhausted every possibility and took to searching through the house for further entertainment.

They spent the evening sorting through old decorations and torn paperback novels. He knew he couldn't forgive her yet, but he also couldn't bring himself to stay mad. She seemed so fragile and lost, and even though he found it damned near impossible to trust anyone, he believed everything she'd said. Once or twice that day, he felt resentment swell inside him, but he pushed it back down and thought about how she'd come back for him in that hotel room, when she could have just left him to die.

Ben had never been good at hiding what he was thinking, but that afternoon he did his best to mask his frustration. He'd made a point to never get attached, but here he found himself smiling like an idiot while Isabel twirled around the room, reenacting a scene from an ancient romance novel. There was something magnetic about her.

They finally ventured into the basement out of boredom but only made it a few feet from the stairwell before turning back, mostly due to Isabel's insistence that they didn't know what could be living down there. For just an instant, when they were in the darkness of that room, she'd put her hand in his and held it tightly. Maybe she hadn't realized what she was doing, or maybe it had been instinct, but for the rest of that evening, he thought about the warmth of her hand against his.

Darkness came on, slowly, languidly, as the moon rose into the sky and cast its pale light inside the house. When Ben and Isabel crept through town, a couple of twilight shadows, Mirrormont hardly noticed.

Ben corrected Isabel when they reached a small housing settlement at the edge of town.

"We're not stealing it, just borrowing it. They'll get it

back. Anyway, stealing is immoral, and so are the people that do it." He cracked the car door and slid inside, hiding his face under the steering column, unable to stop the mischievous smile that spread across it. Ben could feel her watching him as he opened the panel and went to work. His fingers turned quickly, freeing wires from their caps and turning their colors against each other.

"Ready?" he said from the car's floor.

"For what?" Isabel replied just as the engine rumbled to life. Ben dragged himself upright and patted the passenger seat, grinning all the while.

He drove all through the night, Isabel lost in thought beside him. Once in a while, she'd turn and look at him. He almost always knew when she was looking but kept his eyes on the road, his mind already in Detroit. The gauge on the dash kept reminding him they'd have to stop for gas soon, but something about the rush of being in control of his own destiny and the hum of the car's engine as he tilted his foot against the pedal made it impossible to slow down.

"How'd you meet your friend that lives in Michigan?"

"She used to work at the yard I worked in a few years ago, but she left even before I did," Ben said, angling the wheel to the right as the car silently turned onto an exit ramp. "Gas," he added.

"Right," Isabel said, sitting up. "So you think this woman'll know something?"

"I hope so," Ben said. "Cheryl knows a little about everything."

"Can I see that encyclopedia page again?"

"Sure. You got any cash?" He looked up the road to a gas station they were approaching.

"Not yet," Isabel replied, watching him from the corner of her eye. Ben just shook his head, smiling as they pulled up beside the pump. Isabel muttered something about asking for directions and headed inside while Ben filled the tank. When she emerged a second later, she had an armful of snack foods and an enormous grin on her face.

"I don't even wanna know," Ben said.

"Then I won't explain."

"It's like artwork, whatever it is that you do." He turned the engine over and rolled back out onto the road. "Got any cash left over?" Ben glanced in the rearview mirror as the attendant came rushing out of the store, brandishing a bat.

"Looks like he's having a bad day." She shrugged, helping herself to a snack cake as they sped out of the station, making for the highway. "I don't know why he's so mad; I left the rest of his wallet in the bathroom. How about that encyclopedia page?"

Ben lifted himself up off the seat and fished it from his pocket, handing it to her. She read it, front and back, then tossed it back in his lap.

"Why keep a fortune in Echton?" she said.

"Well - would you look for anything in Echton?"

"That's true." She was silent for a moment. "What would you spend it on if you had a fortune like that?" Isabel asked, tearing open a bag of potato chips and offering it to Ben. He dug his hand into the bag, the other guiding the car into the gentle curve of the road.

"Right now, I'm gonna say a soft bed, a beer, and a new pair of boots."

"That's it? Beer, sleep, and shoes?" Isabel reclined

and stared at the ceiling, tossing a chip into her mouth and chewing thoughtfully. "I'd spend every dollar trying to find my mom and dad, I guess."

"I think we're getting closer," Ben said, patting her hand. "I have a feeling."

Isabel sat upright and looked at him. "Do you think Hix is the one putting all this together? Maybe he's the one that hid it and is trying to keep people away?"

"I dunno what to think anymore," Ben said. "Could be he's just looking for it and thought your folks knew something he didn't."

"How long until we get to Detroit?"

"2 days," he laughed.

"Wake me up when we get there," Isabel said, turning on her side, arm wedged between her head and the car window.

Ben just smiled and refocused himself on the road. When they were further into Montana or Dakota, they'd jump another train and see how far that would take them. It felt a little strange. He didn't usually move this fast. It was usually a long trip, then he'd stay somewhere for a while and save up some money, make himself a temporary home, then move on. *Every day is a new day,* he thought, glancing at Isabel who was now snoring softly, the bag resting against her stomach. Forgiveness had always been a struggle, but he found it nearly impossible to hold onto the anger he'd felt when the coin had first fallen to the ground. It had been wrong to hide it from him, but the way she'd come clean made him trust her more, and though he couldn't explain why, he felt his anger soon give way to affection.

Ben finally had time to think, navigating his way east toward something he knew in his heart was horrible and undeniably fascinating. He wondered about Sean McLellan and about Doctor Stanton and his wife, the botanist. He thought about them and their daughter but kept his hands steady, his eyes trained on the asphalt flying by and the sliver of red he could see at the edge of the sky.

TWENTY TWO
UNDER THE MAGNIFYING GLASS

"This time's gonna be better," Isabel said as they walked towards the station.

"Why don't we just buy them?" Ben said.

"Why buy what you can just ride for free?" she said, walking backwards just long enough to wink at him.

"Because what - you've been driving all night, and you're exhausted?"

Isabel patted his arm and grinned. "You're the old pro at this. I'm sure you'll be ok."

Ben sighed. He knew she was right. He'd jumped more cars than he could remember, but he could hardly hold himself upright, and, at the moment, the thought of chasing a locomotive was less than ideal. They slipped around to the other side of the tracks, then into the grain, creeping toward the middle of the train. Moving closer and closer until they were only a dozen feet from the its wheels, they flattened themselves and waited. It wasn't long until the train started to roll, then, racing the surging wheels, their legs propelled them forward, up, and in.

As the adrenaline left Ben's blood and the burning sensation reintroduced itself to his legs and lungs, he realized how truly tired he was. The contents of the car seemed pretty unspectacular, just stacks of stained, wooden boxes labeled FRAGILE. *Filled with art or kitchenware or some nonsense,* he assumed.

"Your turn to keep watch," he said.

"Can I see the coin and page again?"

"So long as you don't hand it back to me in three minutes," Ben said, pulling them from his pocket and carefully handing them over. Isabel nodded her agreement, looking over the face on the page and rolling the coin between her fingers.

"Had enough traveling yet?" Ben said, leaning against the wall of the car, his eyes closed.

"Never," Isabel said, preoccupied.

Ben nodded silently, crossing his arms. "G'night."

She looked up at him for a moment. The pain in her ribs didn't seem nearly as bad, or whatever lingered there she'd grown used to, but Ben looked the same as when she'd first seen him, the new wounds replacing the old. Her heart ached as she watched him slumped against the wooden crate, and she made a promise to herself to take better care of him.

Isabel pondered the coin and the McLellan family for what must have been a long time. She wasn't really sure. All these rides were starting to blend together, and she too found herself nodding off. When the train came to a halt, the air was chilly and smelled of water.

"Chicago! Chicago!"

She heard the conductor shout further up the tracks. Isabel grabbed Ben's arm and shook him. His eyes snapped open, and he gasped, his arm thudding into the box beside him and sending a grey package tumbling to the floor with a horrendous crash. Isabel held on tightly, her finger to her lips.

Ben rose and started tiptoeing towards the door, Isabel in his shadow. He could hear a pair of voices growing closer, one shouting and one answering. A second later, footsteps rang out against the metal walkway, and the door on the other side of the car rattled violently.

"Shit," Ben said, creaking the opposite door open and peering outside. "I'm gonna lead them left. You go right."

Isabel started to protest, but before she could say anything, he was through the door and running across a small field, his middle finger hoisted proudly in the air.

"There! Do something!" one man shouted. A second man appeared from behind the car and took after Ben. Isabel knew she'd only have a few seconds, so she slipped through the crack in the door and between the cars, back towards the station. When she cleared the other side of the tracks, she saw only the back of the man chasing Ben, and a heel sticking out from the other end of the car. She walked, casually, towards the platform and seated herself in the midst of the crowded station.

A few minutes later, the man that had run after Ben reappeared on the platform, his hands on his knees. Another man, who Isabel assumed was the other voice they'd heard, was shouting something at him about doing his job. It was comforting to see them return defeated, but the feeling quickly left her as she realized that now she'd have to find Ben again. He certainly couldn't come back to the station. Isabel stuck a hand under her chin and sighed just as a sinewy hand grabbed hers and pulled her toward another train.

"Yes, why pay for what you can get for free?" Ben said, scowling, his coat now inside-out.

Isabel stood and hugged him quickly.

"Yes, of course. Why would you?"

He led her out into the city, lost in the blur of faces and sound. Isabel couldn't help but stare as people poured around them.

"This is amazing. I've never seen so many people in my life," Isabel said, dodging as a man on a bike flew by.

"From the smell and the skyline, I'd say we're in Chicago," Ben replied.

"Yeah, that's what he was shouting...Chicago." She craned her neck, looking towards the rooftops of the buildings that surrounded them. *I wonder if they're as beautiful on the inside.* She tugged at Ben's arm. "Where do all these people come from?"

"They live here. C'mon." He pulled her deeper into the city until she was sure they were lost, grains of sand in a Saharan storm.

"Chicago is supposed to be where McLellan lived, right?" Isabel asked.

"I had the same thought. I wonder where?"

They walked through the city's heart, winding their way through the streets until they reached a small side alley and ducked inside it.

"Alright, we can probably catch a train from Union station that'll take us to Detroit. It'd only take a few hours,"

Ben said, poking his head out of the alley.

"Is there a library around here? Maybe they have films from the old newspapers or something?" Isabel said. "There has to be something about McLellan here."

"This would be the place to look." Ben nodded, testing the swelling in his face and absently watching the masses of people flow by. "Alright, but let's make it quick."

"You'll only make it worse if you poke at it." Isabel gently wrapped her fingers around his and pulled his hand down.

"Yes, mom," he scoffed, stepping back into the crowd. Isabel nearly lost him as he dodged and wove his way towards a staircase that led to another train stop.

"Always with the trains," she muttered, barely clearing the sidewalk as a car tore by. Isabel caught him at the edge of the tracks.

"Cash?" He held his hand out expectantly. She placed a few crumpled bills in it and unfolded another for herself. "Chances are we're not gonna have to pay, but just to be safe," he added.

The train eased into the station, and as quickly as it'd come, tore off down the track. Isabel flattened herself against the wall of the car, watching out the window as the rows of buildings flew past and melted into a suburban blur.

"Incredible," she said under her breath. The car made several short stops, each with its own high pitched ding. On the third stop, Ben dragged her from the car. He stopped to glance at a map at a bus shelter on the street corner, then pointed down the street and took off. It was only a short walk, a few blocks, before they were at the front steps to an enormous stone building labeled "Public Library." Ben held the door for her.

"Jesus, it's like a castle," Isabel said, wide eyed.

"If you're gonna find something, it's gonna be here," Ben replied, pointing to a room up another small flight of stairs, where a section of long, oak desks were accented by two or three glaring lights.

"You've been here before," Isabel said as he followed her up the steps.

"Long time ago," Ben replied. "I still remember the building, though - beautiful building."

A small, mousy woman seemed to appear from nowhere, dragging a cart of books in tow.

"Can I help you find something?"

"We're researching a historical event," Isabel said.

"These are where the old newspaper films would be, right?" Ben added.

"Oh yes, in this section, and there's an auxiliary section on level three," she chirped. "Anything in particular you're looking for?"

"No, ma'am. Thank you," Ben said, walking toward the section she'd just pointed out.

Isabel lingered for a moment.

"Do you know anything about the McLellan family?" she said. *It was a slim chance but worth asking.*

"Meck-lel-ann." The woman chewed the words. "That's Irish, of course. Sounds familiar." She drummed her fingers on her chin and stared hard at the clipboard she was carrying. "Give me just a moment." Disappearing into a back room, she dragged her cart behind her.

"Well, I guess we'll see what comes of that," Ben said, smirking. "You'd think that in a place this big..." He turned toward Isabel, but found himself alone. As he looked around the room, he just barely caught a flash of her green dress, rounding the corner of an aisle on the opposite wall.

He made his way after her, past row after row of books and long oak tables. There was an air of tranquility about it all, about the smell of the room, and the feeling of the books as he ran his hand along them, enjoying the texture of their bindings. It only took him a moment to find her, doing almost the same thing he was. Her eyes flashed as she skimmed along the rows of books, a single finger dragging against them as she muttered to herself.

"Chicago History," she said, snatching a book from the shelf and cracking it open. Isabel flipped through its pages until she reached the mid 1940's. Her eyes flew over the lines, pausing for a moment, then continuing their path down the page.

"The other two - they were Capone and who?"

"Moran, I think. You find anything?"

"Nothing much, a couple mentions of prohibition and the Valentine's Day Massacre."

"Yeah, my uncle had an old newspaper about that. Total bloodbath."

"Doesn't seem like it was a peaceful time," she said, snapping the book shut and replacing it on the shelf. "If you were a book on Chicago gang history, where would you be?" Isabel made her way back down the aisle.

"There you are," a voice said from the next aisle. Ben leaned forward, peering through the gap between the top of the books and the weathered shelving. The mousy woman they'd first greeted walked to the end of the aisle and shook a small silver canister at him.

"Isabel," Ben called out, struggling to keep up with the

librarian as she strode back across the rooms to a series of angled desks. She disappeared behind one of the desks, and Ben listened intently as a series of strange noises followed.

"You ok?" he said. Peering around the desk, he could see the back of her silver head, immersed in machinery housing.

"What's she doing?" Isabel whispered over his shoulder.

"I think fixing it...or maybe building a time machine so we can see it for ourselves" he replied. A series of soft clicking noises punctuated the muffled bustling of the library, and the screen on the desk lit up, humming softly.

"This was all I could find," the librarian said, reappearing. Isabel leaned forward, her hair falling over Ben's shoulder. The screen flickered, then a magnified block of text appeared and came into focus. The writing in the upper right corner dated it April 23, 1944.

"This help?" the woman asked. Isabel nodded, her gaze frozen on the screen.

"Yes, thank you," Ben smiled and nodded.

"Leave it be when you're finished. I'll take it back out of the projector," she added, vanishing again.

"Terrence Waldrip to testify against Sean McLellan in the murder of Aldrin Mayes," Isabel read aloud. She glanced to the side of the machine, placing a hand on a round, black knob and turning it. The screen shifted, bringing another article into focus.

"Witness Testimony Absent from Trial," she said. "Death Determined to Be a Suicide by City Coroner."

"Nice of him to kill himself in such a timely fashion," Ben said. Isabel snorted and turned the knob again.

"McLellan Case Dismissed. It says it was ruled that without witness testimony, the overwhelming majority

of the evidence against them was circumstantial. Look."
Isabel pointed to a grainy black and white photo of a man
standing between two enormous granite pillars, a second,
younger man by his side.

"Eidsel, maybe?" Ben said,

"Or his lawyer although the resemblance is striking,"
Isabel said, turning the knob again but finding only white.

She wound her way through the library to the counter and, seeing the librarian through a series of windows,
waved to her. She emerged from a back room, a yard stick
in one hand and a crumbling text in the other.

"Is this all you have on the McLellan family?"

"It is. It looks like the other files have been pulled.
Must be on loan to other libraries. I have quite a few books
on Mr. Capone and one about his rivalry with Mr. Moran.
'Deadly Games' it's called, I believe. Would you like to see
some things on him?"

"No, no. That's alright," Isabel frowned, turning back
toward Ben. "Maybe we try another library?"

"We can." Ben paused.

"But?" Isabel said, impatiently.

"Nevermind. I just don't like hanging anywhere too
long." He stuffed his hands in his pockets and looked
around the room, seeing only a few scattered bodies, reading at desks or navigating rows of bookshelves.

Isabel thanked the woman for her help, and the two
returned to the street, finding it much emptier.

"Lunch must be over," Ben said.

"I guess so," Isabel said. This time it was Isabel that
led Ben through the city. She stopped briefly to look over
a city map, then continued to speed past city blocks, only

stopping again to look through a phone book.

"Let's try a little different approach this time. I love this urban grid system. Makes way more sense than country roads," she said, thumbing through the pages.

Ben wanted to ask where they were going but knew it was no use. Isabel had made up her mind. He listened to her shoes clicking sharply against the ground as she walked and kept his eyes on her heels and the occasional splotch of used chewing gum.

"1603 Parkway," she said, stopping in front of a large, old house, marked by eloquent gold lettering that read "Geldhous and Epstein." Its eccentric curves and woodwork made it seem almost Victorian. It seemed out of place, but then again, so did they. She gave the door a few brisk knocks, then stepped back. After a short pause, it creaked open, and a young man in a suit with short black hair greeted them.

"Something I can do for you?" he said.

"I'm interested in legal history," Isabel said.

"Well, that's wonderful. We dabble ourselves." The man said, starting to close the door. Isabel quickly produced the rest of their money from her dress and, holding it between her index finger and thumb, waved it under his nose.

"Very interested." Her voice was crisp, her eyes raised to meet his.

"As you should be!" The young man's voice lightened considerably as he reached for the money.

"Payment comes after services rendered," she said. Ben smiled, watching the two of them. It was a strange thing to see in the middle of a Chicago suburb. A petite woman with a fistful of money in a filthy dress staring down a man in a suit, who towered a foot and a half above her. *If I had to pick, I'd rather fight this kid than her.*

After a moment, he opened the door fully. "On behalf of Mr. Geldhous and the late Mr. Epstein, Welcome to our office. My name is Michael," he said, bowing his head as they entered. The inside of the building was as elegant as the outside was eccentric. Rich, red upholstery covered everything, and the dark mahogany of the floor beneath them shone richly. It was obviously old but had been kept in pristine condition.

"How'd you hear about us?" Michael asked.

"Justa phone book," Isabel said.

"Ok, we get a few of those here and there." He bid them follow him though a long, dark hallway into an enormously tall room filled with thick, leather bound texts. "And what brings you here?"

"We're in a bit of a hurry," Ben said.

Michael nodded knowingly and gestured to a row of chairs at the edge of the room. He crossed the room as they sat down and called back over his shoulder.

"You get into a bit of trouble, eh?" He gave them a knowing wink. "What is it you're looking to get out of?"

"We want to know about a man, used to live here about 50 years ago."

"Oh?" he said.

"Sean McLellan." Isabel watched him carefully as she said it. He turned to face them, then spoke, choosing his words slowly and deliberately.

"Interesting. I didn't realize we'd be ghost hunting."

TWENTY THREE
THE INFORMATION ECONOMY

Michael Geldhouse wasn't sure about the pair on his doorstep until that moment. When they'd mentioned that name, he knew it could be trouble but did his best to rationalize it. *They're already inside, and money is money.*

"Ooph. I can't tell you much, but we might have something," he said as their eyes followed him around the room. He clicked his tongue, rapping his knuckles against books as he passed over monetary affairs and into public domain.

"Well?" the thin woman said.

"Any particular reason?" Michael asked. He couldn't make sense of what they were up to, but it seemed that whatever it was didn't center around legal education.

"Nope, just curious," her companion replied.

When Michael gave him a good look, he noticed the swelling in his face. A bit of dried blood still shone in the hair above his ear. It made him feel incredibly uneasy about the whole thing, but he took a deep breath and forced a smile. They looked just as uneasy as he did, and it actually made him feel a little better. He was never one to take a bet unless it was a fixed one, but from the look of them, he had some pretty decent odds.

"Are you gonna help us? Or watch money walk out the door? Your call," the woman said.

"Easy now, no need for that." Michael jumped up onto a stepladder and plucked a pale yellow binder from a shelf. "That case was one of the first in Chicago to set precedent about the strength of circumstantial evidence in the absence of testimony, but if you're studying this, you probably already knew that."

"Mmhm," she said, leaning forward.

Yeah, I bet, Michael thought. *I bet you know as much about that case as I know about that filthy pillowcase you're trying to pull off as a dress.*

"Right. Well, McLellan had some big-shot lawyer brought in from New York; he just beat the hell out of the prosecutor," Michael said, leafing through the pages. "My pop told my about it; he said they were about to bring Uncle Emile on. They were ready to try anything; the thing was going so badly."

"What happened?" the bruised man said. Michael was silent, looking over the pages of the text. He decided he'd call him "Limps," and the woman he'd call "Patches."

"A little help?" Patches rapped on the arm of her chair.

He jerked his head up and made a face at them.

"You wanna learn about this case, or you want a dancing circus bear? Make a choice, and let me read," Michael snapped. Limps and Patches glanced at each other, then went back to watching him. He made sure to let out an occasional "Hmm" or "Oof" to make a point of his effort. *From the looks of that cash she was swinging around, there's at least $25 there.* If there was anything he'd become exceptionally skilled at in his apprenticeship for his uncle, it was looking busy.

After a few minutes, he walked over, turned the binder towards them and laid it in Patches' hands. He'd throw them a bone. *Why not?*

"The old man, head of the family, Sean, was charged in April, 1944, about three months after his kid got killed in that shootout. Some security guard got brave, took it upon himself to take a shot at the kid, and dad took him out." He paused. "Well, there was only one witness in that whole bank full of people that would say a word about it, and he happened to expire about a week before he was supposed to take the stand."

"Just like that?" Limps said.

"Pop told me they were transferring him, heavy guard and all, and the whole damned envoy got shot up. By the time the smoke cleared, his testimony was, uh, full of holes." He snickered at his own joke.

"We'd read that it was a suicide," Patches interjected.

"Right, a suicide." He raised his fingers in mock quotation marks. "I'm sure that you did read that. In a newspaper?" Michael said. "If you know so much, why are you asking me? This guy didn't do anything halfway."

He gestured to the text in Patches' hand. "Some of the things they say he did, just hearing about it'd give you goose bumps. The transcripts are there, but it says the second time they tried to bring charges against him for armed robbery and murder one, he was smoke in the wind."

"Just disappeared?" she said.

"Right." Michael bowed to her, tapping his index finger against his head. "Smart kid."

He really did remember hearing his father and uncle talk about the case when they'd had too much gin in the parlor room. "Disturbed" his uncle had called McClellan for the calm disinterest he'd shown in the courtroom. It had unnerved even the judge. His uncle said the prosecution liked him for a half dozen murders and a few bank jobs on top of that but hadn't had enough evidence to put it together. In the corner of his eye, Michael saw Limps, who he'd sort of become fond of over the last few minutes, start moving to the edge of his chair.

"What else?" the girl said. "How much money was this guy supposed to have?"

"No one knows for sure. Cops turned his whole place over after he skipped town, but he and every fella he'd put his name in with seemed to vanish into the woodwork, not a penny left behind. Few weeks later, police find what's left of a car McLellan used to own down south, human remains in it, and they find some papers - city coroner files a report certifying his death a few days after that." All in all, Michael remembered seeing a few other cases like it. *If you put enough predators in the cage together, they're bound to eat each other.*

"He used to steal from other gangsters, right? Like Robin Hood or something?" Limps said.

"Not exactly - I can't say for sure. The word was that, yeah, but he was the most heartless of the whole batch. Thought it'd just be easier to take from the ones doing the taking." He waited for a few moments, but neither of them spoke, just stared down at the trial transcripts. "Anyway, this is all really just speculation, but take it for what it's worth, I guess." Michael held his hand forward expectantly. He'd said more than he intended to but nothing he couldn't deny later if someone came after him about it.

Patches peeled off a few bills and gave them to him, her eyes still on the open book. He flipped through the money and sighed loudly.

"This ain't much, lady."

"You didn't give us much," she replied coldly. Limps stood, his eyes almost level with Michael's. Michael had seen that look before, and if there was any person you didn't want to get into a scrap with, it was someone that didn't have anything to lose. Whatever he'd gleaned from his encounter with Limps and Patches put those two squarely in that category.

"Alright, that's fair. Not much to give." He shrugged, adjusting his collar and tugging at the sleeves of his suit. The phone rang loudly in another room, and he gave them his most cordial bow, moving towards the door. Patches rose to follow, but tripped on the carpet and fell into him, recovering immediately, but blushing furiously.

"Sorry, just tired," she said.

Michael brushed off his suit where she'd touched it and faked a final smile. The ringing phone was giving him a headache, and he decided he was done with their little visit.

"Excuse me, I have to grab that. Can you let yourselves out the same way you came in? As always, the house of Mr. Geldhouse and Mr. Epstein appreciates your business, and please return, should you need anything else." He wagged the money at the two of them and winked, sidling through the doorway and into the parlor room.

TWENTY FOUR
WANTED AND WEARY

L aw binder in hand, Isabel returned to plop down beside Ben, biting her lip as she chased her thoughts.

"Well, that was a waste of time," he said.

"Pretty much," Isabel mumbled, combing through her hair with her fingers. "What do you wanna bet Sean and Eidsel hid their stash before they made a run for it down south?"

"Makes sense." Ben stepped out into the hallway and headed toward the door, motioning for Isabel to catch up. "They hide the loot, then try to make their way down south, but Morone or Moran or whoever catches up with them and settles things his way." He knotted his brow, working the ornate lock on the door back open.

"Then he must have left something behind. Some clue about where he left it," Isabel said.

"If he was feeling generous. If I were him, I wouldn't leave a damn thing, so I'd be the only one who'd be able to come back for it. Unless... you never get the chance to come back. Then, I guess it's anybody's luck to come across whatever he left behind."

They emerged into the streets of midday Chicago and headed back towards the train station. The air was thick, but a soft breeze flowing through the city carried the smell of roasting meat and candied almonds. At Ben's suggestion, they stopped for a moment to grab sandwiches, tearing into them as the train eased away from the station.

"Detroit?" Isabel mumbled, her mouth full of what Ben had affectionately referred to as "an Italian beef." He'd insisted that if they were in Chicago, they couldn't leave without one. He reached forward to wipe the crumbs from Isabel's chin and nodded.

"Probably easiest just to jump off this commuter at the edge of town and get on another. It'll take us straight there, maybe five hour ride from here, if that."

"Good," Isabel sighed. "Maybe this time, I'll let you ride in the passenger car."

"Why pay for what you can stea-" Ben froze, leaning forward to squeeze her arm lightly.

"Don't look. The man behind us in the grey coat, I saw him just outside the library after we left." Isabel turned her head just slightly, then laughed as if he'd made a joke and turned to wrap her arms around him.

"He's still watching us," she whispered.

Ben took a deep breath. At the next stop, he stood still until the doors started to close, then slipped out and yanked Isabel through them, clear of the train. Through the window, they watched the man in the grey coat struggle through the crowded train and heard him shouting as he reached the closed door. The man pounded on the window, then reached up and pulled the emergency stop, bringing the train to a grinding halt.

"Run!" Ben grabbed Isabel's hand, leading her down the stairs, through an exit gate, and around a corner.

Isabel threw her arm out, pointing to a storm drain lid across the way. The sound of pounding boots echoed on the staircase above them, and a flicker of gray shot by an opening in the rails, shaking the stairs as the man descended.

"Why not?" Ben muttered, darting past a car and slipping behind a passing bus.

From the honking and cursing behind him, he guessed Isabel had followed just behind, and by the time he'd pried the lid up, she was beside him. She slipped around him and swung her legs into the open drain, her feet ringing out against the rungs of the ladder as she descended.

Across the street, the gray-coated man flew down the final set of stairs, his face shrouded by a small brown hat and his right hand tucked inside the breast of his coat. Ben backed into the storm drain until he lost sight of the man, dropping into the rushing water and cursing as it flowed over the tops of his boots.

"The hell you doin?" A woman in an orange vest appeared at the mouth of the drain. "Get out!"

"What're you waiting for?" Isabel shouted from further down the tunnel.

Ben glanced up, heard a heavy thud, and watched the man in the grey coat replace the woman at the opening of the tunnel. As the man started lowering himself into the drain, Ben took off after the sound of Isabel's voice.

The splashing of the water echoed through the tunnel, and soon it grew so deep that Ben found himself wading after her, brackish liquid flowing around his thighs. He caught her after a minute, her green dress hiked up around her waist, legs working furiously against the current.

"Here," she said, pointing to a side tunnel. They stopped for a moment and heard distant sloshing and cursing from farther down the pipe. Whoever the man was, he was breathing heavily and slowing down. *If we can just keep him moving, he's done for.* Ben was sure of it.

He followed Isabel further, the light growing dimmer as they delved into the drains. When he figured they'd gone far enough, he called for her to stop, listening intently for any sign of the man.

"Is he gone?" she said.

"I don't hear anything," Ben said. "Let's keep it quiet and see if we can get out of this - detour"

She nodded her agreement, holding on to the back of his coat, while they pushed on toward a beam of sunlight, leaking through the ceiling just ahead. As they worked their way to the opening, Ben made a mental note to stay out of dark, wet places and away from pretty girls with warrants out for their arrest.

"You're the one who wanted the bath," he scowled.

Isabel snorted a laugh, then pushed past him and started up the ladder. She moved quickly, and Ben had to sidestep to dodge the water dripping from her legs and shoes. With her back against the manhole cover, she straightened her legs and dislodged it slightly, wrapping her hands around its edge and shoving it to the side. When she had about half of her upper body outside the drain,

Isabel let out a sharp gasp, and her body went rigid. She started to inch back down the ladder but then froze and retraced her ascent.

Muted voices echoed from the street's surface, one he knew was Isabel's, and the other he wasn't sure about until he saw the toe of a black boot sticking out over the edge of the hole, prodding her side. Isabel shifted to the side, and part of the grey coat came into view. *This one might actually be real a cop.* Ben retreated back into the pipe, out of view, as the drone of their voices resumed.

Whatever was going on, they'd been talking for a while when Isabel pulled her legs the rest of the way up the ladder and someone pushed the manhole cover shut. Ben slowly took hold of the metal rungs, pulling himself up out of the water and working his way back toward the surface until he could hear them clearly.

"Well, where is he?" the voice said.

"I don't know. We split up," Isabel answered coldly. "I just told you that."

"Don't you lie to me, girl. It's only gonna make it worse," the man said.

Ben had almost reached the top, and through the opening in the manhole, he could see the man in the grey coat standing very close to Isabel, his arm extended into her ribs. *Either he's a little sick and taking his time, or he wants us both alive.* He couldn't see the man's face because he was turned away, but the way he held himself was almost casual, too confident not to be a professional.

"Let's go for a ride then, eh?" he said.

"How about I just scream?" she shot back.

Ben looked back down the pipe. Maybe a bar that'd

come loose or even a rock, anything that he could lash out with. He spotted a rung that was attached on only one side near the bottom of the ladder and decided that was it. Halfway down, he could just barely hear Isabel's screams.

"Here, take the money! Just don't hurt me, please!"

Take the money? Was he imagining things?

"She's lying!" another voice yelled out. "I'm a cop, you moron. Let go!"

He shot back up the ladder, towards the sounds of feet shuffling on the street.

"Let's see some ID then," a third voice said. Everything was silent for a moment, save the ragged breathing. *They must be right on top of me. I can't see a damn thing.*

"And what badge are we supposed to be looking for? You ain't got shit in your wallet, and the only thing in that coat is a switchblade and that revolver you're waving around like a goddamned lunatic."

"I'm not on duty the - that girl! She's wanted for murder in Ohio, and I recognized her from a dispatch."

"I've never even been to Ohio!" Isabel said.

"Calm down, ma'am. You're not helping the situation."

"He just came out of nowhere and shoved that thing in my face and told me to empty my pockets, and I just ... "

Ben couldn't help but smile as he heard her break into passionate sobbing, which, in his opinion, was a little bit overdone.

"Look here, guy," one man said.

"Officer. Officer Partland," the other man snapped.

"Sure, officer. My partner or I are gonna take you in for a few questions, and if everything checks out, you're good to go."

"Shit, John, hell of a day to be on a bike. If we had the car we could just - " the other man said.

"I know. We'll make it work, we can each hold one until we c'n get a car over here."

"You can't just let her go, you morons!" the man in the grey coat barked.

"She'll be taken into custody...officer. Larry, throw a pair of cuffs on her, would you? I'll take Officer Partland somewhere we can get some ID confirmation for him."

"Yep," the other man said. "Gilbert and Schiff should be around here in a minute anyhow."

For a few minutes, Ben was absolutely still, perched on the top rung of the ladder, listening to the sound of the cuffs ratcheting closed. Isabel's voice was muffled, but he was guessing she was urgently trying to negotiate her freedom when a tremendous crash, followed by a chorus of screams echoed from outside the alley.

"The hell was that?" the officer said, his footsteps growing further away. Then, a series of gunshots echoed against the brick buildings.

"Do not move," Ben heard him shout.

Isabel knocked on the manhole a few moments later. "C'mon. Let's get out of here."

Ben emerged, squinting in the sunlight, just in time to watch her unlock the other handcuff with a thin black pin, which she immediately replaced in her hair.

They ran back into the street, falling in behind a pair of women in dresses and long coats. Ben couldn't resist stealing a glance the other way, where a police bike was on its side and the man in the grey coat was working frantically to break the grip of an officer as two more ran towards him.

Ducking their heads low, Ben and Isabel let themselves be swept into the stream of bodies that passed them.

"I don't think they wanted you dead. I don't think they've ever wanted you dead," Ben said, thinking aloud.

"No? Seems like they're making a pretty good play at it," she replied, pulling him forward.

"Nope." He paused again. "I think if they'd wanted you dead, he would have killed you right then and just been done with it. Whatever Sheriff Hix needs you for - he needs you alive.

"Well, that makes me feel a lot safer."

"It doesn't do much for me," Ben replied.

TWENTY FIVE
IN THE REARVIEW MIRROR

They hardly spoke on the train ride to Michigan, but from the looks they both got, Isabel could tell they were both in dire need of a change of clothes. She'd never been in so many places in one week, and it seemed like every city they passed through was another lifetime.

"Wow," she mouthed as the train wound its way towards Detroit. The city's lights came into view as they rounded a long curve, and she couldn't believe how far they seemed to stretch, like stars in the night's sky.

"I think Cheryl is about 25 minutes from the Grand River stop. We can just drop by when we get into town."

"What's so special about this woman?" Isabel asked.

"I trust her. Anyway, it gives us a place to stay while we find out a little more about this McLellan thing."

"I've got a feeling we'd find out a lot more in Chicago."

"How long were we there? Two hours maybe? Before

we were looking down the barrel of a gun. I've got a feeling anyone who looks into this stuff gets put under the magnifying glass pretty quickly."

"Yeah, I suppose," Isabel said, wedging her arm between the window and her face.

She felt like they'd been running for years, and even when they weren't running, it felt like they were. Her bones were tired, and her feet ached, and she was only pretending that she thought they'd find anything about her family in Michigan. At least it was somewhere, though, somewhere that might be close enough to take a peek at Ohio.

"She's got a daughter about our age," Ben said.

Isabel smiled appreciatively, knowing that at least he understood her discomfort. She knew it wouldn't be long before they pulled into the station, and she'd have to start moving again, so she pulled herself over next to him, her head on his shoulder. Isabel woke to his hand brushing the hair from her eyes, his gaze fixed on the front of the train.

"Couldn't you have just carried me until we were there?" she teased.

"I was wondering if I might have to," Ben said as freed himself from the seat. He wrapped his hand in hers, hoisting her into the aisle, and together they made their exit. Even after they'd reached the side of the road, he kept his hand in hers and raised the other into the air at passing cars until a cab stopped for them.

"Woodward and Brush," he told the driver, sliding in beside Isabel. Isabel leaned across him to read the bright green clock's digits on the dash.

"I thought it was later than that," Isabel said.

"Nah, just a few long days. We get to the house, and

we'll crash for the night. We can see where we're at tomorrow."

"Deal," she replied. Isabel felt too tired even to look at the lights anymore. She settled into the seat, laying her head in Ben's lap. *There's something very comforting about being in total disarray.* In Echton and in Maine, her room had been spotless, everything in its place and the covers tightly tucked around the mattress. This seemed OK now, though. Maybe even better.

The cab's breaks squealed as it began to slow in front of a row of dimly lighted houses. Ben paid the cab driver with the last of their cash and held the door open for Isabel.

"Looks like we have to go scavenging again," he said, watching the car pull away.

"Tomorrow, please. Tonight, I don't think I could steal a cotton ball from a blind man," Isabel groaned.

Ben laughed, surveying the block. Isabel felt uneasy, something about the broken glass and rusted engine parts that pocked the driveway adjacent to them. He turned left and took a few steps forward, then returned and walked a dozen feet in the other direction, pointing to an ancient home with cracked red paint.

"This is the one."

She followed him onto the porch, stepping around an upended tricycle and accidentally scattering a few empty beer cans with her other foot. Ben reached the house first and knocked lightly.

"Cheryl?" he said, peering through the door's dirty glass pane and its spider web of hairline cracks. He tried again, this time a little louder.

"Maybe she doesn't live here anymore?" Isabel offered.

The third time Ben knocked, a light came on inside

the house, and a short woman with thick, tangled blonde hair answered.

"Can I help you?" she said.

"You look even more like her, the older you get," Ben said, his eyes wide.

"Like who?" the woman tapped her foot impatiently, knocking the ash from the end of her cigarette and looking them over.

"Like Cheryl," he said. "You look like your mom."

The woman looked him over, then flicked the cigarette onto the lawn.

"You're a real piece of work, coming here to say something like that," she spat. "What'd we owe you money or somethin'? I ain't got any."

"Janice?" he said, stepping backward.

"Come here again, and I'll call the police," Ben heard her say as the door slammed in his face. He leaned forward and knocked again.

"What are you doing!?" Isabel whispered.

"She's got it wrong, I know Cheryl lives here." He knocked harder until the light came on again, and the woman threw the front door open.

"I want to see her," he said.

"You can't see her," the woman snapped.

"I don't know what happened between you two, but I need to talk to her. I didn't come all this way to have a door slammed in my face," Ben said, planting his foot in the open doorway. Her eyes were hard, and Isabel could hear her teeth grinding, but her expression softened as she studied his face.

Janice lifted a hand to cover her mouth and gasped.

"My God, Ben Richter. Come into the light." She took his hand and pulled him into the house.

"Janice, this is Isabel." Ben reached back, dragging her along. Janice turned quickly and wrapped a calloused hand around Isabel's, shaking it gently.

"Wonderful to meet you. I'm Janice."

As she crossed the threshold, Isabel saw a little girl's head sticking out from a door further down the hall. She smiled and waved, and the little girl waved back.

"Get back to bed, Shelly," Janice called to her. "It's time for little girls to be asleep."

Her tiny curls of golden hair disappeared back into the room as the door shut gently.

"She's beautiful," Isabel said.

"Thank you; my cousin's kid," Janice smiled. She had the same golden locks. They spilled down over her thick shoulders and across a stained t-shirt that was much too large for her. Her smile was beautiful, but she looked so tired, Isabel couldn't help but notice.

"Did you have a fight?" Ben asked, looking around the house. "Where's Cheryl?"

"No, it's... maybe we could wait to talk about it? I'm sorry for how I look. I know I'm a mess. I just wasn't expecting company."

"You look beautiful." He pulled her into an embrace. "It's good to see you."

"Come in, come in." She ushered them inside. "Can I get you a drink of water or some milk?"

"I don't wanna be any trouble," Ben said.

"It's no trouble. Just give me a moment. Please, make yourselves at home." She left them in the living room, flanked by a matching pair of worn plaid couches.

"Well, I remember the house but not the furniture exactly," Ben said, warily. He lowered himself into one of the couches, halfway disappearing in its cushions.

Isabel settled in beside him, taking care to avoid a nearly empty cereal bowl by her feet. After a moment, Janice returned with two large glasses of milk, handing one to each of them. She seated herself on the couch opposite them.

"What are you doing here, Ben? I didn't think I'd ever see you again."

"I'm a little lost as to how I should explain that."

"Try me," she said.

"It's because of me," Isabel chimed in. "He's trying to help me find my parents and thought that Cheryl might be able to help us."

"I see," Janice said.

"There's something going on. Something that these people don't want us to find out about, but if we don't, I don't think we'll find her parents," Ben added.

"Okay ..." Janice said, pulling her feet up under her. She stared at him intently.

"Do you know anything about Chicago gangs?" Isabel said. *Janice didn't exactly look like a historian.*

Janice frowned, shaking her head.

"Not at all. My mother was a bit of a history nut. She might have."

"Was?" Isabel said.

Ben looked to Janice, who's vacant stare had landed on a pile of colorful building blocks beside the couch.

"She's gone? I wondered from the way you looked at me when I said her name."

"She passed early this year. Lung cancer." Her words were short and pained. Ben crossed the room and held her hands between his, looking into her eyes.

"I'm so sorry. She was a wonderful woman."

"She was," Janice echoed. "She asked for you when she wasn't doing so well anymore."

"I'm sorry I wasn't here," Ben said, staring at his feet.

"Hell, she'd rather you hadn't been here, Ben. You know that. I'll give you the note she wrote you before you leave, but also know that she knew you had to get out of this town. She wanted that for you."

"I know," he said quietly.

Isabel pressed her leg against his, just so he'd know she was still there. He pushed back against her, wiping his eyes with his thumb and taking a deep breath.

"Do you think we could stay here tonight? We've come a long way."

"Of course," Janice smiled lightly. "I'll get you some blankets. I have to work in the morning, so I'm sorry if I'm not here when you get up." She stood and grabbed a set of dirty dishes from the side table, carrying them with her towards the kitchen.

"Let me help you." Ben stood and watched her disappear into the other room. Isabel began to get up also, but he gently squeezed her shoulder and shook his head. With an understanding nod, she watched him go.

Ben found Janice in the room that used to be her mother's, staring at her bed, piles of books stacked beside it. He remembered coming there some mornings and shaking Cheryl awake after she'd had too much to drink, and the two of them would go to the yard together, his arms under her shoulders. It felt like it'd been a day, a week at most, a feeling that only grew stronger as he looked around her room, and everything looked nearly the same. The changes were a stark reminder though, scattered oxygen bottles in the corner, a mess of pills on her dresser top.

He'd always known it was sort of a strange match when they'd become friends. She'd been at the lumber yard for as long as anyone could remember, and he was only just starting out, but she was the only one there that treated him like anything but dirt. It wasn't long before the two were inseparable, and in the year and a half Ben worked in Detroit, he'd felt as much a part of her family as anyone. "The son I never wanted," Cheryl always called him.

"I'm sorry to just show up like this." Ben laid his hand on Janice's arm.

"No, it's totally fine. I promise." Janice turned to face him, her face streaked with tears.

They ran down her cheeks from her soft blue eyes, the same eyes he'd remembered Cheryl having.

"It's wonderful that you're back, but please understand that it's a lot at once. I never saw you without her, and it's just been a while."

He nodded, hugging her again and stroking the back of her hair. They held each other for a long while, then Janice finally let go and told him to get some rest. Ben fought the broken closet door open, grabbing a few blankets and tossing them into a pile on the rocking chair. Adding a few pillows, he took the whole stack in one arm and put the other arm around Janice.

"Thank you for taking care of us and for not slamming the door in my face a second time. The second time is usually the one that really hurts."

"You haven't changed a bit," she laughed.

"It's been a little while, I know."

"Ben," she said, "it's been a lifetime."

TWENTY SIX
THE ARMS OF AN OLD FRIEND

That night, Ben slept more soundly than he had in years, without dreams, without waking, and without the endless aching in his chest that wouldn't allow him to be still. Ben awoke to find Janice watching him from across the room and Isabel still fast asleep on the opposite couch. Isabel had thought it more proper, because they were guests.

"How long you been there?" he said, propping himself up, rubbing the sleep from his eyes.

"Just longer than I thought I'd be," she laughed, then disappeared through the door. He stood, careful not to make noise, and followed her.

"I meant what I said last night - about being grateful for your letting us stay here. I can already see you're feeding one extra mouth."

"Her mother'll be back for her next week, soon as

she gets her new place settled out." Janice blushed, shoving her hands into soapy water, glancing back up at him. "My mom always said there was something about you that made her feel like everything'd be fine."

"I dunno about that, but it always is, eh?" He leaned against the counter. "She had a way of knowing exactly what to tell people to help them sort things out."

Janice sighed, gazing out the window.

"I don't even know why. I just felt like if we could get here, maybe she'd help me clear my head. This was just the last place I felt safe," Ben said. As he spoke, he thought about how much Janice looked like her mother and wondered if she'd ever have a daughter with that same broad nose and crooked smile.

Janice nodded towards the phone, wiping her hands clean. "That note she wrote you is over there. I set it out. Can't believe I kept the stupid thing, but she told me to be patient, that you'd be here for it."

Ben carefully tucked the note into his pocket. They both turned to listen as tiny footsteps echoed through the house, coming closer until a mess of blonde hair appeared to hover above the countertop.

"Can I have cereal today?" a quiet voice said. The little girl edged around the corner, eying Ben as she clung to a stuffed rabbit.

"Honey, what are you doing up so early?" Janice scooped her up and walked over toward him. "Shelly, I want you to meet Ben. He used to be a friend of grandma's." The girl buried her face in Janice's shoulder, peeking at him with one eye.

"Nice to meet you, Shelly." Ben extended a hand towards her, long enough for the girl to grab his fingertips.

Janice carried Shelly over to the counter and set her on it. "Not today, baby. Tomorrow, though." Janice poured a bowl of oats and set a kettle on the burner, hoisting Shelly back onto her hip.

"You wanna show me some of those toys I saw yesterday while your aunt makes breakfast?" Ben asked.

Shelly paused for a moment, nodded, then wiggled down from Janice's embrace and ran back to her room.

"I'll look after her for a second. Finish getting ready."

He found Shelly sitting on her bed, carefully combing a doll's hair. The room was sparsely decorated, an old baby crib in one corner and a plastic toy chest spilling its contents onto the ground.

"Did you know this use to be Aunt Janice's room?"

Shelly nodded, glancing around for a moment, then turning her attention back to the doll.

"What's her name?" Ben said.

She shrugged, holding it up for him to see.

"Oh, I see," he said, gently taking the doll in his hand. "Well, she's very pretty."

"Did you come to see Grandma?" Shelly said, picking up another doll from the foot of the short, blue mattress.

Ben didn't know how to respond at first. He just stared at the toy, limp and blank in his hand. He wondered if maybe he shouldn't have come there, if he'd already put them in danger. Ben pushed the thought from his mind, but couldn't help but venture a glance out the window.

"That's a good question – I did come to see Grandma and your aunt. I missed them very much."

"Oh," Shelly said, gently taking the doll back and

bouncing it along the skirt of the bed.

"So, you get to stay with your aunt awhile?" he said.

"My mom says I have to," she replied. "She said I get my own room and everything in our new house."

"You're a lucky one then, eh?" Ben nudged her.

"Do you have your own room?"

"Uh, well," he replied, tapping his nails against the bed's steel frame. "Sometimes, but I've been out looking for something, so I don't have a room now."

"Oh. Are you gonna find it?"

"Yeah, I hope so," he mused. "It's a hard thing to find."

"You just gotta look more." The little girl shook her head and grinned, then hopped down from the bed and trotted back into the kitchen. Ben found Shelly settling herself into a wooden chair at the dining room table.

"Should we wake her?" Janice jerked a thumb at the living room.

"Nah, she can eat when she wakes up. She needs the rest more than anything, I think."

Janice nodded, pushing a bowl of oatmeal in front of him. "I'll eat later, you have this," she said.

"Not hungry," he lied, sliding it back down the table. Janice eyed him suspiciously, then dug a spoon into the bowl and brought a steaming scoop to her mouth.

They ate breakfast together. Janice, Ben, and Shelly. Janice told Shelly about how Ben and Grandma used to work together and that Ben had once kept their house from foreclosing because he sold his motorcycle.

"He left the money on grandma's porch and lied to us about it, right to our faces," she said, pouring him another cup of coffee.

"Don't ever lie, Shelly, unless the people you're lying to are more stubborn than you are," Ben interjected.

The little girl looked on and smiled with them, but seemed far more interested in covering her oatmeal in honey. As she scraped the remnants from the bowl, the sunrise was glowing outside the kitchen window. Janice sent Shelly off to get ready for school and set about clearing the table.

"Still working at that retail store? What the hell was the name of that place?" Ben trailed off.

"Merman's? God no. Working tables downtown. Money's a lot better and lets me keep flexible hours to help out with her." She nodded towards Shelly's room. "You gonna stick around awhile?"

He shook his head, twirling a butter knife between index finger and thumb.

"It would be bad for both of us if we stayed here," he replied. Janice reached forward, looking into his eyes.

"What are you into, Ben?"

"Nothing I can't handle." He gave her what felt like a sincere and reassuring smile. "I'll be ok, I promise."

"You're always welcome here."

"Ok, ok, but no worrying about me," he said.

She kept her eyes on him, then stood and pulled her coat on. "Please tell your friend it was nice to meet her and don't forget the note."

Ben tapped his pocket knowingly, standing to wrap his arms around her.

"Thanks, Jan."

"You're family, Ben. Anytime."

Ben watched them make their way down the sidewalk to Janice's beat up Oldsmobile. He decided he'd wake

Isabel in an hour, and in the meantime, he'd put some thought into their next move.

That morning saw Ben silently pacing the house until he finally found the strength to sit and unfold the letter he'd been constantly running his fingers over. The paper was crisp and white, except a tiny brown ring that ran over its corner. Coffee, he was sure, remembering one of his friend's many vices. His name was scrawled in the upper left corner, and when he'd finished reading the first time through, his eyes lingered on it. He leaned back in his chair and read the note again and again.

Ben,

I hope this letter finds you and finds you well. I've missed our talks, but Janice is under strict instruction to run you out of town herself if you work for the yard again. It never seems like we can find the right things to say when it really counts, but at least we try, right? It seems silly but now that I've so many things to say, I can't find the words to say them. These should count for something. I hope you find what you're looking for or at least a place to rest your head. Whatever it may be, know that I'll be somewhere you are or at least somewhere we used to be. If this comes from my daughter's hands, please hold them for me, she misses having you around the house. (I won't tell her what a bastard you really are.) You made my life a little more beautiful, and I know I at least made yours a little more curious. Sometimes a man can travel the world looking for something and realize he's left it beside the front door.

> *Love, C*

He couldn't stop himself from reading it and from hearing her voice each time he did. The first day they'd met in the lumberyard, she'd called him a lilly-footed princess, then helped him load a flatbed even though she'd already clocked out. He'd liked her immediately. They hadn't known each other all that long, but Cheryl was the closest thing he'd ever had to a mother. She'd taken care of him and loved him when no one else gave him a second glance, and he'd tried to do the same.

Folding the letter and setting it down, Ben rubbed his fingers over the gouges in the table's face and stared down at the letter between his hands. It's lined surface made him think of the note Isabel had pulled from her father's clock and the way she'd clutched at it during their first night in the woods. He smiled, remembering how silly he thought she was for doing the same thing he was doing now, his last memory of Cheryl pinned to the table under his fingertips.

Ben shook Isabel awake, tugging the blanket out from under her and tossing it away.

"What?" Isabel groaned.

"I think I know where your parents are."

TWENTY SEVEN
PATIENCE

B en immediately regretted blurting out an idea drawn
from such a shaky base of evidence. He wasn't sure
about it. He wasn't sure about anything, but when he put
the pieces together, everything pointed to the idea that
the Stantons had never left Echton. He thought about
the house when they'd walked through it, with everything
neatly organized and stored away. Even when they'd entered Isabel's parents' room, it'd all seemed so planned, not
a panicked escape. Certainly not what he'd expect from a
couple fleeing for their lives.

Anyway, he couldn't wrap his head around a reason
why her parents would leave Isabel in a city they were
running from and take themselves to the other side of the
country. She'd never stopped thinking of them, and he
couldn't imagine them leaving her behind so easily. Ben
paced for awhile, then sat beside her as she slept. Isabel

looked so peaceful beneath all those blankets, he couldn't bring himself to wake her yet. He began to wonder if maybe sending Isabel on some wild chase had been her parent's way of getting her out of Echton without a fight. *Had it all been a distraction?*

The longer he thought about it, the more it made sense. Despite a few things he couldn't quite string together, he was starting to suspect that they'd spent thousands of miles chasing their own shadows. If Conrad and Maria had sent Isabel away so they could try to straighten things out on their own, they might still be in Echton, hiding out somewhere. He felt the spark of hope he'd begun to harbor dampen, knowing that the same men who'd been chasing them in Seattle and Chicago were thorough, cruel, and experienced. *Two of those three things are more than enough.*

I have to tell her. He rocked back and forth, his elbows resting on his knees as he thought it all through one more time. Even after all that thinking, he'd simply blurted it out. She sat bolt upright, her hair billowing around her face like a gnarled black mane.

"How do you know where my parents are?"

"What if they never left Echton? Maybe we're still alive because Hix needs something from them," he said.

"That doesn't make sense. If he needed something from them, what does it have to do with grabbing me?"

Ben waited silently, knowing it would only take her a moment to figure it out.

"I'm the leverage," she said slowly.

Again, he waited.

"I'm the leverage. I'm what they need to make them talk. Which means if he has them, they've probably tried just about everything else ...” she trailed off.

Isabel's face grew pale, her eyes glazed over, staring at the stained wooden floor. She was silent for a moment, then started to shake, her fingers entwining themselves in the blanket. Ben sat and pulled her head into his shoulder, his arm around her.

“It's ok, Iz. We'll find them. Everything will be ok.”

She took two short breaths and straightened herself.

“Why?” she said. “Why the letter? I know my father's handwriting. He wrote that note.”

Ben outlined his suspicions to her, reminding her that Seattle was about as far from Echton as she could go without leaving the country. He pointed out the fact that her parents might have known no one would be in Seattle when she arrived, but hoped that the trip would buy them time. Isabel looked on, her expression blank. He wasn't sure if she was digesting what he'd said or even listening at all.

“In Echton,” she repeated. “We have to go back. We have to help them.” Isabel started to stand, but Ben held her in place.

“You need to think this through, or you're gonna do exactly what Hix needs. Say they do have your parents, which we don't even know. If you just go charging in there, they'll have you. They'll have exactly what they want.”

“I don't care what they want. My parents need me.” She attempted to stand again.

“You should care.” He pulled her back into her seat. “Because I don't know if you've noticed, but the guys who've been waving guns in our faces have had plenty of chances but haven't killed us yet.”

“It's not for lack of trying,” she said.

"Trying for me," Ben replied, his hands on each side of her face. "You're the one they need."

Isabel was silent for a moment. It relieved him to see her expression change to the way she always looked when she was thinking something through. Thinking was exactly what he was hoping to talk her into.

"They need something from my parents," she said, steadying her voice.

"And?" Ben coaxed her on.

"What? What do they need? What are they looking for?" she muttered.

"I don't know what it is, but you're the last piece of the puzzle," he added. "So whatever we do next has to be thought through and done very carefully. If you want to protect them, you need to protect yourself."

He knew he hadn't totally talked her out of whatever she was considering. That much he could tell from the way she watched the door, but at least it seemed like they were getting somewhere. If he could keep her talking long enough, at least she'd have to weigh the options before doing something stupid.

"The voices I heard... There were at least three of them," she said. "Maybe Hix has a partner and just uses the Echton police as his pawns. Or maybe there are a few of them that have been looking for the money?"

"I'm not sure about that, but if Hix and whoever he's working with have enough money to fund all of this, the amount of money he's still looking for must be enormous."

"Enough to make it worth his while."

"Right," he nodded. "He's not going to go to this much trouble unless he seriously needs to know something your folks found out. Something worth all this trouble."

"Right," Isabel nodded. "Something my dad found, or found out, that told him where to look for that gold." Her hand absently felt for the coin in her dress.

"Here." Ben fished it out of his pocket.

"Doesn't seem like my parents to look for something like this." She slid her thumb over the ridges at the coin's edge.

"Could have been an accident," Ben offered. "People stumble across things all the time, not knowing what they've even found."

"Knowing my dad, if he found something, he probably couldn't leave it alone until he had its whole life story." She sighed, lying back on the couch.

"The more I hear about them, the more I understand you." Ben nudged her, hoping to draw out a laugh or at least a smile. She snorted softly, the corner of her lip curling upward.

"We need to keep our heads low just long enough to think this through and plan something out," he said.

Isabel sat back, smoothing the dress against her legs.

"Just for a night or two," he added. She looked tense, and he wondered if at any moment she might fly into a whirlwind panic.

"Ok, we wait," she conceded. "But we can't stay here, Ben. We can't risk it. We haven't sat still for more than a minute without being shot at or whatever."

"We?" He glared at her.

This time she actually laughed, sitting upright to lay her hand on his. "I don't know what's keeping you around, but if you figure it out, let me know, and I'll keep doing it."

He laughed too, pulling her to her feet. "Let's go for a

walk. Detroit is a great place to get lost."

"Right," she said, standing beside him. "A hotel?"

"Too public, we need something lower profile, cheaper, more off the radar." He tapped his temple with his index finger. Ben wracked his brain but couldn't decide on anything that would give them the privacy they needed. "We won't know until we look, I guess."

Ben scrawled a goodbye note to Janice, with a special part to Shelly about looking after her aunt and mom, and they locked up the house, tucking the spare key back inside the lip of the porch light. It was only midday, but the sky was a muted grey, an ominous cap to the high-rise buildings that loomed in the distance. Isabel shivered as they stopped to gauge their surroundings, the traffic growing thicker as they moved towards the center of town. They'd been walking for about a half hour when she told him they needed to stop for a moment, ducking inside a small shop while Ben waited on a bench outside.

It was nice to be back in the last place he'd honestly called home. He'd always loved watching the lines of cars flying by and throwing tiny dust clouds up in their wake or sending waves of puddle water crashing over the sidewalk. He didn't feel particularly partial to two wheels or four; he just liked to be surrounded by motion, light, sound. It seemed like only moments ago that the blunt, industrial feel of the Motor City had grabbed him by the collar and swallowed him whole. Now, he walked back into its embrace and smiled at the sweet smell of exhaust mixed with the rain that would surely come.

The moment was shattered by a commotion inside the store and the distinct noise of scuffing feet against tile.

The door flew open and soon Isabel came tumbling out, although Ben didn't recognize her at first, wrapped in a long grey coat.

"I call the police next time!" a heavily accented voice shouted from inside. Isabel sat upright, brushing the hair from her eyes.

"I didn't do anything wrong! I was just looking!" she shouted back.

As the door slammed shut, Ben stood and started walking towards it, cursing under his breath.

"Stop," she whispered, waving for him to follow her down the sidewalk. He caught up to her in half a block, wondering what scheme she'd hatched in the last 15 minutes.

"What?" she said.

"Don't what me. What happened in there? I thought we were laying low."

"We did that last night," she said.

Ben shrugged, holding his hands up.

"I let him catch me."

"You're bonkers," Ben said, shaking his head. "You pretty keen on getting thrown out of places?"

"Well, I let him catch me taking a bracelet, so he wouldn't notice that I was already wearing his coat when he threw me out. I thought we should start gathering supplies, for when we go back, you know?"

Ben sighed, looking over his shoulder at the storefront. "C'mon, the sky is about to turn as dark as your soul."

Isabel landed a well timed poke into his side where she knew his ribs were hurting, then sped ahead, rifling through the compartments of her newly acquired coat and turning the pockets inside out to admire them. They walked through the outskirts of the city until they were surrounded by rows of factory houses.

"I used to know a guy that lived down here although I don't exactly remember it like this." He walked on, looking over the sea of neatly manicured lawns and houses, each a tinted duplicate of the last. "That was something living here showed me. You wanna disappear - just gotta look like everybody else."

"No kidding," Isabel muttered.

"This is where we stay for a few days."

"This?" she repeated, looking around.

"This." He pointed up the street to a "room for rent" sign on the corner. "We scrape together enough cash to stay a few days. Then we make our move."

"You wanna sit here when my parents are God knows where and maybe already in Hix's hands?"

"If he wants you this bad, and alive, it's because you're what he needs. Here's what it comes down to: either we do it right or end up dead, all of us. If I'm gonna go back there, I'm damn sure gonna have a plan."

She crossed her arms. "You've got two days, and less than that if we get something figured out sooner."

"Fair enough," Ben sighed. "Well, we just scrape together a little cash and see if they'll put us up for a week. We might have to sell your fancy new coat," he said.

"Don't be mad," she finally said.

"You've got to be kidding - what'd you do?" he said.

She turned her back to him for an instant, producing a small bundle of cash and a gold billfold clip from somewhere inside her dress.

Ben quickly closed his hand around it.

"That's a great way to attract attention," he said.

"Sorry," she whispered. "It's our emergency fund."

"Please don't tell me you - "

"No, no, no." Isabel cut him off. "I didn't take any-thing from your friends. $10 of our emergency money is actually hidden in their cookie jar. They were lovely. This is from our law council, Mr. Michael."

"You're hopeless." His couldn't help but laugh, send-ing a jolt of pain through his ribs. "I guess we won't be going back for further services from Mr. Giddlestein and Eeples."

"Geldhous and Epstein," she corrected him.

Ben rolled his eyes. "Interesting that when I say we might have to work, money suddenly appears in your hands," he added.

As they walked, Ben pointed out a few for rent signs in the windows of the houses they passed. They ruled out half of them, solely on the basis that Isabel didn't like the look of the house or the color of the paint.

"Plainer is better," Ben cried.

When they finally settled on an acceptable home, she prodded Ben up the drive and to the front door, to inquire about the vacancy. The woman who answered the door was short and impatient, demanding to know their place of origin and to see state identification. He tried to reason with her for a few minutes, but then, realizing she'd be a truly unpleasant host, he excused himself, and they continued down the street.

"Little bit of a disaster," Isabel said.

"Next time, you can try," he replied, scowling.

"So, what's our story?" Isabel said.

Ben glanced up, his eyebrows raised."Our story?"

"Ben, come on. Who is gonna rent a room in their house to a random pair of strangers that look and smell like us? We have to at least pretend to be married if we're gonna share a room."

Ben stopped in the center of the sidewalk, gesturing to a house across the street with a small "Room for Rent" sign in its front window.

"Look. It's perfect, and we're only gonna be here a few days. You're gonna be fine."

Isabel hesitated, running her fingers through her hair slowly.

"We don't even know who these people are, and you wanna share a house with them?"

"They could say the same about us."

Ben faced the house and extended his arm towards it. They walked a few dozen steps until they were squarely planted at the property's edge. It was fairly large and rectangular with a tiny front garden and the same white trim and yellow siding as the two houses on either side of it. It was so plain it almost made him sick.

"What'd you think?"

Isabel shrugged, looking over the front gardens.

"Well, Mrs. Richter, welcome home."

"If they'll have us," she added.

TWENTY EIGHT
CLOSE ENOUGH TO HOME

I get offered one more vacuum I'm gonna beat someone over the head with it, Tom Baylock swore as he made his way through the house to answer the persistent ringing of the doorbell. When he swung the door open, he had to admit he hadn't been expecting what greeted him there. Two exhausted looking kids, couldn't have been older than 25, one with a wad of money in her hand and a finger pointed up at his for rent sign, her face blank. He beckoned them inside and extended his hand.

"Come on in. I'm Tom," he said.

"Tom, is someone here?" Sarah chirped from the other room. She came flitting in, tightly wound blonde curls bouncing on her shoulders.

"Hello there! I'm Sarah, Tom's wife."

"Ben Farnsworth. Pleased to meet you," the young man said, throwing his hand into Tom's.

Kid's got a hell of a grip, Tom thought as he stepped forward to shake the young woman's hand. She had a much lighter touch.

"Isabel Farnsworth," she added, leaning forward to look past them into the kitchen.

"Oh dear, come inside! You must be freezing," Sarah said. Tom noticed Isabel watching Sarah as she moved behind her and saw her jump a little when the door shut.

"Everything ok?" he asked.

"Of course," Isabel smiled demurely. "We're looking for a place to stay, and we saw your sign." Her hand pointed up towards the ceiling.

She quickly explained that they'd just left California, moving east in search of work and were looking for a place to stay for a short time while they searched for apartments. The young man, Ben, hardly said a word, but that was a trait Tom had always valued. *A man shouldn't speak unless he has something to say.*

"I know a working man when I see one," he said, clapping Ben on the shoulder. "You caught us just after church. You hungry?"

"Thank you, sir. We don't wanna be an inconvenience. A man's home says a lot about him. Thank you for letting us into yours," Ben replied.

With that, they were official guests of the Baylock family as far as Tom was concerned. They both looked a little run down, but he figured they were hungry and probably cold. After an enormous dinner, which Sarah insisted on, Tom took them on a quick tour of the house, then upstairs to take a look at the room they'd be using.

"Here you are. Last but not least," he said.

"This'll do just fine. Thank you," Isabel beamed.

"You know, I might be able to use another hand at my shop if you're looking for temporary work," Tom added, looking to Ben. Ben looked back to Isabel, who shrugged and smiled.

"Sure, I wouldn't mind picking up a few hours."

"The airline lost all our luggage, all we have left are the clothes we have on." Isabel added, frowning.

"You poor thing," Sarah clucked from the stairs. "I'm sure they'll have it to you in no time. Let me see if I have anything your size."

"You don't have to - " Isabel started, but Sarah was long gone.

"Can't tell her much, eh?" Tom said, smiling.

"I know that feeling," Ben laughed, avoiding Isabel's gaze, although he could feel it burning into his skull.

It only took Sarah a few minutes to find a pair of jeans and a shirt for Isabel, and another set for Ben.

"These should be just right," she said, dropping the clothes on the bed. "Ben, they might be a little big, but at least they're clean."

"Thank you, ma'am," he said.

"7 AM," Tom said, taking care to give them a big smile as he closed the door behind him. He stood outside to listen for just a moment. He'd never fancied himself an eavesdropper, but he couldn't help but be a little curious. Their voices were muffled, but even after 23 years in a machine shop and 12 in a garage, he still had most of his hearing.

"We didn't even talk about money," Isabel said from behind the door.

"I don't think it's a priority. We'll get to it," Ben

replied, followed by the creaking of springs as someone threw themselves on the bed. "You gonna shower?"

"Yep. Maybe twice," he heard Isabel say.

Tom chuckled as he crept down the stairs to find Sarah there waiting for him.

"Oh Tom, give them a moment. You remember when we were that young?"

"Yes, yes I do. That's why I'm keeping an eye on them," he grinned, leaning on the staircase railing. Sarah took his arm and wrapped it around her waist.

"Honey, how much trouble could those two really get themselves into?"

TWENTY NINE
IF THE WEATHER HOLDS

Isabel plopped down beside Ben, sinking into the bed's soft embrace. *Not a priority.* She considered the words, and the way he'd said them. *It's easy to forget what kindness feels like*, she thought, reaching for the pile of clothes at the edge of the bed.

"Jeans?" she said. "How do you even put these on?" she said, holding them up to examine them.

"One arm at a time," Ben laughed, kicking off his boots and pointing a foot to the bathroom. "Go, or I'm going to."

These should be burned, she thought, gathering her old clothes into a pile in the corner of the bathroom and starting the water.

She emerged, half an hour later, her skin soft and scrubbed clean, a light shade of pink. In the cabinets, she'd found shampoo and even scavenged a spare razor.

"Look at you," Ben said, as she kicked her dirty dress

out of the room, then picked it up with her toes and lowered it into the trash.

"Your turn," she sang, rubbing her calves together, marveling at the feeling. *I'm not sure what feels better, having a shower to use or a bed to sleep in tonight.*

"You look like a cricket," Ben laughed, grabbing the shirt and pants Sarah had set out for him.

In a moment, she heard the water start and sat herself in a rocking chair opposite the window. It felt so foreign to be there. Even though she knew it hadn't been long, any feeling of peace over the last few days had been so fleeting, and being there made her chest ache for her family. She always found herself picturing them locked up somewhere like she'd been. Her father wasn't old, but she knew he couldn't take the kind of treatment they'd given Ben. She'd come to grips with the idea that she had to be careful and patient or this could go terribly wrong, but the comfort of the room she was sitting in quickly turned to painful urgency. If her parents were really in Echton, they needed her now more than ever.

The door swung open behind her, and she heard Ben drop his clothes in the trashcan with hers. He smelled overwhelmingly like soap, the heavy, orange, industrial soap that had been piled beneath the sink and set carefully on the side of the tub. She felt his hand come to rest on her shoulder.

"You ok, Iz?"

She nodded, swaying slightly, her gaze fixed on the window. In its reflection she saw them both, clear enough, but she looked so different than she remembered herself.

"I know you don't wanna wait," Ben said, then added,

"We have to do this right."

"I know... " She scraped her fingernails against the arm of the chair.

"I'll tell Tom I can only stay a half day, then we can put our heads together."

Isabel stared on, expressionless. They were both silent for a while, listening to Sarah bustle around the upstairs, until there was a light knock at the door.

"Yes?" Isabel said.

"Just wanted to say sweet dreams!" she said, followed by the sound of shuffling feet and whispering.

"Thank you!" Ben replied, opening the door slightly to give her a quick smile and nod.

"Maybe we get something Hix wants and put a little pressure on him," Isabel said. "What does a man like that want?" she wondered aloud.

"Money, power," Ben said. "But, more than anything, I think he wants to feel like he has control of things."

The thought of Hix made her shudder. She'd spent a long time watching people as she grew up, trying to consider what made them tick. *There's a certain kind of person that takes pleasure in others' pain. That kind of person grows a vacuum inside their heart, and the pain and hate and the violence they feed it never fills it up.* Yet, she was sure there was something Hix had to feel.

"We pull the supports from under his house and send the roof crashing in. I'm willing to bet that if we give those bastards a little taste of fear, they'll feel something they haven't known in a long time," she said. "We need to make Hix feel like he's losing control of Echton."

Ben lay down across the bed, his feet hanging from

its side. He pulled his arms to his chest and cracked his knuckles, a finger at a time.

"Glad I'm not on the wrong side of you."

Isabel made a face, moving to lie on her stomach beside him.

"We need to do some looking into things, I think," she said. "You go to work with Tom, and I'll tell Sarah I'm going apartment searching during the day. When I'm done shopping, I'll come back, put together what I've found, and we can go over it tomorrow night."

"Maybe start with land records. See if you can find anything there. Be careful about what name you use when you ask about it, though. In Chicago, that guy was on us about a second after we said the name McLellan."

"Might have just been a coincidence, but that's a good point," she said. "I'll ask for the M section or something. I'll figure it out."

"Be careful, Iz."

Isabel could tell from the tone of his voice that he was uncomfortable not being there to look after her. She rolled over, pressing her back against Ben's side and laying her head against his.

"I'll be ok."

The warmth of his skin through the old t-shirt was beautiful, more than the shower, more than the bed. She lay there, relaxed against him and thought about what she should be looking into tomorrow. It was a strange contrast, to feel compassion and warmth at her back and contemplate inflicting pain.

"If we couldn't find anything in Chicago, I don't know how the hell I expect to find anything here," she groaned, rolling back onto her stomach, rubbing her temples. Her thick hair, still damp, fell around her face. Isabel reached a hand up and brushed it to the side, looking to Ben.

"Tomorrow is a different day," he said.

"Tomorrow will be here soon," Isabel countered, watching the slow turning of the second hand on the clock beside the door. She sat upright, looking back to him for a long moment. With one hand she propped herself up. With the other, she grabbed a handful of Ben's shirt and pulled him towards her.

His eyes met hers as they grew closer until she could see herself in his pupils. She tucked her head between his neck and shoulder. Her hand moved under his shirt, gently tracing over the scars that crossed his back like patchwork.

He didn't say anything, just returned her embrace, his hand reaching up towards her face, grazing it gently. She knew it was coming, but it still shocked her when his lips finally touched hers. Ben pulled her on top of him and kissed her again, this time harder.

Somewhere in the distance, a storm began to form. Clouds spun in the sky, turning a sinister gray and holding their contents high about the city. They hung there, blotting out the moon, but never spilled a drop. As the wind picked up, it carried the storm south, past the home of Tom and Sarah Baylock. Deep into the night, they drifted languidly. In their wake, the moon again looked down at the earth and glowed, pale and full.

THIRTY
WHERE SECRETS ARE KEPT

It was a quarter to four when the quitting bell rang. Ben rinsed his hands quickly, squeezing a shot of pumice soap onto them and scrubbing away the grease. As he dried them, he noticed the tiny flecks of black that still clung beneath his fingernails and smiled.

"Ready, son?" Tom said.

"Sure," Ben said, tossing a wad of shop towel into the trash. He wondered if Tom had noticed him tense at the word. It had strangely reminded him of his father's voice, although he'd hardly used it in the same way

The ride back was quiet, the truck rattled softly, and he could just barely hear Bruce Springsteen coming through the battered speakers.

"You did a good job today," Tom finally said. "Remind me of my own son when he was still around."

"Where's he now?" Ben asked.

"South of here. Alabama, I think. Hell, I don't know anymore," Tom chuckled. "Sounds like he and the family are doing well, though"

"Well, I hope he's doing something he loves," Ben replied. It was the best thing he could think to say.

Tom smiled wryly, braking as the light turned orange.

Ben had done his best to keep his head low through the day but couldn't help but notice a few things Tom's mechanics had missed. For the first part of the day, he'd followed Tom around, helping him with little things and trying to ask the right questions, anything that made him seem eager to learn.

From the time he'd been old enough to hold a wrench, Ben had been up and down all kinds of engines but thought it might be a little odd if the kid the master mechanic was was troubleshooting his work for him. During his lunch break, Ben had snuck away to check out a jeep he'd seen a mechanic working on earlier that morning. As he detailed the car beside it, he'd watched the man disassemble the entire oil pump, when it sounded like it was a belt issue in the first place, probably a tensioner alignment problem. The belt wasn't showing it, but it would explain the smoke and rattling and was a hell of a lot cheaper for whatever poor sap owned the car. It'd been bothering him ever since.

Tear the house down to fix a leak in the roof, he thought as he took his chance to search for the culprit, pushing against each spring until he felt the fifth one down realign with the belt. As a pair of footsteps approached, he yanked his arm free of the engine, narrowly avoiding the man as he returned to his station.

"Just checking it out. Beautiful car," Ben said, making

himself busy.

"Just don't touch it," the man muttered, snapping on a floodlight, then turning to root around in a toolchest.

Ben thought about it now as Tom's truck cruised through the city into the beginning of the suburbs. He hoped the mechanic had pulled his head out of his ass. *The smoke doesn't stop coming until the fire is out.* Ben made a mental note to check in the morning.

"You hungry?" Tom said. "Sarah makes a hell of a roast, and the potatoes are even better."

"Starved. Maybe she'll teach Isabel how to cook something," Ben laughed.

They stopped in the doorway as a wave of amazing smells washed over them. He and Isabel both did their best to eat slowly, but having been so long without a home cooked meal, they both helped themselves to 2nd and 3rd plates.

"You must have worked up an appetite!" Sarah chirped, her hands clutched to her chest

"Amazing," Isabel said, leaning back, her hands on her stomach.

"Oh, thank you, sweetie," Sarah replied, blushing. "Did you find anything worth looking at today?"

Isabel looked to Ben and shook her head. "Not much."

"Well, Ben did a hell of a job in the shop. Could make a good mechanic one day," Tom said. "You ever consider it?"

"Crossed my mind," Ben said, smiling down at the remnant of potato on his plate. He noticed Isabel looking at him from the corner of his eye and slid his hand over hers.

"You want a beer?" Tom said, getting up.

"You promised me we'd go for a walk," Isabel interjected.

"When we're back, count me in," Ben said.

Isabel smiled demurely, as she and Ben began to help Sarah clear the table. The light was just beginning to die when they stepped outside. She'd made Ben look at the new clothes she'd bought for them before they left, two outfits each. He missed the feel of his old jeans, but the new ones didn't have any holes in them yet and were definitely warmer. She'd even gotten him a thick, blue zip-up with a fleece lining.

"So?" he said as she closed the door.

"Not much. I looked all day and even looked through the records behind the counter."

"You get yelled at?"

"More than once," she said. "However, I did find something interesting. Actually, it's the lack of something that's interesting."

"Go on."

"Well, I couldn't find anything on McLellan, so I decided to see if there was anything about Echton." She paused, glancing around. "There was as much about it as anywhere else, I suppose, a few records and a little biography, something about its main industry being mining."

"Small town. Probably not much to write about."

"That's what I thought at first, but they've got all sorts of land records for Michigan, Ohio, and some of Indiana stored in the same database, back to 1880. It's really quite an extensive collection, like towers and towers of books. It took me like an hour just to find the E-section in Ohio."

"Jesus woman, don't be cruel. Get to it. What did you find?" Ben interrupted her.

Isabel did her best to look indignant, shoving Ben off the sidewalk into a bush. "It's what I didn't find. There's no record of Echton before 1945. Not a word."

"No record?" he said, brushing tiny green needles from his new jacket.

"No deeds, no ordinances, no regulations - nothing. After 1944 or 1945, there was a bit, as much as there was for anything else."

"Do you think he had it all erased somehow incase, well, maybe if people came looking for the town, and he wanted to throw them off?" Ben said.

"I think it must have happened some time ago, and they tried to cover everything up since then. It would explain a lot, right?" Isabel stopped to look around again but saw no one. She motioned to a bench up ahead.

"And maybe your dad found something about it?"

"I was thinking that or he had to patch up somebody that did," Isabel replied.

Ben slumped on the bench, hunching his shoulders so his coat came up around his ears. *Just like a grouchy tortoise, old man Richter,* Isabel thought.

"So, what do we do?" she said.

"We have to get your parents out of Echton. The rest, we worry about later."

Isabel's eyes opened wide, and she grabbed onto Ben's sleeve, squeezing it tightly. "You mean go back tonight?" she said.

"No - we wait at least one more day. Tomorrow, see if you can't find a land map of that area so we can take a look at it and see how we wanna come at this thing."

"Most of it's up here." She tapped her head. "I didn't spend much time sitting still as a kid."

"All the same. It would help me." He affectionately

ran his fingers through her hair.

"Fine." She crossed her arms. "I'll get you your map."

When they reached the house, Isabel headed up to bed, but Tom caught Ben at the stairs and thrust a beer into his hand. It made Isabel smile, listening to the two of them talk. She'd woken when Ben got up for work at 6 AM, but had promptly fallen back asleep for several more hours. She couldn't imagine how tired Ben must have felt, but thought it was hilarious how obviously uncomfortable it made him to skip out on a beer with Tom.

For Ben, his next day at the shop went much more quickly although it took him almost forty minutes of evading Tom to fix the belt problem on the jeep. When the older man finally caught up with him, he gave him a stern scolding about shirking responsibility, then shoved an old broom into his hand.

"Get sweeping," he barked.

Ben was glad for the mindless work, it gave him time to think about what they could do to get a look around in Echton or at least buy them enough time to figure out what to do with Hix. He knew Isabel would want to rush in, all fire and fury, and burn the city down, but if they had any chance of finding her parents, it would require patience and finesse.

He thought about the shopkeeper Isabel had taken the coin from. If it was the same coin Ben had found the day before, he had to have gotten it from the sheriff or his deputy. *It's easy to trust someone when you think you know them.* If Isabel had spent the last few years with Henry, he'd probably be the first one she'd try to talk to. He took his time sweeping out the shop, taking care to let Tom see him working hard at it and mulling over everything Isabel had told him about Echton. *If I had something I didn't want anyone to find until I came back for it, where would I hide it?*

By the end of the second day, it was like he and Tom were old friends, joking about a raccoon that was trapped under the porch a few months before. Ben claimed it had just been him, searching for snacks. When they got home, Sarah seemed as cheerful as ever, but Isabel was nowhere to be found. Ben asked Sarah if she'd seen her, trying to act casual.

"Not at all. Do you know if she'll be home for supper?"

"I'd assume so," Ben scratched his beard.

They waited for fifteen minutes after dinner was set, then Sarah promised to save Isabel a plate for when she got home. By 6:15, the dishes were cleared, and Ben was beginning to worry. He'd just pulled his boots on and was beginning to lace them, when the front door flew open and Isabel stepped inside, a small hardcover book and a pack of papers tucked under her arm.

"Sorry I'm late!"

Ben rolled his eyes, then stood to hug her. "You scared the hell out of me," he whispered.

"Sorry," she replied, waving to Sarah, whose hands were full of soapy dishes. "Found some good ones today!"

Sarah nodded to a plate of lasagna on the counter. Isabel kicked her shoes off, aligning them with the others, then hurried into the other room and snatched up the plate.

"Thank you so much. I could eat an elephant."

"Well, I hope pasta will do," Tom chuckled dryly.

"I found some options today," Isabel said.

"Leaving us so soon?" Sarah said.

"Just looking at a few things." She took Ben's hand

and pulled him to the stairs, then raced up ahead of him.

"Someone's excited," Ben said, snagging a final bit of pie from the tin.

Sarah smiled and motioned him away, flicking soap at his retreating form.

When he got upstairs, Isabel had spread an enormous map on the bed, with a large section circled in blue on its bottom left side. She told him how she still hadn't found anything that dated before 1945 and that the new maps of the town didn't include a number of things she knew were there, but were a good place to start. Isabel carefully outlined the main drag in town drawing in and labeling each building. She explained that there was only one main road that took you into town, and that north of the city was the forest they'd escaped through before.

When she'd finished with the map, she told Ben that she'd been talking to the records clerk for a long time and that he told her that any official records were probably held at the town hall because they hadn't been transferred for external use.

"If they have those records and even the ones from before '45, it might tell us who knew about the money or at least who's come and gone from the town."

"Annddd," he drew the word out, staring at her skeptically. "That's gotta be the worst place they could possible be."

Isabel sighed, folding the map and tucking it into a pack she pulled from beneath the bed.

"We don't ask. We just take, and don't give me that look. We needed something to store all this in, and it's not like I spent any money on it," she said.

"Give me one more day," Ben said.

Isabel sat, her eyes wandering back to the clock. The relentless turning of its hands exhausted her. She carefully zipped the bag back up and tucked it away.

"I'll tell Tom we're leaving after work tomorrow," Ben added, getting up to close the door. "I'll just tell him on the way back from the shop, and I'll just let him keep my pay to make up for putting us up. We can make a plan and pack that night and leave first thing the next morning."

"They love you, you know," Isabel said quietly.

"As much as you can love a stranger living in your house, I suppose."

"I don't think the fact that you're a stranger is a priority," she faked a smile, slipping under the covers and staring at the ceiling.

"Regardless, they've been good to us," Ben replied, feeling a little irritated. *How is she gonna shortchange a couple that just took us in off the street and fed us for two days?* Tossing his jacket into the rocking chair, he quickly washed his hands and face and crawled into bed beside her.

Something seemed off about the way she moved when he lay down. It had been slight, but he'd noticed something. Ben sighed. He was too exhausted to care. With a swat of his hand, he turned off the light and felt the gentle rise and fall of Isabel's chest beside him until his own breathing slowed and carried him into darkness.

With his alarm blaring, Ben woke with a start, feeling for Isabel but finding only cold bed sheets. He squinted in the dim light and pulled himself out of bed. Quietly, he stalked across the room, and after finding the bathroom empty, he noticed that her extra clothes were gone. Dropping to the floor, he saw clear to the other side of the room under the bed, where the backpack had been.

"Iz?" he said softly. He knew she was gone. The still and lifeless room had already told him that. His heartbeat quickened a little as he walked to the desk, seeing a slip of paper held down by a coin that had grown painfully familiar. Ben turned Sean McLellan face down and picked up the note. In the center of the paper was a tiny clock with pointed hands and a few words scrawled beneath it.

"I'll be where the best secrets are kept."

THIRTY ONE
THE BLIND PLUNGE

Ben did his best to get through the morning at the shop without looking too worried, but his heart felt like it might stop at any moment. He told Tom he could only work a few hours and that Isabel had gone ahead to start negotiating the lease on their new apartment. He knew that if he didn't show up altogether, it would look even more suspicious, and he might get some questions he couldn't answer, and more importantly, trouble he didn't want. Even if Tom was trying to help, he might make it all more complicated. He wasn't sure how far Hix's influence reached with law enforcement, but it was a risk worth waiting a few more hours to avoid.

"It's all very rushed, had to beat someone else into it," he told Tom.

"Alright -" he said, crossing his arms. "You gonna be in tomorrow?"

Ben frowned, avoiding Tom's gaze. Tom went back to fiddling with an impact drill for a moment, then looked up.

"I knew it wouldn't last. Just thought it'd be a little longer than half a week," the older man said, fighting with the chuck. Tom put his hand on Ben's shoulder and sighed.

"Don't worry, son. I know not everything goes according to plan. You come back and see us sometime, yeah?"

Ben nodded, though he knew the chances of seeing Tom and Sarah again once he'd left were almost nil.

"Of course," he said. Ben looked over his hands, the beginnings of blisters on his palms from where the skin had grow soft. It had been good to stay still, if only for a few days. He wouldn't give himself time to think about it. He just had to keep moving. The problem of how to get to Echton loomed just past the door to the shop, but an even more pressing matter was bothering him. He didn't know how Isabel had gotten there.

He tried to imagine her trying to hitchhike or steal a car and settled on the idea that she'd somehow taken a bus or a train to get close, then hopefully been smart enough to disappear when she got within view of the city. More than anything, he was struggling to understand why she'd left without him in the first place.

"What're you doin', kid?" Tom said as Ben punched out and tossed his pay card into the trash.

"I figure we're even after the room and board," he said. Tom squared up his shoulders and shook his finger at him, getting ready for one of the speeches Ben had come to know over the last few days. Before he could even begin, Ben interrupted him.

"I know what you're gonna say, but I'm not taking

your money. You've been more than kind to us, and it's already decided." Ben plucked the card from the dented silver can and tore it into quarters, depositing it back into the trash.

As a compromise, he agreed to let Tom drive him back to the house and said that he'd take a few sandwiches from Sarah, so they wouldn't have to cook that night. When they arrived and Tom told her that Isabel and Ben were leaving, Sarah looked worried at first, but seemed to warm up to the idea. Ben did his best to describe the imaginary apartment they'd be moving to, using his old place in Detroit as inspiration.

"Well, that sounds lovely," she cooed. "A young couple like you should have a place of your own."

He assured her that she and her husband had been more than generous and thanked them profusely before finally stepping out the door, carrying a small feast.

Ben patted his pockets, considering the fact that it'd only taken him a night to go from feeling totally grounded to being thrown back into midair. They'd been nice enough to give him an old duffel bag their son had used in school, and he'd packed it full with the clothes Isabel bought.

He thought hard about what he could barter or sell for a ticket to head down south, and a few blocks from the bus station, saw a neon sign that read "PAWN guns, gold, clothing and antiques." He dug through the bag until he felt his fingers close around the coin.

Half an hour later, Ben emerged from the shop, his wrist bare and his bag considerably lighter. It'd been close to robbery, what they'd given him for all of it. He knew the man at the counter must have seen desperation the second he walked in, and it had taken Ben 15 minutes of arguing just to get enough for a one-way ticket. He headed towards the train station, the coin bouncing lightly at the bottom of the duffel bag, tucked in beside the sandwiches.

"Not done with you yet," he'd told it, before replacing it beneath the only pair of jeans and shirt he'd been able to keep. It was going to a long day, he knew. He was the closest he'd been to Echton since that night he'd stepped across the border into town, but knowing that Isabel was already there made him uneasy. *Where was she now? Had anyone seen her? Was she alone?* His mind flitted through a dozen different situations as he headed to the station and bought his ticket. He'd take it as far as Reinersville, then do the rest on foot.

The half hour before the bus pulled up seemed like slow torture, and given time to think about it, Ben realized that he didn't really know where to go when he got there. He vaguely remembered the forest and that her house had been to the east of the tracks they'd jumped. *Sometimes even having a direction to walk in is a luxury,* he thought.

He rode in silence, for close to three hours, thinking about what he'd say to her. Ben couldn't decide if he'd yell at her, or just hold her until he couldn't anymore. It was uncomfortable, retracing his footsteps to the pace that'd started all of this. Regardless, he knew his time in Echton hadn't come to an end.

He was so deep in thought that Ben nearly missed his stop. Just as the driver began to close the doors, Ben sprung to his feet and called out, taking long strides down the center aisle.

"What's with you people today?" the driver muttered,

adding something about almost being tackled that morning.

When Ben stepped down from the bus, he kept his head tucked low, eyes on the ground. Even thought it'd been weeks since either he or Isabel had been in the town, and the picture of him had been awful, he still felt like every man or woman that looked his way knew something he didn't.

After a few hundred yards, he dug half of one of the sandwiches from his bag and tried to make himself eat but couldn't. He tossed the rest into some tall grass, then cut across a lot and started towards the forest. *The quieter I can make this, the safer we'll both be.* It was comforting to be walking again, his feet on the field's hardened rows. He wasn't exactly sure what meditation or any of that stuff Cheryl used to talk about was supposed to feel like, but this had to be close.

Ben walked northeast, using the lichen to guide his way, then curved east, away from the setting sun. He was losing light fast, and he knew soon he'd have to bed down for the night somewhere. A few acres away, he could see the outline of a shed, its roof half covered in moss, and smattered with golden-brown leaves. *Too obvious, if anyone were looking for me, or worse yet, Isabel, that'd be the first place they'd look.*

He didn't dare approach the building but watched it for a moment to check for any signs of life. Then, satisfied, he moved on. Keeping it to his right, Ben navigated a wide arc around the field. In the fading light, he could hardly see the ground and knew his movements were only growing clumsier and louder. After awhile, he resigned himself to an appealing spot at the foot of an oak tree. Its roots wrapped around a dip in the earth, making a small natural shelter.

Ben sat and forced himself to eat the other half of the sandwich. He'd need his strength to keep this up tomorrow. Before he'd even fully lain down, he knew there was no way he'd be able to sleep, restless as he was feeling. He felt it in his guts, a heaviness when he thought about Isabel without food or water out there somewhere. *How could she be so foolish? She didn't know the first thing about covering where she'd been or finding shelter in a place like this.* If she'd waited just a few more hours, he'd be with her now.

What worried him most was that on her own, she had no one to make her think before rushing into something foolish. When things get personal, your gut talks louder than your brain, he knew from experience. He slung his bag over a branch 30 yards from the tree and settled into the nook he'd found. Pulling dead leaves around him until they covered his lower body, he scooted backwards into the embrace of the tree.

It's no use. Ben's mind was still buzzing. He needed to rest to be ready for whatever tomorrow would bring, but he couldn't shut his eyes without seeing her face. A mile away, maybe two, a train's whistle blew.

"Don't stop here," he told it, "Just don't stop at all."

He lay there, trying his hardest to let the crickets song sooth the burning in his chest. Through the smattering of leaves clinging in the forest canopy, he could see the glow of the moon, where it came down in hundreds of droplets of light, illuminating the forest floor.

Must be close to a full moon, he thought, crawling forward to look around the trunk of the oak. It really was beautiful, the way the light filtered through the dead branches of the trees and cast itself on the ground, a kaleidoscope of splintered shadow and light. At the edge of the light, he thought he saw something blue. No doubt something left behind by hunters as they passed through, but something nagged at the back of his mind. *Hadn't Isabel said this was a preserve?*

Shaking the leaves off, Ben rose into a crouch and moved around the tree. His body blocked the light from above, but Ben's fingers grasped at where he thought he'd seen color a moment before. Whatever he'd grabbed for stung and cut into his hand as he rummaged around in the weeds. He cursed, pulling back for a moment, before carefully feeling around again. His fingers closed around something soft and fine. He rubbed the material between his forefinger and thumb, turning to try to catch a glimpse of it in the moonlight. *Cotton?* He held it up, looking over the finely woven threads and the tiny red splotch at its edge.

Blood. His heart raced before he noticed that his own hand was bleeding from the raspberry thorns the cloth had been stuck on. In the darkness, he couldn't tell if it was fresh or dried - his own, or someone else's. Ben shifted his weight again, holding the cloth up to the moonlight. The wind picked up, sending the blue material fluttering back to the ground.

Ben stepped back, planting his hand firmly over the place it'd fallen. He looked down at the blue cloth trapped between his fingers, then noticed the indentations running beneath him. Cut into the earth, small, pointed shoe imprints ran directly between his knees into the blackness of the Echton night.

THIRTY TWO
SHARP AS SHALE

Sleep never came to Isabel that night, she just stared at the ceiling and thought about how she should be anywhere but somewhere comfortable. Her parents were probably locked away somewhere at the mercy of Sheriff Hix. She was angry they'd mislead her; she could have helped, and maybe then they wouldn't all be upside down. Looking over at Ben, she could only make out the outline of his face and the slow rise and fall of the covers.

For three days she'd been trying to leave, and he kept delaying. Maybe he just didn't want to leave this house. She sat up and pulled her knees to her chest, staring out at the empty street for just a few more minutes until she'd made up her mind. She swung her legs over the side of the bed. Before she left the room, Isabel scratched out a quick note, placing the coin carefully on top of it. It was enough for him to get the point, but if Tom or Sarah found it, they wouldn't understand.

When she made it downstairs, she threw some crackers and other things into her bag, then thought of Tom and Sarah and left a crumpled five dollar bill on the counter. With one foot on the threshold of the door, Isabel looked back and thought she heard Ben's voice upstairs. She wished she had money to leave him, but the bill she'd left on the counter was the last of their emergency stash, and even she'd have to find a way home for free.

Isabel slipped through the door, closing it behind her with a gentle click. The morning cold stung her nostrils and face as she took in a deep breath, adjusting the backpack to fit a little more snugly. It'd been a long time since she'd been up this early, but the driving thought of getting to Echton pushed out the stiffness in her legs and arms and drove back the cold.

She knew when Ben realized she'd gone, the bus station would probably be the first place he'd look, but it was also the fastest way to get home. If he found her, he'd certainly try to stop her from going back, and she just couldn't afford to waste any more time. She rounded the corner near the station and was still working on a plan for getting a ticket when she noticed a bus stopped at the curb, boarding its last few passengers. The letter board at its front window read "Athens, OH."

Isabel had to think quickly. She didn't have time to take the money from someone or buy a ticket even if she had it. She ran to the bus and narrowly made it through the closing doors, the pack bouncing furiously on her back. At a dead sprint, she barely avoided crashing into the driver.

"Christ, lady, all you had to do was say wait," the

driver said, swinging the door shut behind her.

"Sorry," Isabel murmured. She fell backward and practically seated herself on a woman in the front seat. "It's these damned shoes. I'm sorry, ma'am." She looked back at the woman and slid the ticket stub she'd taken from her purse into her front pocket, then pulled it back out and offered it to the driver.

He scratched his chin, looking down at her.

"It's already been punched."

"I was on, then got off for a cigarette. You mind if I take my seat now? My feet are killing me in these damn things." She pointed down to her new shoes. In truth, they were hurting pretty badly. She'd been in a hurry to pick them out and make it home in time for dinner the other night, and this morning had been the first time she'd actually tried to wear them.

The bus driver shrugged and waved her towards the back of the bus.

"Anywhere you want, kid."

"Thanks," she said, weaving her way through the bus.

Isabel found an empty window seat and nestled herself in, using the backpack as a pillow. Guilt quickly bore its way into her, but she did her best to convince herself to stay focused, blinking away tears as the bus pulled away. She was sure she'd see Ben again in a little while, but it was just the way she'd left him, alone in the bed they'd shared.

Now is the time to move. He'll just have to understand she thought, trying tobring her focus back to more pressing issues. *I'll ride this until I'm close to Echton, then sneak into town somehow.* The colored wires Ben had twisted and rewound didn't seem so complicated. Maybe she'd steal a car when she got there and just keep her head down while she scoped things out a little.

The little voice in the back of her mind had begun to sound just like Ben, telling her to be careful and to take it slowly. Henry was really the only one in Echton she knew she could trust, but getting to him would be incredibly difficult. His store sat only a few blocks from the center of town, and even if she could somehow get a car, she'd still be exposed, potentially cornered, if she went inside. She'd call him first, she decided. If the wrong person picked up the phone, she might send up a signal she didn't intend to, but it was an acceptable risk. At least then she wouldn't be putting Henry in any danger, not with a phone call.

The bus rolled along, the diesel engine rumbling through her seat as the feeling returned to her fingers and toes. She started working on a plan, and even though nothing she'd planned in the last month had gone like she thought it would, she began to feel a little better. Soon she'd at least be closer to them, wherever they were.

"Next stop, Reinersville," the driver called out after a few hours.

She thought the time would never come, and even though she knew they still had a ways to go, Isabel gathered her things and slid closer to the edge of her seat. The bus came to a halt just outside the main stretch of town, and she hopped down, heading straight for a pay phone outside the hardware store.

Shaking the backpack, Isabel listened for any loose change she might have missed, then sighed and picked up the receiver. She dialed Henry collect, and when it came time to say her name, she blurted out Harriet, the first thing that came to mind. She listened intently as Fredrick's baritone voice answered and accepted the charges.

"Small's Grain and Grocery."

"Is Henry in?" she asked, trying to make her voice sound high and fluttery.

"He is not. May I ask who's calling?"

"Please tell him Harriet Shale called and will be visiting town and that I'll call again later."

Shale had always been their code word for something bad. Sometimes, when people walked into the store and Isabel didn't like the way they were looking at her, she'd mouth the word, and Henry would let her hide in the back room. It seemed like they were always looking at her like she was something familiar but altogether detestable. She remembered using it but couldn't remember where the term had come from, something about how dark and sharp the rock could be.

"Alright," Fredrick said. She could hear a pencil scratching against a notepad. "Anythin' else? Number he could try you at?"

"Nope, that'll be about it!" she said, trying to sound casual. "Thank you." She laid the receiver back in its cradle and leaned against the wall. *What now?* There was always the chance that if she waited long enough, he'd be in, but the more she called, the more suspicious it'd be.

Weaving her way through a neighborhood in town, Isabel walked back towards the train station and through a backyard into the woods. She slipped inside the tree line, cut north for a bit to get some distance between her and the road, and turned back east. Sticking with the plan seemed like the best idea, and although her house was one of the first places they'd probably check for her, it was somewhere to start, and she could meet up with Ben from there. She wouldn't get too close, just enough to see if anything was happening there and wait to decide her next move.

The skyline told her it'd be winter soon, the landscape looking entirely greyer than when she left. The trees were barren and skeletal. They all seemed like they were reaching toward her as she navigated her way through them, cursing the rigid ground that continued to twist her ankles. She couldn't help but laugh a little, though. After all she'd seen and done in the last few weeks, she still hadn't learned to buy the right shoes. *It could be a lot more miserable.* Isabel tried to imagine pushing through knee high snowdrifts, guessing blindly at the direction of her house. *It'd be a hell of a lot easier to hide, though.*

It was dark when she made out the familiar shape of her family's chimney on the horizon, rising just over the treetops, a half mile ahead maybe. The timing was perfect as the light was finally gone and anyone looking out into the forest wouldn't be able to see her, but Isabel hadn't eaten or drank anything all day and was beginning to feel weak. For a few minutes she stood still, contemplating her next move and listening to the wind rattle the tree branches.

She sat on an old log and opened the bag, fishing out some crackers and a bottle of water. As she ate, she considered her choices, taking her time to think things through, knowing it'd be what Ben would tell her to do. It was probably safe moving up to the edge of the forest, but anything past there, she'd be easy to spot. Her hand closed around the empty cracker sleeve and pushed it into a side compartment of the backpack, as she took a final sip of water. Isabel slung the pack over her back and set off through the forest again.

Using the moon's outline around the chimney as her marker, she walked on. With her eyes on the sky, she forgot to look down and became tangled in a thorny bush she'd walked straight into. Freeing herself, she plucked a stray thorn from her leg, jumping at the sound of thunder in the distance.

"Wonderful," she muttered.

Almost to the edge of the clearing, Isabel crept forward, taking care not to make noise or move too quickly. Rain began to fall, just a few drops that pattered against her shoulders and head. As she came closer to the edge of the forest, she gasped and put a hand up to her mouth. The burnt out outline of the house still stood with two of its sides completely destroyed and the other half a mixture of charred black and blue wallpaper.

A few things dotted the inside of the home from what she could see. Some were half burnt; others looked like they were still intact. Through a hole in the wall, she could see the silvery face of the grandfather clock, glimmering in the moonlight. She watched the house for a long while, straining her eyes for any signs of movement. The rain was beginning to thicken, falling faster and making it that much harder to see. All in all, it was a good thing. She knew this place inside and out, so it didn't matter if it was hard to see. It'd just be harder for others to see her.

Feeling bolder, Isabel took a deep breath and decided to take a chance. She dropped the bag at the edge of the forest, knowing it would only slow her down if she had to run. It made her feel lighter. Her limbs were tingling with adrenaline as she started making her way forward toward the emergency shelter. Keeping inside the forest at first, hidden in shadow, she then began to tiptoe across the lawn towards the opening. The rain was freezing, and she couldn't stop shivering as it soaked her skin and seeped into her shoes.

She made it a few hundred feet, then heard what sounded like a car door shut from the far side of the house. Isabel flattened herself against the ground, not daring to breath. It was hard to tell what it'd been over the sound of the rain, and after several minutes of silence, she thought maybe she hadn't really heard anything at all. Slowly rising to her feet, Isabel continued her perilous crossing. Reaching the tiny opening, she crouched above it and pressed her ear to the smooth metal door. She was greeted only by the soft ringing of empty space.

The door was slick and larger than she'd remembered, and she set her jaw as she started to open it but found the handle had already been set, leaving the door propped open slightly. Her fingers slippery and shaking, she muscled it open, ducking down to look inside. Moonlight illuminated the bottom of the ladder, but nothing around it. The smell of charred wood and plastic drifted up from below, mixed with the smell of earth. Isabel's heart beat against the inside of her ribs as she gazed down at the tiny pool of light where drops of water continued to fall, soaking the cement and beginning to gather.

They can't keep someone out here all the time. There must be times when no one is here to watch the house at all. She desperately hoped that all the bad luck she'd been having had turned in her favor. Isabel tucked her hair back around her ears and straightened her legs, dangling them over the hole, and turned to start down the ladder. Her feet had hardly reached solid ground, when her heart stopped.

In the distance, Isabel heard something clatter, followed by the sloshing of feet through water. She froze, listening intently as they drew closer, accompanied by the sound of someone struggling to clear a stuffy nose and the rustling of a rain jacket. Isabel moved silently, away from the mouth of the hole. Her hands reached back, but found only empty shelves. The footsteps paused near the mouth of the door.

"I know I closed this," a high pitched, nasally voice said. "Who's down there?"

Isabel could see the shape of a head topped by a thin-rimmed bowler hat looming over the opening. The voice was familiar. She was almost certain it belonged to the deputy, the one always following Hix like an ugly shadow. Isabel couldn't decide whether it would be better to wait and see if he came down and take her chances at overpowering him or make a run for the tunnel on the other side of the room and hope it was still open.

"Identify yourself," the voice said, clicking on a flashlight and shining it down into the shelter.

A calloused hand clamped itself over her mouth and pulled her back towards the wall.

"Quiet," a voice in her ear growled.

THIRTY THREE
IN GRASP AND OUT OF REACH

Following the tracks through the forest, Ben ran, catching them with his fingertips whenever he lost the moon's light. It was a lucky break and a curse. If he was following them, anyone else might be too. Once, he made his own set of tracks, leading away from Isabel's, then carefully following them backwards, taking care to vary the path. He knew it'd be useless if anyone who knew what they were doing found the trail, but it was all he could think to do.

It started as a distant rumbling as he walked, peering into the darkness to pick up any other signs of Isabel, but as he followed the trail, the sky began to crackle, and in the distance flashes of jagged light arced to the ground.

Well, sometimes the solution is another problem, Ben thought. It might clear the path behind him, but it'd do the same for the footprints that led him forward. As the first drops thudded into his coat, Ben picked up the pace, alternating between watching the ground and stopping to listen. Aside from the rolling thunder in the distance and the soft patter of the rain against the leaves, he heard nothing.

The leaves grew slick, and several times Ben struggled to keep his footing as the trail twisted and turned. *I thought we agreed you weren't going home, Isabel.* He gritted his teeth. *She's so damned stubborn.* It was slow going, and the rain was beginning to fall harder as the lightning grew closer and thunder shook the ground. Ben was finally forced to stop, realizing he'd completely lost the trail.. He searched the ground, gently probing with his fingers but felt only the outline of his own boot-prints. Cursing, he retraced his steps, but soon realized that in the musty darkness of the forest and with the way the indentations now laced over each other, he didn't know what he was following anymore.

"Goddamnit." He sat down hard against the base of a tree, rain pouring down his face. Ben took a deep breath and tried to focus, but it was overwhelming, the rain and the wind, and each direction he started towards ended up looking the same. A few yards away, he saw an overhang that looked relatively dry, so he made his way to it, slogging through the mud and debris. Tucked under the shelf of fallen wood and compacted dirt, he was sheltered from the wind, and only his feet were in the rain.

He'd just have to wait out the storm or at least wait until the sun started to rise and gave him a little more to work with. The lightning flashed, exposing the landscape for a moment. Further into the woods, Ben thought he could make out the outline of something tall and square, standing above the trees. After the flash, he stared hard at the rectangular outline, barely visible now.

Knowing it was far too rigid and angular to be anything natural, Ben struck out from the overhang, winding around trees and over fallen brush toward the tower, pausing once a minute or so to realign his course. He'd lost the sun, but the moon and lightning together were enough to take him there.

The rain poured on, heavy as ever, but he didn't care; he had a direction, a compass that called him forward. He was drawing closer to the edge of the forest, trying to place his steps well and stay behind the cover of trees whenever he could. By the time he could see the full height of the structure, he'd nearly broken through the rows of trees that surrounded the Stanton's house. *Of course - the chimney.* Ben wiped the water from his eyes and looked up at the dark tower that loomed across the clearing.

"I'll be damned."

From up towards the driveway, he heard the sloshing of feet against wet grass. A dark form made its way across the yard, heading straight for him.

Ben froze, flattening himself against a tree. He didn't dare look back at the yard and put himself in the open again. If the shadow had been Isabel, she'd either decided on being incredibly bold or stupid. He hoped it was neither, and that, like him, she was hidden somewhere along the tree line on the outskirts of the property. Better yet, he hoped she was tucked away in some hidden place he didn't know about or that she'd been smart enough to change her mind and not come there at all.

He finally chanced a peek, shielding his eyes and working his way up through the edge of the forest. The dark outline hadn't really drawn any closer. It stood a hundred yards away, pointing a flashlight at the ground it looked like. As he took a closer look, he made out the open door of the escape shelter they'd hidden in. The figure with the flashlight stood there, motionless for a few seconds, then started to lower himself into the room and shut the door. *No doubt a patrol of some kind.*

It was hard for him to imagine Isabel being rash enough to just walk up to her old house and let herself in to look around. *No way.* She must have come here, seen the patrols walking around, and left. He tried to imagine where she might be now - perhaps back in Reinersville or back in the woods waiting for him to meet her.

Where the best secrets are kept. Surely she meant she was going home, to the place where they'd found the note. Ben looked over the house, searching its broken outline for the shape of a clock. Then, he froze, a shallow breath trapped in his lungs.

Where the best secrets are kept. What kind of secrets would a town like Echton have? His mind flashed to the jail, the courthouse, and finally settled on the town hall. *What if I was wrong? If she isn't here, she must have been looking for a different set of secrets*, he decided.

The bruises that covered his body were a constant reminder of what they might do to her. He started to run again, dodging trees and shrubs on the outside of the property. Once he was closer to the driveway, he made out two sets of vehicles, a black car and a rusted black truck. Either one would do, but it'd all be a whole lot easier if there weren't any people in them.

It was risky, he knew. As soon as he took off with one of

them, it'd be obvious someone had been there, and the town would be thrown into full alert, but as he saw it, he didn't have much choice. Of the two, he decided the truck was the less conspicuous. Anyone in Echton might drive a truck.

Ben slid inside the cab and carefully shut the door behind him. He lay on his side and tore the panel cover from beneath the steering column, feeling for wiring harnesses. He didn't dare turn on the cab light, and in the dark, he couldn't make out a red from a blue. He knew he'd disassemble the damn thing before he made a contact that would turn the engine over.

He popped the door, hoping the moonlight would illuminate the bundle of wiring. It halfway did the trick and Ben resumed his position below the column, tugging the coil apart and ripping the heads off with his teeth. He pulled back, hoping to be able to see the other side of the panel, but it was shrouded in shadow. Waiting patiently, he tensed his shoulders and looked to the sky.

"Come on, goddamnit."

Nothing. The rain had begun to slow, and the sky had grown silent. He felt his chance slipping away the longer he waited. Pushing the door all the way open, he moved over to the car to see if he could find some kind of flashlight or at least a lighter. His eyes traced over the black leather seats, and Ben started to laugh. *I don't know who's dumber, you or me.*

He snatched up a pair of keys from the dash and ran around the other side of the car, sliding into the driver's seat. *A car would have to do.* The engine roared to life, sending the high beams across the field and the wiper blades jumping across the windshield. Ben threw the car into reverse and tore out of the driveway, his hands tight on the wheel, one eye on the rearview mirror and one on the road.

THIRTY FOUR
TWISTED WIRES

As an enormous pair of arms held her in place, Isabel breathed in a familiar scent. Fredrick had always had a distinct smell about him, a mixture of the cologne and soap he used. She stopped struggling and rested her hand on top of the one that covered her mouth as across the tiny room Henry stepped forward into the beam of the flashlight.

"Why don't you put that damned thing down? It's our shift anyway," he called up.

"Small," McCreary snorted. "What're you doing down there? It's Thursday."

"You wanna stand outside in this?" Henry held his hand out to catch some of the rain pouring into the room.

"Great patrol work. You gonna catch anyone hiding in a hole?" McCreary sneered.

Isabel could feel Fredrick's enormous form beside her in the dark, but it still startled her when he spoke.

"Nothing you need to worry about."

He moved around her into the glare of the light, looking upward.

"I worry about everything. That's what makes me good at what I do," McCreary shot back, descending the ladder and sealing the door above him. "Isn't there a damn light in here?"

"You're the ones that cut the power, genius." Henry said, seating himself on the opposite side of the room and gesturing for the deputy to sit beside him. The room was dark, except for the flashlight McCeary brandished like a sword. Fredrick shuffled to his left so his body completely overlapped Isabel's outline. He crossed his arms and kept his eyes forward, towering over the small man. McCeary avoided his gaze, checking each corner of the room, while Henry pulled a lantern from behind him and lit it.

"Hiding down here while I'm standing watch outside like you're supposed to," McCreary said, tapping his foot and sucking at his teeth.

"Told Hix I'd take watch tonight," Henry said.

"Tonight isn't your night. Tuesday..." he wagged a finger at Henry.

McCreary craned his neck to peer around Fredrick, and Isabel did her best to mirror the big man's movements, her feet lightly scuffing the pavement. She didn't dare breathe, but the sound of the water dripping from her dress seemed so loud she couldn't bare it. The seconds dragged by as McCreary sniffled and wiped his nose on his sleeve, turning back to Henry.

"Nobody told me anything. Go home. If I hear or see anything, I'll send word."

Henry had done a good job of keeping his face emotionless, but Isabel could tell he was starting to get nervous. No way could all three of them get out of that room without McCreary noticing. She'd hardly dared to breathe the whole time he'd been in the shelter and was beginning to feel faint. The room seemed so quiet now. Either the rain was dying down, or she just couldn't hear it over the pounding of her heart.

"What was that?" McCreary said, his eyes flicking towards the door.

"What?" Henry said.

"Sounded like an engine. You expecting anyone?"

Henry shook his head slowly, securing his glasses on the bridge of his nose.

"You, come with me." He poked a finger at Fredrick and nodded to the door.

Fredrick extended his hand, gesturing for the deputy to lead the way, and after a second, he did. McCreary disappeared, and as Fredrick followed, Isabel slipped back farther into the shadows, out of sight from the door. When the door finally closed behind them and she heard the two men sloshing towards the other side of the house, Isabel threw herself into Henry's arms and sobbed. He returned her embrace, rocking her gently, her head pressed into his shoulder. After a few seconds, Henry held her at arm's length and looked into her face.

"Where in the world have you been? I thought we'd never see you again."

Isabel shook her head and hugged him once more. She spoke into the folds of his jacket, her voice muffled.

"My family. Do you know where they are?"

"Hix has them locked up. He announced a few days back they're being held for murder."

"Murder? Whose murder?"

"A special investigator or marshal or something was in town a few months back and went missing I hear, and he's saying your folks are on the lamb, hiding out in Echton. Said when this specialist found them, they killed him and that you were involved too."

"Henry," she sobbed. "You know that's not true. It's absolutely not true."

"I know." He stroked her head fondly. "I know it's not."

Suddenly, the door at the top of the shelter flew open, sending a sheet of water and cold autumn air crashing into the room.

"The goddamn car's gone. Get out here now-" McCreary yelled from the yard above but then stopped mid-sentence, his mouth moving but no words coming out.

"She -" was all he managed before Fredrick's hand struck the side of his head. His body crumpled, falling down the ladder as Henry did his best to catch it, letting him down the rest of the way.

"Sorry," Fredrick said.

"Bastard had it coming," Henry replied, looking up.

"The car's gone," Fredrick added simply. "That have anything to do with you?" He pointed to Isabel.

She shook her head, looking down at McCreary. Isabel knelt and held her hand over his mouth, then nodded.

"He's alive," she said. "You can't be here, either of you. You need to leave and tell them I did it or something. Tell them whatever you have to."

"I'm not telling them shit," Henry spat, giving the

unconscious McCreary a kick in the thigh.

She'd never seen Henry lose his temper, and it surprised her now.

"Did you come here alone?" he asked.

"Yes, well, no. There should be someone else behind me. The boy I was with before."

"How far behind you?"

"I really don't know. I think I got a few hours head start on him, but he's fast. I imagine it won't be long."

"You running away from him?" Fredrick chimed in, descending the ladder.

"No, it's complicated, but he's helping me. We just had a temporary separation."

"I knew it wouldn't be long now before you were looking at boys like you look at books." Henry shook his head and grinned.

"Quiet down," she smiled.

Fredrick secured the door and sat down beside Henry.

"Is this place seriously always under watch?" Isabel asked, looking over the shelves, stripped bare.

"Strict orders from the sheriff," Henry scowled. "He's got the whole damned town taking rotations looking for you."

"And tonight just happened to be your night?"

"Sometimes circumstances align themselves with necessity, Mrs. Shale."

"Sometimes you lie to the bastards just to piss them off," Fredrick let out a hearty rolling laugh.

Henry checked his watch, looking up at the ceiling as though he could see through it. "We've got time, but we'll need it to do something about him." He gave McCreary another tap with his boot. "The next shift starts at 2AM, and it's nearly 11 now."

"What do we do with him?"

"Well, we send him on his way and hope he doesn't find his way back before we get some ground underfoot," Henry replied.

"We can't leave," Isabel cried. "My mother and father, I need to find them."

"No one said anything about leaving," Henry corrected her. He turned to Fredrick. "The truck still here?"

"Yeah, looks like someone's been into the wiring."

"Ben," Isabel blurted out, her face lighting up.

"Your friend?" Henry said, standing up.

"I'd guess," she shrugged. "He's got a thing for cars."

"It still working?" Henry asked Fredrick.

"As well as it usually works."

"You have to take me into town with you," Isabel said. "Ben'll be looking for me there."

Henry shook his head. He looked tired, like he'd aged a decade in the short while she'd been gone.

"Let's go," Fredrick said, climbing the ladder in two steps and pulling himself out into the night. He extended an arm down, and wrapping his hands around Isabel's tiny wrists, hoisted her out.

They decided it was best if Isabel rode in the back, beside McCreary in case he woke up and tried anything. If she lay flat, no one would be able to see her over the sides of the truck bed, and with any sort of luck, they could smuggle her into the back of the store.

The ride into town was one of the worst Isabel had ever had. She found herself wishing for the hard wooden planking of a train as the rain picked back up again, spattering her face, and the deputy's head bounced against her legs. He'd been bound at the ankles and hands, an old piece of cloth tied in his mouth as a gag. It'd been a quick fix, but nonetheless seemed like it'd do the trick. She lay in the back of the truck, her head propped upright, with McCreary's own gun trained on him. Isabel just hoped he wouldn't wake before they reached town and secured him with something a little stronger.

She'd forgotten how long the ride was, but at least it gave her time to think. It made sense - about framing her family for murder. Hix himself or one of his men had probably killed the specialist because he'd been looking for the missing gold, and when her parents had stumbled on his secret, they'd been perfect for the fall. *We can clear our names.* She was sure. *We just have to get out of this godforsaken city.* Her father had gone to school with some of the best lawyers in the country, and Hix's authority wouldn't do him much good outside of Echton.

The truck slowed as it reached town, and she did her best to keep McCreary's head from bouncing against the metal truck bed but couldn't help but smile a little when it did. Every pothole or bump sent them both skyward an inch or so, then crashing back down. She tried not to slide or move around, but the slick metal truck bed made it difficult.

As they turned onto the main drag of town, McCreary's eyes began to flutter open. Isabel's mind raced. She couldn't get Henry or Fredrick's attention without sitting up and totally giving herself away, but if their prisoner made a scene, it'd be even worse. She pressed a finger to her lips, staring down at him. His eyes bulged, and he began to squirm, trying to free himself from the nylon bindings. She shook her head and pointed. "Stop," she mouthed.

McCreary just squirmed harder, looking from her, down to his hands, which were growing raw and chafed. He saw the top of the jailhouse go by above the side of the truck and started screaming, although it was entirely drowned out by the combination of the gag and the relentless pounding of the raindrops.

Isabel pressed the gun against his forehead and pulled back the hammer like she'd seen Ben do before. McCreary stopped moving and just lay still, his eyes locked on her finger as it hovered just above the trigger.

"Good boy," she said, giving him a little pat on the head.

They finally reached the store, pulling around the back. Isabel kept the gun trained on McCreary until Fredrick opened the back gate of the truck and tossed McCreary over his shoulder, carrying him inside the stock room. *He looks just like a wet cat,* Isabel thought, watching the look of indignation and discomfort on his face as he was carried like a child being punished.

"We'll take care of him," Henry said.

"What are you gonna do?" Isabel said.

"I'm not sure, but probably more than he'd have done for us." He looked down his glasses at her, wiping the water from his brow.

"Thank you, Henry," she whispered, leaning forward to kiss him on the cheek. "I'll call you again soon. Same name."

"Alright, Mrs. Shale. I'd say after tonight, you have a day or two tops before we reach a point I don't think any of us are looking for."

"I understand."

"Isabel," Henry said, grabbing her arm. "I know where your parents are, but I'm not going to tell you because I don't want you to do anything stupid."

"Like wander into my old house and into a dark room alone," she completed his thought.

Henry nodded gravely. "Know that they're OK for now. He won't touch them if he doesn't have you. Hix knows they're the reason you'll have to come back," he added.

"He's right," she said, embracing him a final time and slipping around the front of the building.

Isabel figured if Hix had people out at their old house, he probably had them everywhere in town. She wrapped the dress around her hands, squeezing the dark blue fabric until the water ran from it. It fell back to her legs, sticking against them. If Ben wasn't at her parent's house, he was probably somewhere else he thought she'd go. She felt another wave of guilt surge over her as she took a deep breath and wiped the rain from her face.

Making her way back around the feed store, Isabel ducked under the window so even Henry wouldn't know she was going further into town. She tucked her hair under the collar of her dress and crawled under a broken piece of fence that separated Henry's store from the insurance offices next door. The town hall was only a few more buildings down. If she could make it there, she could at least look for a car that matched Fredrick's description.

Stealing a car from the Echton law enforcement could hardly be considered "laying low," but Isabel had to admire Ben's courage. She'd always considered herself a pretty smart girl, but she was starting to realize in the last week or two, even smart people can have bad ideas. With one foot up on the trim of the City Bank and Finance, and the other on a piece of drainage pipe, she pulled herself up and over another fence, falling softly to the ground on the other side.

Isabel crossed the final stretch of ground, sliding through a narrow brick walkway and over a pile of scrap. As her ankle cleared the end of the pile, it sent a piece of sheet metal crashing down behind her. She froze, listened for a moment, then shuffled along the brick wall on the other side of the lot and peeked over it. Then she realized why no one had taken notice of the loud noise in the alley.

Across the lot, she saw three figures closing in on a large black car, partially tucked behind the fence of the city hall building. Her grip tightened on the brick wall beside her, and her whole body tensed.

"Iz," a voice whispered from further down the wall. She knew the voice immediately, relief flooding over her as she crawled towards it.

"Are you ok?"

Ben reached for her.

"You do that again, and I'll ..." he whispered.

"You'll what?" she mouthed.

He just shook his head and glared at her, putting his hands on either side of her face and kissed her. They both turned to watch the car through the bushes as one of the figures crept up behind it, and the other two came at it from the front.

"Mouth breathers," Ben said. "You can hear them from a mile away."

"Those mouth breathers are about to take our ride out of here."

Ben held the keys in the moonlight and swung them back and forth before sliding them under a bush.

"Option B isn't pretty, but it could work."

He pointed to their left a few blocks over, and as Isabel turned, under the next streetlight, she saw exhaust rising into the air from a truck with an empty cab. He lowered his eyebrows, nodding towards it. Isabel nodded in return, and they both crawled along the wall as close as they could get to the truck.

Ben was the first one over the wall, and he set across the street at full tilt, making for the open truck door. Isabel struggled to clear the wall, her already torn dress snagged on a sharp edge in the brick. She tugged at it savagely, ripping the fabric, then holding the rest of the dress up around her legs so they could move freely. She first noticed something was wrong when Ben started slowing 20 feet before the truck, his hands coming up to cover his face. Then she saw him, George Scray, the owner of Scray's Diner.

George's ebony skin blended into the darkness, but she could see the shotgun he had trained on Ben, jabbing it at him like a spear. She heard shouts from the other men around the corner and their footsteps against the pavement as they ran towards the sound of the struggle. Then, something strange happened. She was halfway to them when George glanced at her, running across the street, and tossed Ben the gun. Ben almost dropped it, he was so surprised. Then George said something to him that she couldn't make out. Ben was still for a moment but then he threw a right hook into George's jaw and dropped him, jumping into the driver's seat of the truck.

Isabel rolled over the side into the bed and pounded

on the rear window.

"Go!" she shouted.

For the second time that night, Isabel found herself bouncing against the metal rivets of a truck bed, speeding through Echton. As they cleared the main drag, Ben opened the back window, and she crawled through it, squirming into the front seat.

"What the hell was that?" she said, working to right herself in the truck seat.

Ben shook his head and shrugged.

"He told me to hit him."

"He what?"

"He had me, dead-center, and he tossed me the gun and told me to hit him."

Isabel just shook her head in disbelief. *They were neck deep in a town that'd been hunting them in 24 hour shifts, and they'd finally been cornered. It didn't make sense.*

"Speaking of what the hell was that," Ben added.

He told her how he'd followed her footprints to her house and his trip into Echton to look for her. Isabel held onto his arm and explained what Henry had told her about her parents being framed for a murder and how Henry and Fredrick had saved her from McCreary. He made a face when she mentioned the name and smiled when she told him about how he looked, slung over Fredrick's shoulder as he was carried into the back room of their shop. She told him that she couldn't imagine what Henry had planned for their prisoner, but that it was probably cruel but not deadly.

"Take a right up here; we'll head south. I know a place we can hide out," she added.

"This a better idea than going to your old house?" He

furrowed his brow, keeping her in the side of his vision.

"Yes," she said, scowling at him. "Fine. You were right."

"Damned right I was," he replied.

They drove on for a few minutes without speaking, their bodies soaked from the rain but warm where they pressed against each other.

"I can't shake this," she finally said. "Can you make any sense of what happened back there?"

"Seems like we have more friends than just Henry," Ben said, letting himself smile at the idea. It was good to have something to smile about.

THIRTY FIVE
OUT OF SIGHT

Rolling through the back roads of Echton, the truck rattled and sputtered up the inclines as they climbed further into the hills. Ben felt like he could trust Isabel, but after 25 minutes of what seemed like blind turns, he'd begun to wonder exactly what she had in mind. On the other hand, if he'd lost track of his own whereabouts, anyone else would probably have a hard time finding them. After about 40 minutes, Isabel pointed to what looked like the iron bones of some great beast, poking above the trees as they rounded a bend.

"Lumber mill?" Ben asked.

"Used to be an ore mine. My father took me up here once when I was younger to show me what the people in the town did for work."

"Not exactly my idea of a good field trip," he said, remembering the time he'd spent building fence lines around company land in Florida.

"They opened another mine, about 15 miles east of here because this one wasn't producing. Pull in there." She pointed to a collapsing wooden shelter, tucked away beside two elevator shafts, each chained shut and marked with a no trespassing sign.

Ben yanked the brake into place and killed the engine. He nudged the door open and hopped down, looking around. The wooden support beams, which were dotted with random nails and hooks in some places, looked solid enough. The roof was caving in from the back forward, and he could see moonlight coming through it in some places.

"You don't think anyone will come out here?"

"Doubt it. This place is a graveyard," Isabel said.

Looking over the rusted machinery and scraps of rusted metal that littered the ground, Ben had to agree.

"That drive we used the only way up here?" he asked, pushing an overturned crate out of his way.

"Yeah, I think so," Isabel replied, climbing a set of stairs that led to some kind of loading structure and looking back the way they'd come. "There's some kind of office up here, but the windows are all broken."

"How long ago'd this place go under?"

Ben followed her up the steps and looked out over the camp. It was all so still and lifeless, like a breathing, moving, creature had just taken its last step and collapsed. Isabel began to shiver, and Ben wrapped his arms around her.

"We get a few hours of sleep here. Then we'll be back in touch with Henry and be that much closer to your parents."

"Yeah, but ..." she protested, face buried in his coat.

"Nothing you can do right now. Things are only

gonna get hotter with McCeary disappearing. We've both seen what it's like in there."

"Yeah, but the longer we wait, the greater the chances that something might happen to them."

"Here's how I figure it, Iz: I think Hix is arrogant, and that might make him stupid. Once he realizes his right hand guy is gone, he's gonna set the whole town out looking for him. When they go out looking, we go in looking."

"That actually might work." Isabel looked up at him, her hands busy smoothing her dress.

"Thank Fredrick. He's the one that clubbed McCreary. Either way, I think we call Henry in a few hours and see what he thinks. You really trust him?" He looked down at her.

"I do."

"Good enough. It helps to have someone you can trust who's living in the middle of people you don't."

"That's true."

He could see her mood beginning to brighten from the way her body softened against him. It was good to see that a girl with so much on her mind was still in the fight.

"What do we do now?" Isabel said.

"We sleep," Ben replied, walking back down the stairs.

"Where are we supposed to sleep out here?" she called after him.

"The truck seats recline, I think."

Ben talked Isabel into at least resting for a few hours before they went looking for a phone. He did his best to drift off, but with the constant sound of her body rustling around next to him, tossing and shifting, he doubted he'd had a solid five minutes.

"You alright?" he finally asked.

"There's no way I'm gonna sleep right now."

"I figured as much," Ben said, covering his eyes with the inside of his elbow.

"I'm gonna go for a walk," she said, nudging the door open with her foot.

Grabbing the steering wheel and pulling himself upright, Ben jumped out to catch her before she reached the edge of the shelter.

"We shouldn't go anywhere alone."

Isabel nodded, grinning. "Wanna go for a walk?"

Ben sighed, then took her hand, and they headed towards the other side of the camp.

"Where do you think the nearest phone is around here?" she said.

"Public phone? I'd say probably in the next town over, but I'm betting Hix has warrants and maybe even men in all of those towns, depending on when he realizes McCreary's missing."

"What if we ask someone to use their phone?"

"Who would we ask out here?" he said, looking around at the thick evergreen foliage and down the overgrown path they'd started to descend. Far ahead, he saw an opening where the trail spit out onto the road.

"People usually lend a hand here if you ask them," Isabel said. "They're not all bad."

"That's a nice thought," Ben said, "but you can't even ask them. What if they recognize you?"

"I agree. That's why you're gonna ask."

Ben didn't like the idea of approaching a random stranger's house and asking to use the phone. *Awkwardness aside, I have no idea what I'm walking into.* Yet, like a lot of other situations, he didn't think he had much choice in the matter. They were running out of time and options. If they were going to get into Echton while the manhunt for McCreary was in full bore, they'd only have a day, maybe less, to figure something out.

He and Isabel walked for awhile and sat at the edge of where the hill opened to the road below, overlooking a long valley. Greenery ran to the horizon, split by a dirt road and dotted with the occasional house and the flow of the early morning traffic, miles away.

"I don't wanna kill anyone, Ben," Isabel said.

"I don't either." He stared off into the distance, grinding tiny grains of sand between his fingers.

"Thank you - for helping me," she said softly.

He nodded slowly, tossing a piece of rock between his hands. Ben exhaled slowly and tossed it to her. "Take a look at this, and tell me what you see."

She held it for a moment, giving her fingers time to explore its face before angling it towards the rising sun.

"It's a fossil," she replied. "You can see the imprint of a shell and all the tiny ridges. My mom used to collect these. We'd find them near the coast sometimes."

"And?"

"There's no reason it should be here," she said. "I've never seen a fossil in Echton."

He plucked the rock from her palm and held it up to the sunlight, leaking through the trees above. "Sometimes, we end up somewhere a long ways from where we were made and in a place we never thought we'd be in," he said. "Sometimes, the hardest thing to realize is that even if we can't make out a reason for why we're here, or why things are the way they are, it's just because we haven't put the pieces together yet."

Isabel laid her head on his shoulder.

"Things go faster if you can see the big picture while you're putting the pieces together," she said.

"You're the one in charge of the maps," he smiled warmly. "What time do you think it is?"

She looked up at the sun, just beginning to peek over the tree line at the other end of the valley.

"5 or 5:30 maybe."

"Too early for a house call?"

"Half the people around here are up at 5AM or going to bed at 6AM, depending on the shift."

Ben stood and dusted his pants off, offering her his hand. "Let's see if some folks will let us use their phone for our broken down car."

"You mean the one that's just out of sight of their house?" Isabel laughed, giving him a gentle nudge.

"Right. I think you'll need to stay with the car though."

Isabel made a face before setting off down the hill, pointing to a light blue farmhouse a half mile up the road. Ben caught up and walked beside her until they'd come into sight of the house. Isabel promised to make herself scarce while he was gone. She made him repeat Henry's number four times before she was satisfied, even though he insisted he'd just be able to look it up in the phone book if he forgot.

"Be back in a sec," he said, trotting up towards the driveway. He'd felt fine about the idea with Isabel by his side, but as he took the long walk up to the farmhouse, he felt his confidence wane. Ben scratched his beard absently, stopping just a few steps from the porch. He was still standing there when a little girl opened the door and waved to him.

"Hi sir," the girl said, her voice soft. "My gran'ma wants to know if you're alright?"

Ben looked around, walked up the steps, and knelt down in front of her, looking her in the face.

"I could use your help," he said, forgetting everything he and Isabel had rehearsed. The little girl's face was pale, with large brown eyes and thick black hair that fell over her shoulders. She took his hand and walked him inside, where a woman stood from where she'd been watching them.

"Ma'am, could I use your phone?" he said. She was older, greying at her roots, and she wore an apron and dress, fraying at the collar and shoulders.

"Of course," she said, scooping up the girl. "I'm Tara." She gently took his hand and shook it.

"Thank you, Tara. I'm Ben."

Their eyes met for a moment. He thought it was a little strange, the way she looked at him like he was an old friend, just stopping back in for a visit. Tara led him into the other room and showed him the phone, but in the process of getting inside, Ben had completely forgotten Henry's number. He looked around for a moment at the cluttered counters and sink full of dishes.

"I'm sorry about this mess," she said, collecting plates from the counter and tossing them onto the already towering pile. "It's my daughter's house. She's at third shift still."

"It's no different at my place," he smiled. "Do you have a phone book by chance?"

She dug an ancient phone book from beneath a pile

of papers and handed it to him, her other arm holding the little girl to her hip. Ben flipped through the pages until he came to Small's Grain and Grocery. Feeling her eyes on him, he paused to look up. She just stared back and smiled, the little girl twirling Tara's hair around her hand.

"I'll let you make your call," she said, as she walked back into the living room, leaving Ben alone in the kitchen.

He punched the numbers in slowly and deliberately, keeping an eye on the living room door. She seemed nice enough, but he couldn't afford to trust anyone.

"Small's Grain and Grocery," Henry's voice buzzed on the other end of the line.

"Hey John, it's Barney Shale."

"Oh, Barney. You still coming to town tonight?"

"Car's broken down out here. Maybe you could come give us a lift," Ben said, stretching the phone cord to get a better look at the next room.

"Sure thing. Where you calling from?"

"Out by the old mines. Lady out here was nice enough to let me use her phone."

It actually eased his nerves a little, having something to say that was true. As he leaned a little farther, he saw Tara gazing out the window, slowly rocking the little girl on her hip.

"Alright, what do you need?"

"Just a few gallons of gas, I think," Ben said. "Better bring the cables, though; I'm not sure what's wrong with it."

He retreated back into the kitchen as far as the cord would allow him to and lowered his voice.

"The old mine, south of town, tonight." He returned his voice to the normal volume, faking a hearty laugh.

"Alright John, take care."

"Be safe," he heard Henry say just before the other end of the phone went dead.

Ben hung up the receiver, walking sheepishly back into the living room. "Thank you. I think we should be alright. He's gonna come get us."

"Us?" she said.

He stared blankly at the door, then shook his head and looked back at her. "My wife is back with the car." Ben patted his pockets as if he'd forgotten something. "I'd better get back there. You never know."

"You need a ride or anything?" Tara said, setting the little girl on the couch.

"We'll be alright, but I appreciate it," Ben replied, heading for the door.

The screen door groaned as he swung it back open, and for a moment, he swore he heard his name.

"What's that?" Ben turned back towards her.

"Hmm?" she replied.

He held her gaze for a moment, then let the door shut behind him. They both stood there, the breeze whistling through the mesh in the doorframe.

"Stay here a minute," Tara said, moving back into the kitchen and returning a moment later with a pie. She nudged the door open with her knee and offered it to him.

"Please. It's the least I can do."

"I - thank you, but I..." He tried to read her face.

"I recognize you from the posters at the church, Benjamin. I'm not sure what you're into, but I've got a feeling it ain't somethin' you ever did wrong. I'll pray for you."

Ben wasn't sure if he should thank her or just turn

and make his escape. It wouldn't take long to get away from the house, and he didn't like the way things were shaping up inside it.

"Please, take it," she said, pushing the tin into his hands. "Looks like you could use a sweet anyhow."

Tara smiled gently and the little girl waved from behind her. Ben walked down the steps and out onto the road without looking back, the pie held loosely in his hands. When he reached the bushes where Isabel was hiding, she emerged and joined him, staring at the pie.

"Now where'd you get that?"

"I'm really not sure what happened," he said, "but there's at least one decent person in Echton."

"Oh?"

"Not much else I could say to explain it, but it sure smells good." Ben turned back towards the house, watching it shrink into the distance as they made their way up the hill, back towards the mining camp.

"You talk to Henry?"

"Yeah. He's gonna meet us tonight after he closes up shop," Ben replied.

"You think it's OK to eat?" she said, eying the pie and biting her bottom lip.

"You gotta trust someone, sometime, right?" he said, handing it to her. "Some girl told me that once."

"Someone around here has to be telling the truth," Isabel smiled.

THIRTY SIX
MUTUATAS VITA

It was nearly dark when Isabel heard the rumble of Henry's truck twisting its way through the back roads to the mining camp. She and Ben had spent the day talking strategy, and she'd taken the map from her backpack and pinned it up on a piece of plywood in the machine shop. The room wasn't ideal, but it was getting colder as the sun went down, and at least they were sheltered. Once they'd cleared away some of the scrap lumber and swept the broken glass into a pile in the corner, it wasn't so bad.

Without a watch or a working clock, it'd been torture, waiting all day for the sun to go down and tell them it was nearly time to meet. When she heard the shifting of gravel under tires down the hill, Isabel rushed out to meet the pair of headlights filtering through the evergreens. Ben insisted that they run up the hillside a short way and hide as the truck approached. Perched atop a fallen tree, Isabel started to get up as she saw Henry get out of the passenger's side and Fredrick from the driver's, but Ben grabbed her arm as another person started to emerge.

"Who's that?"

She shook her head, peering down at them.

"Mrs. Shale?" Henry called from below.

Isabel looked to Ben and answered, "Yes, dear. My associate would like to know who your guest is."

"A friend," a female voice said.

"It's alright, Iz," Henry added.

Ben held his breath to listen, and before he'd let it out, Isabel had already started down the hill.

"Good, let's do that," he muttered.

They walked in front of the headlights, their breath thick in the air around them. Ben beckoned them to follow him into the shop, where he relit a gas lamp Isabel had found earlier. The five of them circled around its light, the pinned up map on the wall beside them.

For the first time, Ben got a good look at the third person that had come in the truck. She was rail thin, wrapped in a worn denim coat and had on what looked like a home-knitted cap. Her hair poked through it in some places in knotted silver locks, and her skin was a deep brown like worn leather.

Henry stepped forward and hugged Isabel, then turned to Ben. "Thank you for taking care of her," he said, squeezing Ben's hand heartily. "This is Kathryn Estalgo, I've known her since..."

"The beginning of time," Kathryn said, smiling. "It's a pleasure to meet you both. Henry's told me all about you, and I insisted that he bring me here."

Isabel found it surprising how vibrant Kathryn

seemed when she spoke. She looked ancient, but the way she moved made Isabel feel like the elderly one.

"What's this?" Henry said, holding up an empty pie tin, smears of blue with crumbs caked on its bottom.

"Breakfast, lunch, and dinner," Isabel laughed.

"Thank you for coming out here," Ben interrupted them. "I understand you're risking yourselves for us. It's not a small thing to ask."

"It's worth it," Fredrick said, his enormous shadow casting Ben's face in darkness.

"Thank you," Isabel said, touching his arm. "Will you tell me where they are now? I'm not going to do anything stupid, Henry. I need to know."

Henry sighed, and Fredrick nodded to him, opening his mouth to speak.

"I'll tell her," Henry cut him off. "I have a suspicion they're in a back room of the jail somewhere. Hix won't tell us where he's keeping them, but I always see that weasel deputy of his sneaking around there a few times a day. It's the only thing that'd really explain it."

Isabel clasped her hand over her mouth, remembering the noises that had haunted her when she'd been confined to the same dismal quarters. The vibrations she'd heard and the feint yelling into the night.

"That's where they kept me, and there were noises I heard. You mean?"

"We don't know that," Ben said. "Could be we were inches from them, but we could have been miles too."

"They must have known," Isabel said, taking a few deep breaths and trying to keep the aching in her throat from leaking through her eyes. She bit her lip to distract herself from the idea. Anything else would be better, anything except the thought that she'd been only a few feet from her parents and left them in Echton to chase an apparition. *I should have put it together,* she thought. *I should have looked at the evidence and realized that they'd never leave me alone like I left them.*

"It won't be long now," Fredrick said.

"You will see them again. I promise you," Henry added, leaning forward to wipe a tear from her nose.

Isabel blinked furiously, gesturing to the map and Ben, who was poised beside it.

"We've been talking about this all day, and I think we might have some ideas," Ben said, looking to the area they'd outlined and sectioned off, marked with dust from a stray piece of charcoal.

"What'd you do with McCreary?"

Henry grinned, placing a hand over his mouth. "We had a little chloroform left in medical, so we encouraged him to get a little shut-eye and sent him out with the returned produce crates."

"Where?" Isabel said, choking out a laugh.

"Well," Henry paused, looking at his watch and stifling a smile. "He should be on the east side of Indiana by now and in Nebraska by tomorrow."

Ben snorted, clapping Henry on the shoulder.

"How long until he wakes up?" Isabel said.

"Well, we left him some air holes so he should be fine. Somewhere in the Midwest, I'd think," Henry said, laughing. "That gives us a day or two before he finds his way back."

"Anybody asking questions?"

"Hix is raising hell," Fredrick said.

"Thought he might be," Ben replied. "Any search efforts going out?"

"Just small stuff today, but I've heard they're organizing something big soon. They've been going door to door all day long. Won't tell anyone what they're looking for, though. I'm thinking they're afraid to let anyone know they're not in the whole. Half the morning, I had the bastard in my back storage room, and John Dixon is in front asking if I've seen anything suspicious," Henry chuckled.

"What'd you tell them about last night?" Isabel chimed in, trying to keep her voice steady.

"I told them we handed off the shift to him when he came out there and told us the schedule was wrong and that I haven't seen hide nor hair of him since," Henry said, looking to Fredrick.

"They asked a lot of questions about you an' him." Fredrick nodded towards Ben. "But I guess they figured we're too stupid and too old to pull something like that off," he chuckled.

"I made a hell of a show about hatin' you after you stole my truck when you left town," Henry winked. "Made it clear I was no friend."

"Any idea when this thing, something big, is gonna happen?" Ben said.

"Tomorrow or the next day, I'm sure of that," Henry said. "They've been everywhere inside town today. I'm guessing they'll be moving to the woods and outskirts tomorrow, which is gonna take a lot more manpower."

"That's what I was hoping," Ben said, returning to the map. He outlined their plan, adding that whatever day the biggest search was going to be on would be the ideal time for them to steal into town. When all of Echton's residents were out searching for them, they would be inside Echton looking for Isabel's parents.

"Only problem is, someone gets word that something smells funny in town, we're right in the thick of it," he concluded. "We get stuck inside town, there's almost no way we're gonna get out outside of handcuffs or a coffin. "

Fredrick nodded solemnly, producing a pencil from his coveralls and drawing an outer line on the map, sketching a wide circle around the border of the town.

"They'll start on the outside and go in I'd guess. Try to chase you into someone else if you slip away. This is where you're gonna find the most trouble," he said, pointing to two spots he'd marked with an "X." "The jailhouse will be nearly empty, but the city hall and the church are a kind of makeshift dispatch and'll have folks on deck or on guard 24 hours a day."

Isabel groaned, tracing the line with her index finger. She turned to Ben.

"Sometimes you have to take risks," he said, quietly. "I don't like it. I don't think any of us like it, but the only options we have are gonna put us right in the heart of this thing."

They agreed that either tomorrow or the next day, whenever they were called to look for McCreary, Ben and Isabel's plan would fall into place.

"The day after tomorrow'd be better," Ben said, pacing the length of the shop. "Anything you can get us about positions, times, or numbers would all be helpful."

Henry agreed that, regardless, they'd meet the next morning and either update the plan or move into action. It was growing late, and he'd been glancing at his watch with increasing frequency. After a few more minutes of discussing the simplest way to get them into down, he jingled the keys in his hand and nodded towards the truck.

"Speaking of it, we have to go, or they'll know something's off. Mayor Hatley flagged us down on our way out, and we told him we were just making a run to see Kathryn's family, south of town."

"Is he involved in this?"

"Not of his choice. He's a fool, a harmless fool, but it never took much to twist his arm," Henry replied.

After a moment of silent pondering, Isabel dug inside Ben's bag and produced the coin, setting it carefully on the table. From the moment she produced the coin, she could tell its very presence made Henry and Kathryn uncomfortable.

"What is it?" Ben said. "We know it has something to with all this."

Fredrick stepped forward and picked up the coin, looking it over. Kathryn's eyes were wide as she took the coin from him and closed her hand around it.

"It has everything to do with this," she said, looking up at Isabel. They were all silent for a long moment until Fredrick spoke up.

"What is it?"

"Where did you get this?" Kathryn replied sharply, looking to Isabel.

Isabel blushed, a deep crimson red, but Henry gently wrapped an arm around her shoulders.

"It's alright, Isabel."

"I took it. I'm sorry," Isabel whispered.

"Ah, I see," Kathryn said, eying her.

"What happened?" Ben said.

"Started about 40 years ago. A line of black cars rolled into town," she said. Kathryn paused, setting the coin back on the table. "It was summer - I remember - when a whole mess of men and a few women and children came in, in a big group, like I said before. They said they'd traveled from a long way off and were only looking for a hot meal and a place to rest before they moved on."

"It was obvious they were trouble from the minute they stepped out. They stayed for that first night, and we all spoke in whispers and talked quietly, too polite to say anything about it. Well, that day turned into a short while, and then the days started to pass, and they showed no sign of picking up and going.

All they did was fight and steal from the folks that already lived here," Henry added, shaking his head.

"Who were they?" Isabel asked.

Kathryn paused, running her thumb over the face of the coin as if she hadn't heard her.

"They took over the hotel, the bar, and soon, the hall. At first, we sat by silently, hoping they would figure out we didn't have anything to give and just move on and leave us be."

"No one knows what shithole they climbed out of," Henry said tersely, "but the bastards wouldn't leave. They took over everything. We just lay quiet, like if we held our breath long enough they'd go poof and disappear."

Ben was silent, watching Kathryn's face as she listened to Henry, her lips tightly pursed, as though all the world's secrets might tumble out if she opened them.

"There was a man - hardly a man - maybe a few years older than you." She pointed a finger at Ben. "Born here to a miner and a school marm. Both passed away before he'd hardly finished school, God rest their souls. He found himself a job as a deputy under Sheriff Halsted."

Henry nodded his agreement. "Quiet kid, I remember. Seemed like a good one."

"Halsted and his other deputy buckled, you see," Kathryn said. "But for whatever reason, this one didn't roll over as fast. Brave or stupid, I don't know what the difference is half the time."

"What was his name - the deputy?" Ben said.

Kathryn scratched her head, fending off a shiver, and tightened her grip on the jacket.

"Gabriel Spears," she said. "Everyone just took to callin' him Spears. Didn't know him well, kind of kept to himself, but I remember the name."

"What happened?" Isabel interrupted her.

"They killed him," Henry said, shaking his head sadly.

"Killed him?" Isabel said, leaning forward.

"He stopped one of 'em from going after the woman that, uh, used to run the bank. Her name was Patricia." Henry sniffed, rubbing his eyes. "Patti."

"Who was she?" Ben asked.

Henry stared back blankly, and Kathryn laid her hand on his arm, squeezing it lightly.

"She was my wife," his reply came drifting back, and his eyes turned to Fredrick. "I'm sorry, son. I just couldn't tell you. I didn't want you to live with it."

Fredrick sat down hard, sending up a cloud of dust from a workbench, his hands on his knees as Henry went on.

"She musta been walking home, and one of em came up on her, drunk, caught her in the alleyway. So, Spears hears it, runs in there, and scared him off, but when he's helping her up and walking her back into the street, they shoot him. Shoot him and her both," Henry spoke softly.

Fredrick's eyes looked moist and Isabel pulled him into an embrace, releasing him after a moment.

"Everybody rushed over an' he pointed that gun right at me next - Fredrick in my arms - and told me my son was next if I moved. They died in the street. All of us there, and none of us did a damn thing about it," Henry spat. "Scared as hell. No one wanted to see their family hurt the same. Who could blame 'em?"

"My God," Isabel murmured. "I'm so sorry."

"It's alright," he wiped his nose with his sleeve and sat on Fredrick's other side, one hand on his son's shoulder. "I'm sorry, Fredrick."

"The man that'd led them there - tall man with thick black curly hair - it was his son that'd fired the shots, and when he heard what happened, he came out, him and all the rest of them," Kathryn said. She paused for a moment, watching Henry and Fredrick. "He pulled a rifle from one of them cars and just kept firin' it into the air until we're all silent, just watching him."

Isabel could hear Henry's teeth grinding.

"He said something to one of the others, and he come back with a chest a few minutes later. Then he walked over to Spears' body and stood next to it, emptied the chest out on the ground and told us to come grab one. Nobody moved at first, but he trained that rifle on the mayor, Bernie Krantz was his name, and said he'd be dead at the count of three unless we'd all come forward and take a piece, one of these," Kathryn said, holding the coin up, its polished surface gleaming in the lantern light.

"A token he gave to those that owed him something. That's what he told us. He said, ' This is blood money, and it's on your hands. Blood from this man and this woman, and it will stain them.' Then he held one of those coins up."

Kathryn held her hand up, the coin clutched in it. "And he pointed to it, told us that as long as we wanted to live we'd carry that coin, and as long as we carried that coin, we'd do as he said."

"Everyone in Echton?" Isabel said.

"It's a symbol we were made to live with. A reminder of what he could take from us," Henry replied. "Almost the entire town was there that night, come in for the jubilee. Anyone that wasn't knew the story, though. Word spread quick. There was just too many of them."

"How many of the people that were there that night are still here?" Isabel said.

"Every one that ain't in the ground," Kathryn looked through a broken window into the darkness.

"Even the man that gave you the coin?" Ben looked on intently, the charcoal he'd been holding crumbling in his clenched fist.

"It was quiet after he said what he said. No one made a sound. It was awful the way he smiled, looking around the circle of us there, knowing he had us pinned there under the weight of each other. His eyes were dark as night. I swear, it was almost like you could feel the cold in his soul when he bent down, pulled the star from the kid's chest, and pinned it to his son's."

"The man that still wears it," Kathryn said.

THIRTY SEVEN
DESPERATE MATTERS

They spent the night in the truck, tucked inside the crumbling shed and hidden from view by a sheet of plywood Fredrick and Ben had dug up from somewhere to use as a makeshift door. She'd always been fond of Henry, but now her heart ached every time she had to watch him leave. It reminded her that whatever happiness she'd known there had been so quickly taken from her. Isabel was restless with more to think about than ever before. Her parents in sight but so far from her.

Ben seemed calm, like he already knew what was going to happen. He just shut the door to the truck and carefully locked it, laying the seat back until he was facing the sagging roof.

"What'd you make of it?" she asked him after awhile.

"Not sure. Guess I'll have to think about it," his reply drifted back.

She took it as a sign that he hadn't been able to sleep either, so Isabel turned on her side and looked over at him. "Do you think it's true, what Henry and that woman told us?"

Ben sighed, turning on his side to look back at her. "Hix fits the bill," he said, rubbing his temples.

They were silent for a while, and Isabel found herself nodding off. If only for a bit, she'd let herself rest. She must have slept for a little while because she dreamt of awful things and woke clawing at the door and Ben's leg. She tried to focus, to talk herself back into reality.

"You don't think he hurt them much, did he?" she found herself saying.

"What's that? No...no I think they're gonna be just fine. Your parents sound tough as nails, and if he wanted you, he'd be focusing on that, right?" Ben said.

"Yeah," Isabel said, turning over. "I just can't stop thinking about it."

"It'll be day soon anyway," he said, glancing at the rearview mirror where he could see the first rays of sunlight spilling over the tree line. Ben sat up to stretch his back, twisting from side to side.

"I wish it were a year from now, when this is all over, or a year ago, and I could stop it from ever starting," Isabel said, laying a hand on his.

Ben nodded, popping the truck door open and swinging his legs around.

"Where are you going?" she said.

"Big day," he smiled. "We should get ready."

He walked around the old mine, gathering a few things he'd put together and tossing them into a pile on the table beside the map. The cold morning air prickled his nose as he inhaled, and for the first time in awhile, he was grateful he hadn't traded out his old boots for something else. As he gathered, Isabel watched, neatly organizing everything and emptying out their packs.

"Where'd I put that rope?" he called over to her.

Without looking up, she pointed to a hook on the other side of the room and collected a few metal rods, laying them out neatly on a part of the table she'd cleaned off.

A few minutes later, she could hear a soft scraping noise echoing through the clearing. She followed the sound a few doors down and poked her head inside another shop to find Ben behind an enormous circular stone, scraping away at the edge of a piece of metal.

"What're you making?" She stole up behind him and put her head on his shoulder.

"This is iron, and although the edge isn't all that great, it's sharp enough, and if you need to start a fire, it'll be helpful."

"I don't know how well my parents will take to the woods if we have to hide there."

"I don't know that it'll really be a choice," he said grimly.

He slid the blade across a piece of cardboard, half slicing and half ripping the corner off. Isabel leaned forward and scraped her thumb against its edge sideways, yelping as it nicked a tiny cut.

"What're you doing?" Ben frowned, putting his hands around hers. "I just said it was sharp."

"I just wanted to see," she said, pulling her hand back and sticking her thumb in her mouth.

Ben leaned forward to kiss her fingers, then wrapped the iron in burlap and tucked it under his arm.

"So, what's the first thing you'll say to your parents?" he said, walking back towards the shop. *Anything I can do to keep her busy. I'd want someone to do the same for me.*

Isabel followed, still holding her thumb tenderly.

"I'm gonna ask them to consider moving," she said, kicking an old cardboard box.

Ben laughed, pushing a last few items into the bag, including the last of the food from Tom and Sarah.

"As soon as we're out of here, I'm going to buy my mother a flower for a new garden and a book for my father."

"A book about what?"

"Something that doesn't feel anything like reality," Isabel said, leaning against the countertop.

Ben set the two bags beside each other carefully and leaned against the window, looking back toward the way Henry would be coming. In a few hours, they'd either be headed into town, hidden beneath a layer of tarp and greenery or waiting for another day to pass. He wasn't sure what to hope for. *It'd be good to have another day to think it through, but it's torture for Isabel, and I've already lost her once.*

"Now what?" Isabel said.

"We wait," he replied, settling himself so he could watch the countryside as the world woke up.

Time passed slowly that morning, more painfully than Ben had ever remembered. It was nearly noon, judging by the sun, and they hadn't seen any sign of Henry or Fredrick. He was beginning to grow nervous and couldn't stop himself from pacing the floor, kicking the wall as he reached it and turned around.

"You're making me anxious doing that," Isabel said.

He stopped and exhaled, his hands busying themselves checking and rechecking their packs.

"I don't like this."

"I'm sure there's a reason," Isabel said. "Henry would never just leave us here."

"It's the reason that I'm worried about, not that he forgot about us," Ben replied. "I've seen Hix and those others give out plenty of reasons."

Isabel frowned, tapping her toe against the crumbling concrete. There!" Isabel cried, racing outside.

Ben hopped up and walked out to stand beside her in the bright sunlight.

"See it?" Her index finger extended, following the large shape of a truck moving up the road, coming in and out of view. Ben pulled her back inside the overhang as it approached. It was Henry's, he knew, but he didn't trust the truck if he couldn't see the man behind its wheel.

After a few minutes, the truck broke the clearing and rolled to a stop. A pair of shaky legs emerged from the driver's side and dropped to the ground, closing the door behind them.

"Isabel?" Kathryn's voice said.

Something is wrong. Only one pair of footsteps. Something is wrong. Isabel peeked out of the building, then gasped and ducked around the plywood cover, running out towards her. Blood was dried on the side of her face, and she walked with a limp, hobbling towards the woodshop.

"Ben!" Isabel shouted, but he was already sprinting towards them, and he helped Isabel catch Kathryn, gently letting her down beside the truck.

"Kathryn," he said, cradling her in his arms. "Are you alright? Can you hear me?"

"They didn't get to us," she said, her voice nearly a whisper. "I made it."

"What happened? Where are the others?" Isabel blurted out, doing her best to stay calm. "You're OK now," she said, dropping to her knees, stroking the old woman's face.

"McCreary. John Stark found out they had him," she said, reaching a shaky hand inside her coat and producing a small gold star, which she pressed into his hand.

"What is it?" Ben said.

"Take it. This way they'll know you."

"Who'll know?" Isabel said.

"When the time comes, you'll understand." She smiled and relaxed her head against his arm. "Go. Henry said he'd draw them off for you as long as he could so you'll have your chance."

"Where is he?" Isabel said.

Ben lowered his head to listen to the faint breathing that still moved from Kathryn's mouth.

"She's still breathing but barely."

The angle her arm lay at told him that it was broken in at least one place, and the blood dried on her head and neck led straight to a gash in her temple.

"They know," Ben said, looking up into Isabel's face.

"Kathryn, are you ok?" Isabel shook her lightly, holding her breath as she waited for her to open her eyes.

"She's still alive, but that alone's lucky, judging from the look of her." Ben shook his head sadly, looking up at the still running truck.

"Here."

He traded places with Isabel, so Kathryn's head was in her lap, and tucked the star into his pocket beside the coin as he ran to the truck, opening the door to look over its contents.

"Old rags and a few tools," he shouted.

"We have to do something for her," Isabel moaned.

"Keep pressure on that cut," Ben said, snatching up his other shirt and tossing it to her. "That should stop what's left of the bleeding. If we can get her stable, we can at least hide her somewhere."

His mind flashed to the woman who'd given him the pie. *Stranger or not, it'd at least be a decent house we could leave her in. Anywhere is better than here,* he thought. *The further we can get her from ourselves, the safer she'll be.*

"Help me carry her to the truck." He slid his arms under Kathryn and lifted her carefully, maneuvering towards the opposite truck door.

Isabel ran ahead, opening the door and moving back towards him to grab Kathryn's feet. Together, she and Ben hoisted her into the truck, and Isabel slid in beside her still form to hold it upright. Ben jumped into the driver's seat and turned the key, cursing the truck as it turned over but didn't start. On the third try, Ben coaxed the engine to life, his foot carefully working the gas.

He threw it into first and started toward the farmhouse, following the curve around the hillside until he spotted the house and sped towards it, sliding to a stop in the driveway. Ben ran to the door, pounding on it. The door shook and was finally yanked open, revealing the woman he'd seen the day before.

"Help," Ben gasped, pointing to the driveway.

She looked from him to the truck, then called back into the house, "John! Jack!"

A teenage boy and an older man appeared, their faces and clothes as worn as hers. The two of them followed him out the door and back onto the lawn, where Ben threw the truck door open and helped Isabel lower Kathryn from the truck into their waiting arms. They carried her inside without a word, and as Ben watched her legs disappear through the open door, the woman stepped forward and touched his shoulder.

"Please help her. She's been good to us," Ben said.

Tara hesitated, staring hard at him. "I knew it was only a matter of time," she finally said.

"Thank you. She saved our lives," he replied, heading back for the truck.

When he put the truck into reverse and glanced back at the door, she'd disappeared.

Isabel looked to Ben for an explanation as they pulled back onto the road, but he kept his eyes forward and slammed his foot to the floor.

"I can't explain it because I don't know. I just know that that's the best thing we can do for her right now."

"And what about Fredrick? What about Henry?"

Ben cracked his knuckles against the steering wheel and turned hard-right as the wheels struggled for traction against the dirt road.

"We make it count."

THIRTY EIGHT
TEARING THROUGH THE GEARS

"None of it's gonna work now. You know that," Isabel said as the truck sped towards Echton.

They passed back through the mining camp, stopping for only a moment to throw their packs into the truck. Isabel couldn't understand why Ben was so quiet. It made her more nervous. Together, they sped through the narrow roads, sending plumes of dust and rock shooting off into the trees as the tires spun.

"Then we change the plan."

"To what?" she said, her voice growing shrill.

"That's the real question," he replied, cutting a hard left past an old farmstead. "We have probably-" Ben glanced at the spot on his wrist where his watch used to be, "15 minutes to think about it."

Isabel's feet tapped rapidly as she watched the trees fly by. She wracked her brain for the best way to get back into the town without being noticed. The way they'd planned would have to do. It was the only way. They'd just give the store a wide birth. It worried her to wonder about what Henry was doing to draw their attention away or to think about 'them' chasing him. She tried to concentrate on navigating.

"Take a left up here." She pointed to an aluminum sign, peppered with holes.

"What's next?" Ben said, his right hand rummaging through the duffel bag.

"A right in a half mile or so," she said. "Why?"

"Hold this," he released the steering wheel and used his other hand to fully open the bag and pull out a short crowbar. Isabel jolted forward, grabbing hold of the wheel as the truck started to veer from the road.

"Here?" He put his left hand back on the wheel and started to veer right.

"Next one."

"Got it."

Isabel could see the spire from the church in the distance and knew they'd be coming into sight of the town in only a few moments.

"We have to go further west to get farther from Henry's shop," she said.

"West - you sure?"

"No - east, we should stay east. If he's leading them somewhere, it'd be west or north, away from where he knows we are." Isabel swept her hair out of her eyes, pulling it back tight against her head. *THINK* she screamed inside. *You've got to think, or we've lost already. If we can get in and out, there's still a chance to all meet up in the next town or even further away.*

"Drive to the back of the jailhouse, and I'll get out. I

need ten minutes, just drop me and circle back around it."

"You said you weren't gonna go alone." Ben kept his eyes on the road, but it was obvious from the tendons standing out in his forearms that he wasn't thrilled with the idea.

"Plans change, right? I need you to trust me."

He pursed his lips and exhaled loudly.

"Trust me," she said again.

"Fine," he shot back. "How do I know you're ready to be picked up?"

Isabel pulled a piece of white cloth from her bag and held it up. "I'll throw this over the side of the fence, so you can see it when you drive by."

Ben nodded, taking the cloth in his hand to examine it and tossing it back to her.

"If you're gone more than ten minutes, I'm coming in."

The tone of his voice told her there wasn't any further he'd be pushed, but she wasn't going to budge either.

"You circle twice, and if you don't see it, then something is wrong."

Ben frowned, accelerating down a hill as they neared the outskirts of the city. They were silent for a few minutes, each watching the handful of cars and houses they passed as Isabel helped him navigate the border of the town.

"Tell me when we're close," Isabel said, dropping to the floor of the truck amid the clutter.

He lowered his eyes as a single black car flew past, watching it in the rearview mirror, but the car didn't slow or turn around.

"Jesus," he muttered.

"What do you see?"

"Big yellow building. There's a cross street here – Brixton, it says."

"Take a right on the next street. Should be Ruven St.," she said, feeling the car take a slow right turn.

He started to relax a little, but his heart stopped when he turned the final corner into town and saw another black car parked up ahead outside the jail. Ben slowed the truck to a crawl and squinted, trying to see through its dark windows.

"What is it?" Isabel whispered.

Ben shook his head and rolled forward until they were only a few feet from the jail's fence line. He nodded quickly and motioned for Isabel to get ready, then reached across and cracked the door. She slid through the opening, taking her backpack and the crowbar with her, then flattened herself against the fence and slipped out of sight.

As Ben pulled away, he watched the jail in the rearview mirror, slowly letting down on the gas as he pulled into the intersection. He couldn't help but wonder what kind of trouble Henry and Fredrick had thrown themselves into, and soon, he knew.

At the far end of the road, he saw a cluster of cars circled around the grocery, the outlines of men moving around in front of them. He pulled the truck to the side of the road and listened carefully. They were shouting something at the front of the store, and although he couldn't make out what they were saying, he had a good idea. One of the men fired at the shop's far window, then jumped behind a car as a bullet hit the ground in front of him, showering his legs with dirt.

Ben jumped at the sound of tapping on the truck's window and looked over to see a young boy standing beside it, his head barely above the door.

"I'm s'posed to yell if I see anyone around here that I dunno," he said, looking Ben over.

Ben smiled, pulling the star from his pocket and flashing it to the boy.

"It's alright. I'm here to keep an eye on things."

The boy screwed up his face and stared back at him.

"My dad says you're all down here to take care of a situation."

"Oh?" Ben said, knowing that if he didn't get going soon, someone who wouldn't be convinced by a shiny piece of metal would discover him.

"Yep," the boy nodded.

Ben nodded too and tried to keep his face straight, not knowing whether to go while he still could or hang on a little longer and see how it unfolded. *We can't just leave them in there. As soon as we have Isabel's parents, we'll make a second run through town.* He told the boy to keep up the good work and gave him a quick wave as he pulled ahead and made for the edge of town.

Knowing that Isabel would need a little extra time to get her parents ready to jump inside the truck, Ben made a wide arc around Echton. When he felt he'd gone far enough, he pulled into a side alley and started to make his way back towards the jail. He'd made it nearly halfway through when he saw a short man with a ragged silver goatee and a rifle step into the mouth of the alley. Ben glanced backwards. It'd be a long shot to reverse out the way he'd come in, and with the man only a dozen feet ahead, he didn't like his chances. He rolled down his window as he neared the road and stuck his head out.

"Somethin' I can help you with?"

"This's Henry Small's truck," the man said, his finger tapping the side of rifle.

"Not the last time I checked," Ben faked a laugh, hoping it'd sounded genuine.

"Sure it is," the man said, peering in the window. He stepped back and pointed the rifle at Ben, who waved a dismissive hand at him.

"Take it easy," he said. "We caught up with that lady't took it and dropped her. Vinnie told me to take it back to the jail and leave it there."

"You John Stark's boy? I swear you look just like 'im."

"C'mon now. Imma hell of a lot prettier than that crusty old bastard," Ben said.

The man squinted at him, brushing the trigger with his index finger, but then broke into a wide, toothy grin.

"What the hell'd you do with her?"

"Left her in the old mine. That's where we found her. Ain't nobody gonna miss her neither." He leaned out the window to spit, watching the other man's face. Ben knew he was no actor. *If Isabel was here, she'd put me to shame.* It didn't matter now; he just hoped it would be enough.

"Alright," he said. "Better get over there. Things ain't got any better. Riggs' been hit in the shoulder by a stray, Johns just told me on his way over."

Ben gave the man a short nod and eased the truck past him. He exhaled, not daring to look back until he'd gone a few hundred yards. When he finally glanced in the mirror, he saw the man had returned to a chair outside the back of the shop and was still watching him.

It took him only a few minutes to get back to the jail,

and as it came into view, he could clearly see the white rag Isabel had thrown over the fence. He idled up next to it, and only had to wait a moment before she was in the truck with him, hunched down on the floor.

"Where are they?" he whispered.

"Nothing there, just empty cells and an idiot who fell asleep in his chair." She set the small bottle of chloroform from Henry back into the bag and tossed a rag beside it. "He's sleeping better than ever now. Didn't even wake up when I broke the locks in the two back rooms," she whispered.

Ben glanced into the rearview mirror. He hadn't realized he was biting his lip until a tiny drop of blood rolled down it. Without a doubt, soon, someone would realize something was wrong, or someone would find the broken locks.

"Where the hell have you been?" Isabel added.

He shook his head, pressing forward towards the street. "Talking my way through this death trap."

She gave him a half smile and laid her hand on his knee. "We have to go to the city hall. It's the only other place they'd be."

"Where is it?" he whispered back.

"Take a left at Main, then drive a quarter mile, and it'll be on the right side. There's a drive where you can drop me off, and you can circle around again."

"Bullshit," he replied. "I'm coming inside this time."

She hardly had time to argue. In a matter of seconds, they were pulling into a driveway 40 feet behind the city hall's tiny parking lot. Ben killed the engine and slid the sharpened metal piece from the bag, unwrapping it carefully. Isabel watched the windows on the second story of the building for any signs of movement but seeing none, started towards it, keeping her head low. Ben followed behind her, trying to quiet the sound of his boots against the pavement.

They reached the shrubs behind the building, and Isabel pointed to a pair of boots propped up atop the railing on the other side. Creeping toward the street, Ben looked back to find her moving toward the back door, eyeing the lock that secured it. He tossed her the blade, and she caught it silently, slicing through the screen door and carefully undoing the first lock. She lost sight of him as he walked toward the front of the building but heard half a yell followed by a sharp thud.

Isabel tried to open the lock with a bit of wire she'd fashioned into a hook, but it was no use. The keyhole was nearly rusted shut.

"Open, you bastard," she muttered as she dug the claws of the crowbar into the soft wooden doorframe and pulled, splintering half of the frame with a loud crunch. She paused to look around before continuing until she'd completely freed the lock and pushed the door open.

In the next room, she heard the sounds of a struggle and rushed in to find Ben wrestling with a much larger man who had him cornered against a bookcase. Ben had his hands sandwiched over the man's mouth and nose but was quickly losing color in own his face from the pressure of the larger man's fingers around his neck.

Isabel thought quickly, pulling the last of the chloroform from her bag and stealing up behind him. Raising herself on her toes, she poured the last of the liquid over the man's head and sent it streaming down his face, into his mouth and nose.

Ben's eyes were wide as he continued to struggle until the drug began to take effect. The man's arms went slack, his eyes rolling back into his head. Gasping for air, Ben grabbed him by the collar of his police uniform and did his best to lower him to the ground silently, finally dropping him and stumbling backwards.

"Sorry," Isabel mouthed. "Are you ok?"

He nodded, clutching at his throat and taking shallow, rasping breaths. With one hand on his neck still, he motioned to a back room. Isabel wasted no time, jamming the bar between the trim and the door. She wrestled with it for a moment, but the wood around the lock would only break away in tiny bits, leaving the mechanism untouched. Ben pushed past her with something in his hand and slammed it into the door, pushing the lock inward. With two more swings of the hammer, he'd freed the door. Isabel jumped over the broken wood and twisted brass and ran into the room, throwing herself into the still form of her father, her other hand reaching towards her mother.

Tears streamed from her father's eyes, and she threw her arms around his neck, undoing the piece of cloth that covered his mouth. Ben moved to her mother, untying her gag as well and, moving to her hands, quickly realized that without the proper tools, he'd never be able to remove the handcuffs that bound them. He looked to Isabel, who he could see had just come to the same realization.

"My Isabel," her mother sobbed. Isabel ran to her and hugged her tightly, her father pulling against his restraints, trying to follow.

"It's alright now," Isabel said, untying the ropes around her ankles. "Everything is gonna be alright. This is

Ben," she whispered, pointing back to him. "He saved me, and he came here to help me save you."

"The records! If there are more, we need to take them all with us," her father said, his voice hoarse. "We need it all."

"The records?" Ben said, looking around them.

"The records can prove it if they haven't destroyed them already," her mother said, watching the door. "Have you been to the house?"

"Floor plans, maps, alarm systems, false identities, it's all there," her father said, rising to his feet and struggling against the rope that bound his handcuffs to the wall.

"Stay still! I'm trying to undo these knots," Isabel snapped, struggling with her mother's restraints.

"Explain later! We have to go," Ben hissed. "We can do the cuffs later, we have to get out of here."

"What's the rush?" said a voice from the door. "You only just got here."

Ben looked up to a see a thin man in a dark suit, a smile playing across his lips, revealing a row of jagged teeth.

He recognized him immediately. He'd never really gotten a great look at Hix in the first place, but the curly silver-brown hair and sharp cheekbones and nose brought the realization to him like a thunderclap.

"McClellan," he whispered.

THIRTY NINE
A WALL AT YOUR BACK

Henry knew he'd never been good at hiding anything, so he did his best to stay clear of anyone that morning. Even the ones he trusted. He shut the door to the shop and tacked up a hasty note about falling ill. He and Fredrick had been trading off turns sleeping at home and taking watch at the shop. No sign of McCreary coming back yet, and no sign was a good sign. He wondered if they should have just kept him here under their watch. *Too much of a liability,* he thought. *If anyone were to find him here, or if he were to escape, we'd be done for. He's not a bad man, just a stupid one. We can't just kill him. We also can't afford to have him anywhere near.* He wished he could get Isabel and Fredrick out of Echton as easily, but that couldn't be helped.

Hunkered down in the back room with a cup of coffee, Henry heard Fredrick's long, heavy strides behind the store and watched the door handle jiggle and swing open. They hadn't spoken about it, hadn't said a word about his mother on the way home, but he knew it must be burning at the front of Fredrick's mind.

"We oughta toss it," Henry said, poking a finger at the gun belt they'd stripped from the deputy and hid behind the ice chest.

"Ought to," Fredrick's reply came back. "Won't matter much soon. We'll have to get on outta here as soon as Isabel and her folks clear out."

"I suppose you're right," Henry sighed. "Hell, we might even need a gun."

He thought about how he'd begged Fredrick not to come back all those years ago, but he'd softened in his old age. Henry didn't really ask questions, couldn't afford to ask them, but things were getting worse. Sadly enough, he'd been living with that sickness so long, he'd grown used to all of it, but like sicknesses often do, it continued to spread. Before the Stanton's even knew what Echton was, he'd seen it getting worse. Late at night, Hix's men would call him up and tell him to get to the store. He'd slip out or make some excuse to Fredrick, but it was always because someone needed to be patched up. Then, it was just after Doc Henderson had died, and they said a Navy man, a former medic, was the one for the job. It was as close to hell as Henry could figure, being forced to help the ones who'd killed his wife, under the threat that they'd kill his son.

It continued even after Conrad Stanton assumed his role as Echton's new doctor. Until Hix felt like he could keep Stanton under his thumb if he needed to, he wasn't gonna take any of his men to him. His plan panned out for a short time, and after awhile, Hix was sending them all to Conrad, but there was a critical error in his plan; he hadn't taken enough time to measure up Conrad Stanton. Mayor Hatley had come to Henry one night, his face black and blue. He said Stanton was starting to ask questions, and that Hix had told Stanton to play ball, but he wouldn't. It wasn't long after that Conrad and his wife had gone missing "Armed and dangerous." Hix had called them.

Hatley said they just had to lay low, had begged Henry to cooperate, or they'd hurt his daughters. Henry felt like he'd died again that day, like so many days where he'd stitch them back up, or do his best to fix whatever they'd gotten themselves into. They'd made it clear that speaking up was a death sentence, so he kept his head down and buried his anger.

It didn't stop the suspicions from churning inside him, though. The scars, the marks - injuries that could only be bullet wounds. It wasn't that often but more than just a coincidence, and new faces kept appearing as the old ones stopped. Occasionally, they'd slip him a few 10 or 20 dollar bills. *Blood money.* Hix made him keep the coin on his person, but the money he kept in a box under the porch, and prayed every time he added to it that he'd never have to open it again.

He heard them whispering about different cities, different jobs, "arrests" as they called them, always in the same hushed tone. They talked as if it was all business and he was guilty by association, like he would be implicating himself if he ever actually listened. He was listening. To every word. He never asked for this and promised himself that before this was all over, they'd be taking it back.

That morning it felt closer than ever with Fredrick's towering frame beside him and the stillness that filled the air. It was comforting to have his son with him even though he wished he weren't there. Isabel was practically his daughter, and if there were two people he could pull from this mess, she and Fredrick would have been in another country. He didn't have that luxury now.

"You alright?" Fredrick said.

Henry nodded, groaning as he straightened his legs.

"Son...I'm sorry you had to find out that way," he said. "Your mother was a beautiful woman. I -"

A sharp rapping noise rang out from the front door. Henry motioned Fredrick to sit down and went to answer it.

"Thought you were sick," a voice said as he pulled the door open.

"Mr. Stark, what can I do for you?" Henry said, holding his gaze. He recognized the man from a few weeks ago; when he'd set his left arm in the front room of the jail. It'd been a nasty break, and when he looked closely, he could see the outline of the brace under the man's coat.

"You're to report in an hour, bring a rifle if you got one," Stark said sharply.

"Report for what?" Henry feigned surprise. He looked back, catching a glimpse of the back door opening and heard Kathryn's voice say something to Fredrick.

Stark peeked over his shoulder into the back room, then carried on. "We're going out north of town, someone'll explain your duty when you report."

Henry looked on blankly, furrowing his brow.

"Just be at the town hall in an hour, you and him too," Stark pointed back at Fredrick, who'd stealthily made his way to the front of the store and was standing behind Henry.

"The town hall," Henry repeated, frowning.

"Just be there. Don't ask any stupid questions." Stark sneered and turned to walk away.

"How do you know McCreary isn't just lost somewhere? Or left town to look after something?" Henry called after him. Stark turned, his good hand resting on the handle of his sidearm. Fredrick's hand closed around Henry's arm pulling him backward.

"I never said anything about McCreary," Stark said, walking back towards the store and starting to push his way inside.

Fredrick yanked Henry back and shoved his palm into Stark's chest, sending him tumbling back out the door. He pushed the thick door shut and slammed the deadbolt home as the first bullet hole punched through it, missing his shoulder by inches.

FORTY
THE ANGLE OF REPOSE

"I haven't heard the name out loud since my father passed, some fifteen years ago," Hix said, circling them menacingly.

Through the opening in the door, Ben could see the room start to fill with uniforms and suits, all standing between them and their only chance of escape.

"Why stay here?" Ben said, trying to stall Hix. *Think, think, think,* he repeated the word to himself. *There must be a way.*

"Why here is a damn good question," Hix snarled. "I hate this town, hated it since the day I got here, but now it's mine. I own it." He words dripped like venom, and the corners of his mouth twitched, rising as he spoke.

"My father used to always say, how'd he put it... Eidsel, my boy, don't ask for what you can just take." Hix drew his gun from its holster and flipped open the chamber to examine the bullets. He snapped it back shut and waved it over them, coming to rest back on Ben.

"Got a whole family of murderers and thieves, it seems," he said, "and I believe it was this one here's been assaulting my officers."

He doubled Ben over with a hard punch in the exact place his ribs were broken. *Lucky guess.* From the other side of the room, Isabel gasped and ran to him, but Ben pushed her back. Hix produced a paper from his vest pocket and started to read aloud.

"Robert Tiller – Taxation Specialist from Indiana; John Barden – Federal Marshall; Arnold Flickton – Ohio State Patrol. The list goes on and on. Twelve counts of murder or accessory by our count, maybe more we haven't discovered yet," he smiled. "However, I'm sure if we work at it, we can get a full confession from our suspects, unless they're killed in an escape attempt."

The way Hix glanced up at Isabel as he said each name made Ben's stomach churn. He set his jaw, glancing back at the barred windows behind them.

"Vinnie!" Hix barked.

A towering trenchcoat pushed its way through the crowd and into the doorway.

"Yeah?" Vinnie said, smiling at the four of them, trapped in the back half of the room.

"This the kid that took the hearing outta your ear?"

Vinnie turned his head towards Ben, where a white bandage was carefully secured over his right ear.

"That's him."

"Let's add a few counts of assaulting an officer of the law and resisting arrest," Hix said. "I've got a few more here'd love to take a chunk out of you." He stepped forward, looking Ben in the eye. "It's too bad I want you for myself.

I'm gonna kill you; I'm gonna kill your girlfriend and them too." He gestured to Isabel's parents. "I'm gonna remind the people in this town who's holding the reins. How about that for a last thought? I'm going to kill all of them, slowly, and painfully." The words were like a noose, tightening around Ben's neck.

"Listen, I can tell you where the files are," Conrad said hastily. "Let Isabel and the boy go, and they're yours."

"You'll tell me either way," Hix sneered.

That was it, Ben realized. *That's why he needed Isabel, so her parents would tell him where all the files were, all the evidence of their dirty work that Isabel's father had gathered.* Hix strode over to Isabel and ran the back of his hand down her face. She tried to shy away, but he grabbed her by the hair and pulled her close, turning to look back at Conrad.

"You're gonna tell me exactly where you hid them. It won't take all that much convincing." He released Isabel, turning to Conrad and firing a shot into his leg.

Conrad gasped in pain and staggered backwards. He struggled to regain his composure. Pulling against his restraints he yelled, "Do whatever you want with us, but let them go. They don't know."

"Actually - it sounds like they know more than you do," he said, stepping around Ben as he moved toward the back of the room. With the gun pressed against Conrad's chest, Hix touched the tip of his boot against the wound and pushed. Conrad groaned in pain, stumbling.

"If there's one thing my daddy got right, it's that he knew when to get the hell out. It sounds like these two've been doing their research. Just like her old man, right? A daughter not unlike her father." He gave Conrad a hard kick, knocking him to the ground. Hix stepped back, wiping the top of his boot against Conrad's slacks and turning away.

"You'll rot before we tell you anything," Isabel spat. "People know we're here, and they'll come looking for us."

Hix didn't seem to hear her. He just paced the length of the room, tapping the barrel of the pistol against his brow.

"There's not a single one of you's not guilty," he said, whirling around and cracked the butt of his pistol against Maria's head. She crumpled like a burnt leaf, falling to the ground with a thud. Isabel screamed and threw herself on her mother. Behind them, Conrad struggled toward his wife, but was cut short by the ropes that bound his hand-cuffs to the wall.

"Coward!" he yelled.

Hix smiled, straightening his suit jacket and walking back towards the door.

"My father dragged me to this shithole town and told me we'd just stay long enough for the heat to die down. Little over forty years we've been here, with a few new recruits," he chuckled, gesturing to the other men in the room. "Every one a loyal soldier, and they've been well rewarded for it."

Vinnie snickered, cracking his neck.

"Things around here happen the way I say they happen," he went on. "And it looks like we just caught a break, captured four at the same time." Hix ran a hand through his hair and gnashed his teeth. "Murderers and thieves living among us."

"It'll never hold up," Isabel snapped.

"Ain't a witness in this town who'll testify otherwise."

Ben, who'd been silent, looked over the cluster of

bodies that crowded the rest of the hall. He counted 12, maybe more if some were still outside.

"I think you're afraid," he said.

"Of you?"

Hix came closer until Ben could smell the acrid stench of coffee and old cigarettes.

"That they'll stop listening to you," he replied, struggling to keep his voice steady.

Hix raised the pistol and cocked it, pushing the muzzle into Ben's forehead. Ben didn't move, just stared into the dark brown of Hix's eyes.

"Show me how you did it, all those years back. Show me how you killed that kid in cold blood, shot him in the back."

"You don't know anything about cold blood," Hix said. "I did what had to be done when my old man was too weak to do it."

"You're only a coward," Ben yelled.

If he could get them out of the house or at least most of them, maybe Isabel and her parents could somehow escape through the back. They'd only need a few minutes, and that chance, however slim, was worth it. He looked at Isabel, at the beautiful light in her eyes, swollen from crying. She held his gaze until he turned away, facing the sheriff again.

"How about it? There must be a pair on you yet, something other than tar and smoke?" Ben pointed to the gun in his hand. Why don't you give me one of those, and we can have it off, just one to one."

Hix snorted, massaging the hand he'd hit Maria with. "I'll be back for you as soon as your friend's dead." He gave Isabel a crooked smile, waving the gun towards the door.

"You can't!" Isabel screamed, throwing herself at him.

Hix was too quick, bringing a boot up into her stomach, and as he pushed her back, he brought the back of his hand across her face. She fell beside her mother, who'd begun to stir, clutching at her head where she'd been struck. Ben felt his hands clench involuntarily, and it took every bit of his will to keep from doing exactly as she'd done. *Keep it together. They'll have a shot if I can change shift his attention for even a few minutes.*

Ben tried to focus on Hix, but kept Isabel in the corner of his eye. She wasn't moving, but he could see the faint rise and fall of her chest as she lay, her mother struggling to be closer to her.

"Come on!" Ben yelled, staring at Hix.

Hix just smiled, watching them on the ground.

"Where you belong," he said, turning to walk from the room as Vinnie's thick fingers wrapped around Ben's arm and dragged him in Hix's wake.

When they cleared the front door, Vinnie threw him forward, sending Ben crashing down the steps and out onto the road. Ben shook his head, trying to clear it, and looked around. *I have to stay sharp - only for a few more minutes.* He was shocked when he realized how many people stood around the town hall, their attention on him. Among the crowd were familiar faces. He spotted the man who'd let him go two days before, his eyes carefully watching Hix and the men that poured from the room.

They gave Hix a wide birth, splitting in two, opening the space around them. Ben pushed himself to his feet, wiping a trickle of blood from his mouth. Hix tossed an old revolver towards him, skittering across the dirt. Ben stared at the gun, then back at the gathering crowd.

"Pick it up," Hix growled.

Ben looked on, his eyes glossy. It was one of the few times he'd felt truly weightless. From his pocket, he drew the gold star and closed his hand around it. Hix made a face, spinning the chamber of his revolver.

"Doesn't make a difference to me," he snarled, then turned and shouted to the crowd. "Don't you dare shut your eyes!"

The men from the town hall walked around to the front of those who'd gathered, placing themselves between the wall of people and the two figures framed against the midday sun.

"Remember this day!" Hix shouted to the crowd. Then, without warning, he jerked his hand upward, loosing a bullet into Ben's left arm.

Ben had never felt anything like it, the searing pain that tore through his shoulder and into his chest. He dropped to one knee, the star falling from his hand into the dirt. *Stand up, you have to stand back up.* He pulled himself back to his feet, if only for a few more moments- as much time as he could take. A murmur ran through the crowd, rising in volume as it went, and Ben followed their eyes to the door of the town hall. At the top of the stairs stood Isabel, looking down at them with her clenched fist held outward.

"Glad you're here to watch," Hix said.

"I have something of yours," she shouted.

Her voice was steady, but Ben could see her shaking. He kept his eyes on her as she swung her arm towards them, the coin flying from it, glittering in the sun before depositing itself at Hix's feet.

"I won't hold it for you anymore," she added.

Ben glanced at the pistol and kicked it away, cradling his left arm and shifting his weight. His vision was starting to blur. *Run!* he thought as he watched her. *Get as far from this place as you can.*

"Do what you're good at," Ben spat, struggling to keep his legs under him.

"With pleasure," Hix said, walking towards him, raising his aim as he drew near. He cocked the hammer back and trained the sight on Ben's chest.

Ben felt it, the coldness that crept into his bones and threatened to take him as the barrel of the gun filled his vision. At first, he thought he'd imagined it, when he heard the clank of metal against the ground. He looked down and realized another coin lay between them, halfway hidden by the dirt.

"Who threw that!?" Hix bellowed, sweeping the gun in a wide arc. From his other side, a second coin flew through the air, landing beside the others, and was followed by a third and fourth.

"Next one to throw dies," he yelled, whirling around to face the direction the last coin had come from.

"No!" someone said from the back of the crowd, and another coin was lofted, striking Hix in the chest.

"Take it back," a woman yelled from behind him, hurling a coin at Hix, narrowly missing him.

Hix nodded to Vinnie and waved a hand in the direction of the sound. Vinnie turned to walk towards the woman who'd spoken, but as he tried to move through the crowd, three sets of hands wrapped around his uniform and pushed him back into the clearing. Another man stepped forward, throwing a hard right cross into his jaw, sending him reeling backwards. The man glanced at Ben, then grabbed the front of Vinnie's uniform and pulled him into the crowd, where he disappeared under a flurry of blows and rising dust.

It seemed to happen so slowly, but in a fraction of a moment. The people of Echton swallowed the men Hix had arrogantly paraded in front of them like the sea takes a sinking ship. They vanished in a frenzy of blows and strikes, sinking beneath furious screams and muffled impacts. The sound of gunshots echoed against the buildings, and the brawl continued to grow, enveloping them.

It took Ben a second to realize that Hix wasn't watching him anymore. The sheriff stood, horrified as man after man was brought to the ground, disappearing under the waves of people that seemed to appear from nowhere. Amid the crowd, Ben saw Fredrick pushing towards them. Blood stained the front of his shirt, and he was limping. He kept his gaze focused on Hix, grabbing a uniform by the arm and tossing him backward. More men in black uniforms and plain clothes with stars on their chests appeared from the alleyways and buildings in town, but they were eclipsed by the men and women that continued to pour into the square, sweeping them away into the madness.

Hix stood alone at the center of the street, a dozen paces from Ben, waving his pistol wildly, firing the rest of the chamber into the crowd. His eyes were wide, searching for any path of escape. They landed on the open door to the town hall, and he ran toward it, fumbling with a handful of bullets as he tried to reload. He made it only a few paces when Fredrick's huge hand closed around the back of his collar and brought him to a sudden stop, slamming him against the ground. With the other hand, he grabbed the gun from the squirming sheriff and tossed it away.

Pinned under Fredrick's weight, Hix took a knife from his belt and sunk it into Fredrick's thigh. Fredrick grimaced, pulling the blade back out and pitching it into the crowd, the blood from his chest and leg dripping onto the immaculate blackness of Hix's suit. Above the din, Ben could see his lips moving, but he struggled to hear Fredrick's voice.

"You owe your life," was all he could make out as Fredrick hoisted Hix into the air, his hands wrapped around Hix's neck.

Ben shuddered as the sheriff's legs kicked wildly and his hands clawed at Fredrick's thick arms. The grocer's hands only tightened, taking the color from Hix's face as it contorted into an awful grimace. Finally, his arms and legs went slack, hanging loose at his sides. Fredrick slammed his limp body to the ground.

"Where's Henry?" Ben shouted to him.

Fredrick closed his eyes and shook his head. Reaching into his pocket, he produced a gold coin and let it fall onto Hix's chest, tears glimmering as they rolled down his face. He mouthed the word "go" to Ben and pointed toward the open town hall. Ben passed him, grabbing the keys from Hix's belt, and met Isabel at the top of the stairs. Together they moved through the building towards her parents. Her father had propped himself upright, and both he and her mother were as far forward as their restraints would take them. With his good arm, Ben undid Conrad's handcuffs first, careful to be gentle with the cuts on his wrists, then set about freeing Maria.

"Isabel," she murmured weakly.

Conrad, Maria, and Isabel dropped in a heap in the middle of the floor. Ben watched them, leaning against the wall, trying to slow his breathing and keep his arm still.

"What's going on out there?" Conrad said, looking towards the door as Fredrick walked through it.

"A storm," Fredrick answered for him.

FORTY ONE
SEEDS, WATER, SOIL, AND TIME

The door to the grocery was already propped open as Isabel pushed her way inside, wrapping her arms around two brown bags on the counter. On the wall hung a picture of a grey-headed man, finely dressed and smiling. Beside it was a portrait of a young blonde woman, dressed in white, a warm smile on her lips. The plate beneath listed Patricia and Henry as the founders of Small's Grain and Grocery.

"Pretty shoddy service around here," Isabel called toward the back room.

In an instant, Fredrick appeared, grinning. Isabel set the supplies back on the counter for a moment to hug him before re-collecting them and making her way toward the door.

"You know, we could probably use a hand around here," Fredrick said.

"I told you, I'm not gonna ask him until his arm's better." She shot a knowing glance back at Fredrick, then pushed the door open with her foot.

Ben was waiting for her outside the store, behind the wheel of her father's car. She thought it suited him well, having new clothes and finally being clean-shaven.

"Jesus, thought I was gonna die of old age out here."

Isabel made a face, then set the bags in the back seat, sliding in beside him.

"We'd better get back. You're looking pretty gray."

Ben laughed, turning the car around. *This drive seems like it keeps getting shorter*, he thought, knowing that every time they made the trip, it felt more like home.

They pulled up the driveway, where the frame of the Stanton house had been resurrected in new timber, fresh snow topping it in tiny mounds. Tom Dawkins, the man who ran the mill's lumberyard had insisted on donating it, and they'd hardly gone a weekend without at least a dozen of Echton's residents showing up to help build the house back into a home. In the meantime, the Stantons had taken to living in the emergency shelter. The bunks they'd set up were less than comfortable, but for now, it felt like home, and Ben couldn't argue with that.

Isabel hopped out, grabbing the bags before Ben could make his way around the car, and bustling off towards the shelter in the middle of their yard.

"Just missed everyone," Conrad said as they descended the ladder. *He's moving better every day*, Ben thought. The limp in his stride was hardly noticeable.

"Sorry," Ben replied, blushing. "I wanted to see the old mine again. Thought it might not make a bad workshop, given a little fixing up.

Conrad patted him on the shoulder, smiling warmly

as Maria rose from her stool across the room and came to hug them both.

"Kathryn was asking about you again," she said. "Seems like you made quite an impression."

Ben snorted a laugh as he lay back on his bunk, his good arm behind his head. The other was healing nicely, Conrad had told him, but it still hurt like hell whenever he moved it.

"You get a lot done today?" Isabel asked her father.

"Not as much as I'd like to. Seems that Mr. McCreary finally decided to poke his head back into town a few days ago. George Scray found him hiding behind the diner, and we had a talk with him. I don't think we should expect any trouble, but it still worries me a little."

"How's your project coming?" Ben asked.

"Yeah, who's gonna file the report?" Isabel said.

"Already done," Conrad said. "The Mayor and I went into Akron last week to voice our suspicions. I figure by the time they come out to investigate, maybe another day or two, there won't be a trace of Hix-"

"McLellan," Isabel corrected him.

"McLellan or the others in the whole town."

Isabel stood over his shoulder and began to read aloud. "Discovery and confrontation of federal felon - McLellan. Index, evidence, dates...blah, blah." She flipped through the pages. "You're going to give them this?"

"No, no. It's just to keep everyone on the same page. Make things easier for all of us," Conrad answered, straightening the loose pages and setting them carefully on the table.

"You don't think they'll come back?" she said, retreating to the bunk to lay beside Ben.

"I don't think so," Maria said.

In this whole mess, it was one moment Isabel looked back on proudly. Practically the whole town had come out for the release of McLellan's men. The handful that hadn't escaped or been killed were released from the jail and marched to the edge of town, where they were given strict instructions to leave and never return. After seeing what had happened to rest of them on that day outside the town hall, she figured none would bother to chance it.

On the corner of his desk, Conrad kept the box with the files Hix had been keeping, floor layouts and security plans for First Federal Bank, Independent Investments, Government Bond Facilities - the list went on and on. Conrad told them how he'd grown suspicious after a member of the city council had come into his office with a broken arm and bruises on his neck that looked like finger marks. The man claimed he'd already filed a report, but it didn't seem to add up, so Conrad had started looking into things.

He explained that as he asked about the records, he was met with increasing hostility until Hix himself stopped by late one night and laid it out for him. "Don't ask questions you don't want answers to," he'd said. "Just do your job and fix them up."

Well, Conrad did as he was told, but that's when he'd begun to put things together. Hix must have told the boys he was ready to cooperate because from then on, injuries he had to treat just got worse. Men he'd never seen with wounds they couldn't explain or didn't bother to. He stayed quiet, fixing them up and compiling records of each one.

He'd written Isabel the note to keep her clear of it if something happened to them. What he hadn't known, until he'd woken to his and Maria's arrest, were the consequences of the game he'd been playing. He'd taken to hiding all the paperwork under a loose floorboard beneath the clock, a bargaining chip in case anything happened to him. When Hix and his men took them into custody, that's where the records had stayed.

In their firebox, they'd been one of the few things that had outlasted the flames, and the medical records he'd been keeping, paired with the work logs they'd taken from the sheriff's office and the floor plans they'd recovered from the back room of the town hall, outlined it all pretty well.

"This was the perfect staging point for anything in the Midwest, any robbery or heist or whatever sort of scheme they wanted to plan," he explained to Isabel and Ben. "An alibi whenever they needed one and a badge to hide behind."

"Jesus," Ben said, " and no cop would think to accuse another cop."

It all seems to fit, but where does the trail end?, Conrad wondered. If there was really a stream of dirty money flowing into Echton, all that cash had to end up somewhere.

He turned back to Ben and Isabel. "So anyone who finds out about this little hit and hide business, the disappear," Conrad said.

"It makes sense," Isabel nodded. "But Hix was smart... I'm guessing he knew Echton would be in for a little more attention than he wanted if he made us disappear, so he tried to kill our name first."

"Tried," Ben said, smiling.

It took time, but Isabel could see the town healing and actually beginning to thrive. They buried their dead before the first snowfall, each grave marked with a beautiful white cross. She wasn't sure what they'd done with Hix or his men who died that day, but she didn't particularly want to know. Whatever had become of them, she assumed they were far under the ground or water.

"You alright?" Ben said.

She shivered, wrapping herself around him.

"I'm ok."

"We can go see Henry tomorrow if you want?"

"Ok," she smiled. "I'd like that."

"I would too." He stroked her face, then sat up.

Ben knew it would be awhile before he stopped looking over his back or started trusting the sound of another person behind him. Yet, in all the madness and deceit, something beautiful had found them. He saw it whenever he met the eyes of someone passing through town or worked beside them as the frame of the house rose back into the sky outside their shelter. The fear that had so deeply rooted itself in them was beginning to loosen its hold. It was obvious in the way people spoke and looked at each other.

Looking over at Conrad, who was reading a book at his desk, and Maria, on the other side of the room sorting and putting aside ingredients, he didn't really think anything at all, but the feeling of calm from simply being with them never failed to amaze him. There, with Isabel Stanton beside him, in the warmth of that room, he was content to stay.

A knock echoed on the metal door of the shelter, and as Conrad mounted the ladder and opened it, Ben heard Fredrick's voice float down towards them.

"Found this tin under the porch when I was redoing the lattice. It's full of this stuff. Must be a thousand dollars in here."

He and Isabel were silent, listening intently to the sound of rustling paper.

"I'll be," Conrad said. "See that mark on the corner? These came from a federal bond facility. Here are a few more with a whole different mark."

"There's something else," Fredrick said, sifting through its contents. "Something my father tucked away at the bottom of it."

"Did you hear that?" Isabel whispered.

Ben nodded and rose, walking over to the stairs where the two men were standing, looking over a piece of parchment as they unfolded it.

"What is it?" he said, feeling Isabel's body press against his back.

"I don't know what to make of it," Fredrick replied. "Just a bunch of squiggle lines and X's and numbers."

They were all silent for a moment. Then, Isabel slipped around Ben and took it from him, turning it on its side.

"I know this," she blurted out. "These, these numbers are locations or latitudes or something. I've seen this pattern before."

"This is us." She pointed to a faded letter "E" at the top of the paper. "It's -"

"What?" Ben said.

"A map," she whispered. "It's a map."